BUTTERFLY KISSES

COURTNEY DAVIS

5 PRINCE PUBLISHING
5PRINCEBOOKS.COM

Published by 5 PRINCE PUBLISHING & BOOKS, LLC

PO Box 865, Arvada, CO 80001

www.5PrinceBooks.com

ISBN digital: 978-1-63112-373-3

ISBN print: 978-1-63112-374-0

Cover Credit: Marianne Nowicki

04232024.1

To my husband who never judges any of my ideas and supports all my efforts in making my dreams come true.

ACKNOWLEDGMENTS

Thank you to Cate Byers for her continued amazing editing help, you make me a better writer every time we work together.

Thank you to the team at 5 Prince Publishing for continuing to give my stories a chance.

OTHER TITLES BY

COURTNEY DAVIS

BUTTERFLY KISSES

CHAPTER 1

Sachi nearly dropped the tray of macaroons she was taking to the window display when she spotted him across the street. Black button-up and crisp jeans. His dark hair was short and shaggy like he'd missed more than one haircut, and a decent enough stubble was on his face that she could see it from where she stood, staring.

"Fuck me," Sachi whispered as she watched him pause and look around. She knew every face in this district, and he was definitely new. If he was wandering about on his own it meant he was a supe; humans only came through with tour groups to gawk and buy souvenirs, confident of their safety in numbers. Her bakery, *Butterfly Kisses*, was a hotspot for those tourists, they weren't afraid of a butterfly shifter, probably because most of them didn't realize that butterfly shifters were vampiric, and that she also happened to be half witch. Her long lilac hair and bright blue eyes screamed innocent and sweet. Of course it helped that she kept her fangs hidden behind a soft smile.

Her business partner, Fern, wasn't scary at all. A vegetarian supe who could shrink as small as an inch and grow only as tall as five feet. She was a fairy with short blonde hair and big green eyes, though she did have a snarky attitude.

As a result, no human walked into their establishment with fear for their lives and it made for great tips most days over her last almost ten years in business. Sachi did most of the baking, but Fern helped and was great at decorating. Her small size lent itself to intricate design work with frosting that they had become known for.

"Oh, what's that?" Fern asked. Her silver fairy wings vibrated with excitement as she came up to the window with a box of cupcakes ready for delivery.

"I'm not sure, but I want to find out," Sachi admitted with a giggle.

"Looks delightfully dangerous. Vampire?" Fern had a thing for bloodsuckers, maybe that's why they'd always gotten along so well. Fern's family lived in the huge oak tree outside Sachi's mother's house so they'd grown up together, spending their high school years flying around and getting in trouble with the local boys. Their friendship had stayed strong even after graduation.

"No way, the sun's not even down yet," Sachi pointed out.

Fern shrugged, "They've been working hard on fixing that problem. Lance told me they think they have a lead with some kind of sunscreen lotion, but the tests haven't been successful for more than preventing complete combustion. They come away with nasty burns every time." Lance was Fern's vampire boyfriend and another old high school friend. Along with Sachi's high school sweetheart, Cash, the four of them had been great friends. She hadn't stayed with Cash after high school, but Fern and Lance had been on again-off again all that time, currently on.

"Too bad you're not single." Sachi gave her friend a wiggle of her eyebrows, *she* didn't have a boyfriend. "Well, I guess I'll deliver those in his direction." Sachi pulled her hair out of its usual worktime bun and smoothed the lilac curls, letting them fall around her shoulders. "Do I have any flour on my face?"

"You look great," Fern assured her and opened the door, handing her the cupcake box. It was a congratulatory gift for a witch friend of theirs who'd just given birth to triplets.

Sachi sashayed out of the *Butterfly Kisses Bakery* thankful she had dressed in a sundress today rather than shorts. Wearing a dress always made her feel flirty and this one was short enough to show a lot of leg but cut high on the chest for modesty with cute cap sleeves to be appropriate for work and perfect for approaching 'tall, dark and stranger' to see what he was doing in her little district. She tried to seem casual, waving at neighbors and old friends without stopping as she hurried across the street. She noticed more than one local supe giving him a second glance, a new person in town, not human, was hard to ignore.

She slowed her pace so she wouldn't seem too eager as she got close and put on her most welcoming smile. "You look lost," she said sweetly behind him.

When he turned, she nearly lost her breath, he was even more handsome up close. His eyes weren't just dark, they were black, and he had a wide smile revealing perfect white teeth of a normal size. Not a werewolf then. She subtly took a deep breath, searching for a hint and tasted a bit of magic. Warlock perhaps.

"I suppose I am," he said with a little laugh. His voice was deep and pleasant, making her think of dark rooms and passionate embraces. "I was supposed to go to *Moses' Bar*. This is the street, but I don't see a bar." There was a bit of frustration in his voice, obviously he wasn't used to being lost. Probably the type who always liked to be in control, and that appealed to her more than she'd ever realized as a tingle ran up her spine.

"*Moses' Bar*," she whispered, trying to keep her thoughts out of the bedroom. "Umm, gosh, I don't know it." She ran her eyes up and down the man, he was tall and broad shouldered, maybe worked out occasionally but definitely didn't take it overboard. He was leanly muscled, more like a martial artist than a body-builder. It's too bad he was looking for Moses, but that confirmed

3

her warlock assumption. "Maybe it's the other Lilac Street, it ends up there; see," she pointed to where the street hit the riverbank. "Gnomes built the damn grid here, so it doesn't make any sense to anyone else. Lilac Street picks up again about ten blocks south of here. Good luck." She waved as she hurried away, daring to glance back after half a block. He was already gone, no doubt heading south.

"What a waste of a pretty face," she sighed, anyone looking for Moses was bound for trouble, good thing the handsome man would never find him.

"Who was that hunk?" Maureen, an elderly fairy asked from her usual spot outside the little tailoring shop she'd owned with her husband for a hundred years or more. She was rocking back and forth in a chair designed for someone the size of a human toddler, its well-worn light blue paint faded and cracked. She had a smile on her wrinkled face as she nodded to a young fairy who flitted forward and whispered in her ear before flitting back off to help a customer. One of her great grandchildren, Sachi was certain.

Sachi stopped and gave the woman her full attention, anything else would be considered rude in the town where everyone knows everyone and they love to talk about each other. "Don't know, just a stranger passing through. He won't find what he's looking for and he'll probably be out of here before the roads close for the night." She wondered where he was from and where he'd go once he realized he wasn't going to get what he wanted here.

"Stranger, huh? Too bad, I wouldn't mind seeing him walk up and down the street regularly," she laughed.

Sachi nodded agreement and moved on before she could get caught in a long conversation with the fairy. Maureen was sweet but she did love to talk.

Sachi headed on toward Witch's Row; it was actually State Street, but no one called it that. Every witch in the district lived on that street and they'd made it their own. Every house painted black, every house had a cat, also black, and the smell of magic was so heavy there it was a wonder any human dared to visit the shops that sold fake love charms and sage to repel nonexistent ghosts. They had the real stuff, too, of course, but it was reserved for other supes, and kept in the back. Giving humans real spells that they couldn't invoke was a waste of energy and money, and witches were resolutely unwasteful. They never did anything unless it benefited them in some way, and they always collected on their debts.

"Definitely a warlock," Sachi said as she stepped onto Witch's Row and inhaled the scent of magic. That's what the guy was, she was sure now. He'd smelled like spells done recently but not today, just faint enough that he might only practice on occasion. More than she did though. Her father had been a good warlock, but he had failed to teach her how to stir up spells and harness her inner magic. She could do some simple stuff, but nothing like the witches who had been practicing since they could talk. Some days she wished she knew more, others it didn't matter. She could bake a hell of a cake though and she enjoyed her shifting abilities. Being able to spell well would have just been icing on the cake.

Her mind brought up an image of the handsome stranger. *He could be the cream filling*, she decided with a smile.

They didn't get a lot of warlocks in this district since the witches had such a huge presence and they really only allowed men in their lives for one thing, and it usually resulted in a pregnancy. Her own love life had been bone dry for a while now and it had really started to irritate her lately. She knew she was attractive, her body was slim, but she had enough curves to show off when she wanted to. She got hit on daily, mostly by dumb humans though and she would never consider dating one. A human and supe relationship wasn't against the law but it was highly frowned upon and could never lead to a life together. Humans couldn't live in supe districts and supes weren't allowed to live outside of them. There were lots of eligible men in the South Texas District however, so her dry spell was mostly her own fault, she just wasn't interested in any of the guys around here, she needed fresh meat. Nearly every supe she interacted with here was someone she'd known all her life and as a result, she knew way too much about them.

She pictured the warlock she'd met on the street and a little tingle erupted in her. Maybe she'd see him again, but if she did, he might be mad that she'd sent him on a wild goose chase. Not to mention she wasn't interested in being involved with whatever he wanted Moses for. The last thing she needed was a dangerous one-night stand. Her footsteps faltered as the idea of a little danger sent an unfamiliar thrill through her body.

Or maybe she did.

Sachi sighed heavily. She *was* half witch; it was in her DNA to love 'em and leave 'em. She hadn't done much of that in her life though, it was hard in a small community like theirs where everyone had an opinion about what everyone else did. But an out-of-town sexy supe who would want to be gone in the morning, that was sounding more and more perfect. She was starting to really regret sending him in the wrong direction.

"Oh look at her!" she heard a little human girl exclaim as a group of tourists walked down the steps of a well-known witchy gift shop.

Sachi smiled and waved. She was used to the attention, her coloring was always a favorite of human children.

"Mommy, what is she?"

"Oh, umm…" the mother said, obviously embarrassed by her child's curiosity.

Sachi just laughed and showed the child her cupcake box with the *Butterfly Kisses* emblem on it. A light pink and lavender butterfly sitting on top of a fancy-looking bright pink frosted cupcake. "I'm a butterfly and I like to bake delicious treats," she told the girl who promptly squealed with delight and demanded her mother take her to the bakery.

"Yes, I've heard of that place," one of the other tourists declared. "Delicious eclairs." She leaned close to the mother of the child and whispered, "And it's safe."

Sachi straightened from the crouch she'd been in to talk to the child. "Best around," she agreed, pretending she hadn't heard the whispered comment.

"Okay, Caroline, we'll stop by and bring something home with us, but you can't eat it until after dinner, you'll spoil yourself on all the sugar you've had today," the mother said.

"Enjoy the rest of your day, ladies," Sachi said to the group and hurried on down the street. She was glad her bakery had a good reputation with the tourists, she'd worked hard to change the image of the building to not resemble the bar it had once been.

Sachi walked up the steps of a two-story house with a little red sign out front that proclaimed *Penelope's Potions*. A sign hanging under it said *Closed*.

The grey front door had a shockingly bright pink and blue banner announcing that both a girl and a boy had arrived. It contrasted with the entire street and made Sachi laugh, witches went all out for births, it was one of the only times they used the colors light pink or baby blue.

Sachi knocked and opened the door without waiting for an answer. She'd gone to school with Penelope, and they were still good friends. Good enough that she was fairly sure the witch wouldn't throw a curse her way if she opened the door uninvited, but she still hesitated before stepping across the threshold. One thing you learned quickly in any district was that the threshold of a house was sacred and crossing one uninvited was not only bad manners but could lead to bad luck and curses too. Especially on Witch's Row.

"Pen?" she called softly, not wanting to be the cause of any waking babies.

"In here!" Penelope called from a hidden living room. "I hope you brought cupcakes; I'm starving."

Sachi hurried in, shutting the door behind her. She walked through the front room which was set up as a little store full of dried herbs, crystals, and mostly fake potions. A black cat was curled up on a bed atop the counter, he opened one green eye and looked at her judgmentally. "Good evening, Tom," she said to the cat. She didn't offer him a pat, he didn't like her and she'd been scratched more than once by the feline. "Of course I brought cupcakes, Fern decorated them with mauve and yellow since you had yourself a mix," she called into the house.

Sachi went through a door that said *Employees Only* and down a short hallway. This part of the house was Penelope's safe space and Sachi felt a shift in the air around her as she entered it. There was definitely a spell that separated the public space from the private. The air smelled different too, much more pungent in both magic and herb scents here.

Penelope was in a small living room, sitting on a couch with two babies in her arms and one in a bassinette at her feet. They were all sleeping, and they all looked exactly the same. Squishy and bald.

"Adorable!" Sachi squealed immediately, knowing it was her duty to delight over newborns, but in reality, she wasn't very impressed with infants. She liked when they got old enough to have personalities, but babies were just crying, pooping things that she didn't understand.

"Here take this one, I want a cupcake." Penelope held out an infant to Sachi.

Sachi took it and sat in a chair. "They're lemon lavender."

"My fave," Penelope gushed as she unwrapped one and began eating. She looked good for having given birth less than twenty-four hours ago. Her long black hair was freshly braided, and she was beaming with new mom glow which was a nice way of saying exhausted but happy about it.

"Who am I holding?"

"That's the boy, I'm calling him Johnny for now, but I might go with Dimitri instead."

Sachi couldn't help laughing at that, one name would help him blend with the humans outside of the district and the other would proclaim his supe status. "A warlock, huh?" Sachi touched his round cheek and felt his energy, it was so subtle, mostly feeling like Penelope's still, but it was there, a little touch of magic all his own. Similar to what she'd felt with the handsome stranger. Warlocks weren't as powerful as witches, the magic passed on the X chromosome so the males only got half a dose. That didn't mean they couldn't become powerful, it just meant they had to work harder at it, and most didn't. "I met a warlock today."

"Really? I didn't think any of the girls were entertaining this month, it's a bad moon for procreation you know."

Sachi didn't know, but she nodded agreement. She didn't track things that didn't apply to her, and children were nowhere in her near future. And having no boyfriend meant protection against children wasn't even a thought she needed to have. "He was on the street outside my shop, I gave him directions south."

"South?" Penelope asked with surprise. "He was looking for a werewolf den? This close to the full moon? Is he suicidal?"

Sachi shrugged and changed the subject, not wanting to admit she'd sent the poor guy on a wild goose chase. She asked about the birth and the other babies' names—both girls, Veronica, and Victoria. Penelope cheerfully told her every painful detail of the birth and admitted she hadn't called the father yet, but she would before they turned one, she assured Sachi. The intricacies of warlock/witch relationships were delicate. A warlock father could demand to take a son as soon as it came out of the womb and there wasn't much to stop him, so it wasn't unusual for the witch to not divulge the birthdate and sex of the children until the first birthday. Sachi looked down at the young warlock in her arms. He would probably leave the South Texas District within the year, and maybe never return. Sachi wanted to ask her friend how she felt about the coming loss of one of her children but didn't. It was the way things were, and talking about it wasn't going to make it less painful.

"Do you have someone coming to help you? Three's a lot."

"My mother hired a nanny. She's supposed to start tomorrow."

"What about tonight?"

"My sisters are coming over, we'll be fine." Penelope gave her a wide smile. "I know you want to run away; you can't fool me. Do you want to take some wolfsbane with you?"

"If you don't mind. I can run out back and pick it myself." Wolfsbane cookies were in high demand around the full moon, it kept the young werewolves from shifting before they were ready to handle themselves, and pregnant werewolves from shifting in the dangerous later months of pregnancy, so mothers flocked in to pick up cookies from her shop in the days leading up to it.

"Help yourself, you know where it is," Penelope said around a mouthful of cupcake.

"Thanks, I'll be right back," Sachi said and laid the little warlock down in a nearby bassinet before hurrying out back.

Penelope had an amazing witch's garden in the back of her house with herbs and medicinal plants, even some that Sachi knew were poisonous. Penelope shouldn't be growing them, it wasn't legal, but Sachi didn't care, she wasn't a snitch. They got more than stitches in The South Texas District, and anyway, even poisons had their place in spell-casting and strong medicines. Sachi went out and snipped a bundle of wolfsbane and some lavender, then headed back inside to say her goodbyes.

She couldn't stop herself from giving her opinion about the

names. "Veronica, Victoria and Johnny? Please, name the poor kid Dimitri, he'll thank you later."

Penelope laughed and said she'd consider the input. "My father's name is Dimitri I think, so it fits," she shrugged because not being sure of your father's name was normal for witches.

Sachi knew she'd been lucky, her own warlock father bucking tradition not only by having a child with a butterfly shifter, but also by continuing to live in the same district and playing a minor role in her life despite her being female. It had been a point of contention between her and the witches growing up, which was why she'd turned down the opportunities to study magic with them in school. Penelope had been the only witch who dared befriend her, at least until her father had died. Now the witches were all perfectly friendly. She supposed because they didn't see her as having something they didn't, any longer.

It also hadn't helped that in high school she'd been head cheerleader dating the captain of the football team. Witches weren't exactly full of school spirit, and they'd seen her as a stuck-up bitch. Maybe she had been, though she liked to think they'd been wrong in their assumptions.

CHAPTER 2

The sun had set by the time Sachi left Penelope's house and she walked back to the shop in the new dark. The streets were quiet in their in between time and no one stopped her along the way to chat. Human tourists were all gone for the day and the nighttime-loving supes hadn't yet emerged from their homes to do their daily activities.

Butterfly Kisses, like most shops in the district, was open to please the majority of customers both nocturnal and diurnal. For her, that meant she opened around eleven in the morning and closed a couple hours after sunset. She was lucky, she got to run a bakery without the godawful early hours that usually were associated with baking.

She hoped Fern had started the end of day clean-up tasks without her if they hadn't been too busy the last hour. Sachi was looking forward to laying down in her hot apartment and reading up on spells after work. Encountering that warlock today had given her the urge to cultivate that part of herself a bit. If she ever wanted to date one, she'd be horrified to admit how little she knew about that part of herself. She was too embarrassed to ask even Penelope for help learning. No witch worth her shit needed lessons in stirring spells at the age of twenty-eight.

When she walked into the bakery Sachi wasn't at all surprised to find that not only had Fern not yet started to clean up, but there were at least ten other fairies flitting around the shop, and she could smell something baking in the back. Her dream of an early night of reading was going up in smoke.

Sachi watched three of Fern's siblings pull a chocolate chip cookie from the case and drop it into a box on the floor. You'd think Fern would have had them size up to a more reasonable height before trying to help, but at least someone was watching the front of the shop while Fern was in back making a new mess.

"Sachi! We're helping," Fern's siblings said in unison as they dropped another cookie in the box.

"I see, try being bigger than the box, that would help," she said with a laugh and turned to the young vampire mother who was waiting patiently. "Good evening, Miranda. How are the kids?"

"It's Val's birthday tonight and he wanted your cookies. Wouldn't settle for anything less, the kid woke me up at three in the afternoon, he's so excited," she groaned. "I'm not sure how I'll make it through the party tonight without a nap."

"I'm glad he likes my cookies, next time tell him that I don't bake them until five, so no use getting up before then."

Miranda gave Sachi a thankful smile as she accepted the cookie box from a now three-foot-tall fairy girl. "You're welcome to come by tonight if you aren't busy. Val would love to see you and Stavros is going to be there."

"Oh, thanks," she said with a tight smile. She'd had a brief, hot, love affair with Miranda's brother, Stavros when he'd come to town for Miranda and Randy's wedding. Thinking that it was safe to have a couple night's stand with an out-of-town vampire. It had ended badly when he'd offered to move to this district and Sachi had shifted into a butterfly and flown out the window leaving her clothes and purse behind. He could have taken his bat form and chased her, but he hadn't, and he'd left town without telling his sister that she'd rejected him so harshly, which she appreciated.

"He's a nice guy," Miranda said seriously. "And still single. He'd love to see you."

"Oh," was all Sachi could say to that.

Miranda gave her a pleading look then waved and left.

"Fern!" Sachi yelled when the door closed behind Miranda. "What the hell are you cooking this late?"

"Seraphina got dumped," a three-inch fairy said as it flew up into her face and then away again.

"Great," Sachi grumbled as she went back into the kitchen.

"Oh, hey Sach," Fern said with an apologetic smile. "I just needed to cheer up Seraphina, she broke up with Franklin again."

"He told me my wings are fat!" Seraphina scream-cried as she stuffed a peanut butter cookie into her mouth. She'd grown to her full four feet and sat on the counter as Fern made a mess of the entire kitchen, baking peanut butter cookies and cupcakes with red and black frosting, apparently.

Seraphina had short red hair and bright pink wings. She was dressed in a black and white striped spandex minidress and knee-high black boots. Her makeup was running down her face and she looked like the most goth fairy Sachi had ever seen. Usually, fairies dressed in pastels and bright colors. Sachi was guessing this look had most to do with the species of Seraphina's boyfriend; vampires tended to wear leather and black everything.

"Well maybe dating a vampire is a bad idea," Sachi offered softly. She'd met the kid a couple times; he was captain of the basketball team and swim team, a real full-of-himself asshole. Maybe he'd grow out of his attitude, but she doubted it, most vampires thought pretty highly of themselves.

It was thought that butterfly shifters and vampires had some distant ancestor in common, somewhere along the evolutionary road they'd separated into two different species; those who sought the light and those who sought the dark. However, they both shifted into flying things and drank blood. Most vampires liked to pretend they were something completely different than butterfly shifters, but she didn't believe that.

Sachi dipped a finger into the black frosting waiting for the cupcakes. The sugar content immediately registered in her brain as if she'd already stuck it on her tongue. A fun little trick she got for being a butterfly shifter. "Why black? And it's over sweetened too."

"Don't eat that!" Fern yelled and grabbed her hand, forcing her finger away from her open mouth.

"What the hell?" Sachi hissed.

"These are for Franklin, revenge cupcakes," Fern explained.

"Revenge cupcakes?" She frowned at Fern, she could lose her business license if Fern was cooking up poison cupcakes in here.

"It's just a little something to give him the runs, don't worry, it won't kill him," Fern said with an eye roll.

"Right, nothing to worry about, just poisoning a minor is all," Sachi grumbled.

"*You* aren't doing anything," Fern said. "Seraphina is going to leave them in a plain box on his doorstep, he'll never know they were baked here."

"He better not," she snapped as she thoroughly washed her hands.

The sound of tiny fairies saying *oohh* at the front of the store had Sachi hurrying back to the front expecting a customer. She froze when she saw the tall, dark, and very handsome warlock standing at the counter with a look of frustration on his face.

"You," he accused, recognizing her right away. His face hardened into anger, and she felt her throat close a little.

"We're closed," she managed with confidence, as if she had no idea why he was upset with her. She pasted on a friendly smile and walked to flip the sign, it was early to close, but whatever he was here for, she didn't want another customer walking in on.

"Yeah, closed, magic boy," one of Fern's brothers said, flying up into the man's face without fear.

The stranger swatted at him. "I need Moses," he insisted angrily.

The entire store went silent as a tomb.

"Out! Everyone out," Fern ordered, coming out of the back, pushing all her siblings along. A swirl of colorful fairies erupted in the room and headed for the door. A few of Fern's brothers gave the warlock the most withering looks they could manage, at the size of seven inches or less. He didn't seem bothered by the show of threat, just watched with annoyed curiosity as they swooped and tittered and went out the door Fern held open. Seraphina in tears, clutching a box of poisoned cupcakes to her chest, was last to leave.

Fern turned when everyone else was outside. "Should I stay?" She asked, eyes flicking between Sachi and the stranger.

"No," Sachi said with a shake of her head. Something told her that tall, dark, and dreamy wasn't a threat to her. "Make sure no one sees Seraphina make her delivery," she said sharply.

"Call me," Fern ordered, then looked at the warlock, her silver eyes flashing with anger. "If anything happens to Sachi, I'll get Penelope to curse your balls."

"Yikes," the stranger said and put up his hands, then yelped and grabbed at his head.

One of Fern's brothers hadn't left, apparently, and he'd swooped down to pluck a hair from the warlock's head, adding credit to the threat of a spell. The tiny fairy boy was out the door before anyone could stop him and retrieve the hair. Fairies were hoarders by nature and Sachi was willing to bet that the boy would hold on to that hair for the rest of his life in case he ever needed to use it.

The warlock glared after the fairy, then spoke calmly to Fern. "I don't know Penelope, but I swear I mean Ms. Mercher no harm, I just need to speak with her father."

Fern nodded and left.

It took Sachi by surprise to hear him call her Ms. Mercher. She covered it by moving back to the kitchen, she had a lot of clean-up to do, and now with no help.

The man followed as she'd assumed he would.

"So apparently you know who I am," she began as the door that separated the kitchen from the storefront swung closed behind him. "But you have yet to introduce yourself," Sachi accused and started gathering up the dirty dishes.

"My name is Jax Lintel," he said as if it should mean something to her.

"Never heard of him," she was happy to admit and raised an eyebrow at Jax. "My father is dead though, so you're out of luck."

"I'm sorry to hear that," he said with a flat tone and a pass of something angry on his face that he quickly covered. "That does change things a bit," he mumbled. "I suppose. You must be in charge then?"

"I own the bakery, inherited from him. I can't see how you'd need me for anything you thought you were coming to see Moses for, but if you insist on staying to chat, you can help me clean since you scared away the twits who made this mess." She eyed him sideways and appreciated him all over again as she set a stack of dishes in the sink. She was still trying to decide if she thought he'd be a good one night stand choice.

Jax was a sexy male with his touch of brooding and mysterious, even an edge of danger. It was too bad he was obviously into something dumb and illegal. She let out a little sigh as she set a pile of mixing bowls next to the sink. Probably not a good one night stand choice.

"Are you in the habit of poisoning your customers?" he asked, holding up a bottle of laxative Fern had obviously used in the cupcake frosting.

"Only ex boyfriends," she said with a grin. "How did you know I was Moses' daughter?"

"When I figured out that this was actually the place I was looking for, I assumed the cute little vixen who'd sent me to the middle of werewolf territory must be connected to Moses, and when you were here, I connected the obvious dots." He winked at her, and she felt a little thrill crawl up her spine.

The reaction surprised her, she didn't usually go for that kind of male bravado.

"But you're not a witch," he continued thoughtfully. "You don't smell like magic and your look is..." he dropped his gaze over her pink and white striped sundress. "Not witch," he finished with a laugh.

She laughed too, because he was right, she didn't dress like the witches. She preferred light colors and a little frill even. She was a creature of the sun and air and she embraced it. "What *do* I smell like?" she asked, wondering if he could pinpoint it. A lot of people couldn't if they'd never met a butterfly shifter. They weren't common to all districts, especially if he was from a northern one, he might have a hard time. Butterfly shifters were not cold weather supes.

His dark eyes swept up and down her body again, making her heat a bit under his scrutiny, but she'd asked for it. He leaned close and inhaled deeply. His eyes drifted closed, and his lips parted slightly. It was a very intimate gesture, and she felt her body lean toward him involuntarily. Her eyes locked on his parted lips, and she found herself wondering what they tasted like. Her tongue dipped out and wet her own lips in anticipation. His gaze locked onto the gesture then back to meet her eyes.

"Sugar, vanilla, and cinnamon," he said softly, each syllable pushing his breath toward her nose and filling her with the scent of him, all magic and male.

She bit her lip to keep herself from groaning. She liked his scent, a lot.

"I'm guessing that's from your bakery," he continued. "Lavender and wolfsbane, also probably the bakery. You're not a fairy, too tall, and your eyes aren't silver. I spotted a sharp tooth in there, but you were out in the daylight. Your purple hair must be natural because your eyebrows match." He pulled on a strand and lifted it to his nostrils, inhaling. "Pollen and blood. The only creature that smells like that is a butterfly shifter. You're a rare creature."

She smiled wide and nodded, feeling lightheaded at the small contact. She wanted him to wrap his hand in her hair and tug her head back, attack her mouth with his and... fuck, she had to stop those thoughts before she jumped him right there. Maybe it had been way too long since she'd gotten laid, and her body had decided to take its care and keeping into its own hands. Her thoughts briefly turned to Cash, but she pushed them away, that was a complication she didn't need. But this man, he smelled like magic and male, and it made her insides twist in the most delightful way. He was just passing through, that was as uncomplicated as it could get.

"Of course I guessed that from the name of your bakery, your delightful scent only confirmed my suspicions," he added with a sly grin.

She stepped back, cheeks reddening at the compliment and wiped the counter again. "My mother is a butterfly shifter. I take after her mostly." She turned back and gave him a little smile, hoping he couldn't read the lust in her eyes.

His gaze dipped to her mouth, and she smiled wider, flashing her fangs. He didn't look intimidated, interested maybe, or was that just her hopeful thinking?

"Half butterfly shifter and half witch," he mused. "I knew Moses had a child, but I didn't realize he'd chosen outside his species for the mother. I suppose I should have guessed, otherwise he never would have been allowed to remain in the same district."

Her mind flipped back to why he was here, and she clamped her lips shut. She needed to remember that this guy was bad news. "I am not into whatever you think my father was into." Her father had been a good man, but he'd run a bar and he drank too much. Rumors were rampant that he dealt in black magic deals from the basement, but she tried not to listen to those. He'd been a decent father for a warlock and that's all that mattered now that he was gone. Jax looked at her questioningly but didn't say anything. "Ms. Pearl," she added when the silence stretched too long.

"Who?"

"I'm not Ms. Mercher, I'm Ms. Pearl, Sachi Pearl. I never took his name." She shrugged. She'd been lucky he was in the same town as her and took a minor interest in her, but she wouldn't go as far as saying they were close, and he'd obviously not cared enough when she was born to insist on her taking his name. When she'd gotten a knock on her door at eighteen telling her he was dead and she was the proud owner of *Moses' Bar*, she was sad, but not surprised and honestly, she hadn't spoken to him in weeks before that. She scrunched up her nose as she tried to recall what her last interaction with him had been. It was all fuzzy in her head now and she got a prickling at the base of her skull as if her mind was fighting her effort to remember.

"How long has he been dead?"

"Ten years, and if he owed you money or something, I'm not taking responsibility. You're shit out of luck because other than this building, he didn't leave me any inheritance. I don't sell black magic, and I'm not interested in buying anything you're selling."

Silence met her words. She washed and rinsed, wondering what he was thinking, why he was here, and how soon before he would leave?

"You don't smell like magic," he finally said.

"Didn't we already establish that?"

"You're not practicing?"

"Nope."

"Why?" he demanded, the level of concern in his tone confused her.

She paused and looked at him, now really annoyed. "I don't know who the fuck you are or why you're here, but I don't owe you one damn explanation. I may not cast spells, but I know how to throw a punch."

He didn't look concerned with her threat, and she was regretting telling Fern to leave. If he was a practiced warlock, he could nail her ass to the wall with barely a thought, not to mention the fact that he was a fit male, and she was an average strength female. She wouldn't be able to defend herself from him easily. She could turn into a butterfly in an instant and try to fly faster than he could spell, but she didn't really want to take that chance. She put her hands into the bubbly water and gripped a spatula, maybe she could smack him with it.

"I think you are going to need my help," he finally said with a sigh.

She was surprised by that. "I'm not into whatever my father was into," she said again firmly. "Whatever you heard about *Moses' Bar*, just forget it. It was all lies anyway," she said softly. "It was just a bar; he was just a drunk and I certainly don't need your help with anything."

She hated being reminded of what people had thought of him, she tried to remember her father picking her up on the occasional Sunday morning and taking her for ice cream, going to the park and fishing in the river. He'd tried to teach her to fight when she was a teen, because he said she looked too delicate. She had all her mother's butterfly features. She supposed he was mostly right, the only thing she'd inherited from him were the thick red lips. Her nose was small, her eyes were big and blue, she had pale skin that held a sort of internal sparkle which kept her away from much makeup. Overall, not very threatening.

"Your father was thought to be a very great man," he said, but something in his tone made her think he didn't agree with those who thought it.

Sachi turned to give him a sardonic look, "No one thought that." Maybe he wanted to seduce her before he headed out of the district. That thought made her belly warm and her annoyance and anger started to shift back to desire. Maybe she wanted to let him.

A look of confusion took over his features. "What did you know of your father's work?"

"He owned a bar, and I turned it into a bakery when I inherited it."

Jax shook his head, his dark hair catching the light as it moved. It was nearly black, but not quite and she liked the way it laid in a messy careless fashion around his face. "You inherited more than that." He narrowed his eyes on her, boring into her with intensity as his next words filled the space between them. "This is the Portal Keeper's house."

CHAPTER 3

Sachi pursed her lips and raised one eyebrow. He was insane, of course he was insane because a normal cute warlock looking for a good time couldn't have possibly stumbled into her life. "I think it's time for you to leave." She might be able to overlook, even embrace, the danger of a black magic warlock for a night or two of fun, but a psychopath who believed in portals, not so much.

Jax took a deep breath and gave her a serious look. He moved into a wide stance and put his hands on his hips, obviously trying to give off the impression that he knew what the hell he was talking about and stating that he had no intention of leaving. "My predecessor worked closely with your father, even assisted in keeping this Hell portal closed ten years ago."

She started to laugh, a little hysterical maybe, but it was better than thinking too much about the insane man she was alone with. "Okay, there were definitely some crazy rumors that went around about my father, but a portal to Hell, that's a bit out there, don't you think?"

He scoffed at her. "Where do *you* think this district's Hell portal is?" he snapped.

"This district doesn't have a Hell portal why the—well—why

the *hell* would there be a Hell portal here?" She threw her hands up in exasperation.

His face creased into a look of concern. He opened his mouth, then closed it and cocked his head. He stared at her unspeaking for long enough to make her nervous.

"Your father was Moses Mercher?"

"Yes," she said with a barely disguised *duh.* "We covered this already."

"And he owned this building, which was a bar, *Moses' Bar*?"

"Obviously. A bar, nothing more. He was a warlock and a mostly absent father. He was known to drink too much and rumors about black magic went around town though I don't give them much credit. No portals to Hell have ever been mentioned, no dealing with demons."

A look of great concern came over his face as he considered her words. When he spoke his words were careful and slow as if he were speaking to someone he thought was a complete idiot. "Each one of these districts is really just a safely guarded portal and the supes who live in the district are tasked with protecting it."

She glared at him and spoke back with the same slow, *you're an idiot* tone. "What are you talking about?"

"How do you not know this?" he snapped.

"Am I being punked right now? Is a camera crew about to jump out of the oven?"

He shook his head and ran a hand through his hair. "Unfortunately, I am completely serious, but…" he paused and looked her up and down again, this time there was no appreciation in his gaze, just calculation. "How long have you lived in this district? Are you, well… are you allowed to be alone? Do I need to call someone to come pick you up? Does your mother take care of you?"

She narrowed her eyes and jabbed a wet and soapy spatula in his direction, tired of his attitude and crazy claims. "I've lived here all my life and being alone is fine. I'm not some kind of simpleton, though I'm starting to wonder what hospital *you* escaped from." She dropped the spatula in the sink and lemon scented bubbles splashed up on her. She wiped at them angrily.

"Are you fucking kidding me? How did your father not explain? He was a Keeper, for God's sake." Jax snapped back. "Every other district is very aware of their true purpose and your father was in charge of the South Texas portal. It is here in this building, it has to be, and it's almost time to do the closing spell."

Sachi had heard enough, she shoved at his chest, catching him off guard and getting him to step back. "You need to leave. I don't have time for this shit. I'm tired and hot and look at this fucking mess I still have to clean up." She pushed on his chest again, but he didn't budge. She knew a couple self-defense spells and she started to call magic to her hands, she could stun him enough to give him pause if she had to.

His face was stoic, his tone determined. "Where's the basement?"

"Excuse me?" She took a step back.

"Show me the basement, I'll prove it to you."

"Right, like I'm going to walk down into a basement with a stranger whose obviously some kind of fanatical. Do I look like a big breasted cheerleader in a slasher movie?"

His eyes looked her up and down and he raised an eyebrow. "Well, not the big breasted part, no, but I can definitely see you with a couple pompoms and a short skirt." His lips quirked up and his eyes slid half closed as if he were imagining just that and he liked what he saw.

"Go team," she hissed, not letting his sexy charm trick her into making stupid decisions.

He sighed and crossed his arms over his chest. "Either take me to the basement or I will find it myself." He shrugged. "I am not leaving, Sachi, I have an obligation here and even if you don't help, I'm going to make sure the portal stays closed. I'm going to make sure the people of this district stay safe. Then I'm going to put someone in charge here who knows what the fuck is going on." His tone was serious, his voice stern and it definitely felt like a threat.

She narrowed her eyes at him and crossed her arms over her chest. Why the hell did she want to believe him? She hoped it wasn't because of his cute face and wide shoulders, because she could find that lots of places and it wouldn't involve possibly falling into the hands of a serial killer or escaped mental patient.

"Fine," she snapped and started for the basement, annoyed with herself. She called a little magic to her palm, she could jolt him, she could bite him, and she could shift and fly away, she wasn't completely helpless, she reminded herself.

Jax followed but he didn't crowd her, and she appreciated it. No doubt he could sense the magic she was holding; a smart warlock wouldn't get close to the promise of a strong jolt from a witch. She wondered if she should alert the police to his insanity once she proved him wrong. Probably he shouldn't be wandering around the district if he was this delusional.

"Where?" she demanded as they reached the cluttered basement. She'd moved everything of her father's from the bar and apartment above it, down here, unable to bring herself to just toss it even though she hadn't touched it in at least nine years. She looked around with a sigh, knowing it needed to be taken care of, but she didn't come down here often, so it was easy to forget about it all. This one last connection to the father she had so few memories of, it was silly to keep it.

Jax picked his way carefully around the piles of boxes. "A Keeper was picked for each portal; the honor is usually inherited by their children. Their job is to stop the portal from opening on its ten-year cycle and monitor for disturbances. The rest of the supes in the district are there to support, to keep humans from discovering what we're hiding, and since we all came out to the humans it was basically demanded of us to contain ourselves anyway, so this arrangement made sense."

Sachi was following him now, trying not to admire his tight ass in his jeans. "Then why hasn't anyone ever mentioned it?"

"I don't know," he admitted grudgingly. "There is something strange going on in this district." He paused and looked at a drain on the floor. "What's that?"

"That would be in case the basement floods," she didn't add the *obviously*, but it was there in her tone.

Jax snorted and kneeled near the small drain grate. He reached out and touched it with one finger. The world shifted around them, the floor shivered and lit up with a bright gold light. The small drain was suddenly a gaping hole shimmering with white light rimmed in red.

"—the fuck?" Sachi let out on a breath.

"This is a portal, and it is not fully closed like it should be," he said in a serious tone. "The white light is us, warlock energy sealing it in place, the red is leaking demon energy and it means something definitely could have escaped." He turned to look at Sachi, his face stone cold and unreadable. "This is bad and probably why you don't seem to know that it's the only reason this district exists."

"What? No, that's not possible," Sachi said, incredulous, she didn't want to believe what she was seeing.

He sighed dramatically and motioned to the pool of light. "Take a look, Sachi, this is not normal." He said it as if she were an idiot and it pissed her off.

But she had to admit there was something weird going on and an odd prickling in the back of her mind told her she needed to remember something. She stared down at the floor and forced her mind back, tried to think of any time her father had mentioned a portal of any kind. She came up blank, not just that she couldn't remember him saying anything, it was something more. It was as if there were holes in her memory, she could remember her father, looking up at him from the kitchen table and him talking to her mother about something important and then... nothing, the memory completely cut out. "My memories have been tampered with," she whispered.

"I'm starting to think so, too," Jax said, "And not just yours unfortunately, I think the entire district might have been spelled to forget about the portal and the possibility of demons." Jax stood up and waved his hand. Just like that, the floor was back to normal.

"I've walked over that thing a million times, why didn't I fall in?"

"It's partially closed, that helps, but also the glamour that hides it from the eye is strong enough for your feet to believe it. You won't fall through if you don't know it's there." He tapped his head. "The power of suggestion is a strong magic. I suggest avoiding it now, at least until we get it closed fully."

"I'll put up a sign," she said dumbly. "I'll remind everyone that there's a portal to Hell in the basement so it's a no-fly zone," she said with a little hysterical laugh and covered her mouth with a hand as panic started to spiral through her.

"I'm afraid it's a little more complicated than that. The only thing that has enough power to make an entire district forget what it's here to do, is a very powerful demon and it must still be close. We need to find it and make sure no others have escaped. Sachi, where was your father killed, and when exactly?"

"Ten years ago this month, right here actually," she said with a frown. She didn't like where this was going.

He looked at her with a touch of sympathy. "I think whatever came out of that portal last, killed your father."

His words made her head spin, it was all too much. "I need a cookie," she said with a tight smile and walked upstairs.

She had shoved three peanut butter cookies into her mouth before she was ready to turn and face him again. He was sitting on a stool, watching her with an intensity that made her uncomfortable.

She wrapped her arms around herself as she took a steadying breath. "My father died in a drunken stupor, bashed over the back of the head by someone trying to rob him," she whispered. "He was a good man, but he owned a bar and his clientele wasn't exactly the most honest." She repeated the well-known history.

"Or is that just the story the demon wanted you to believe?" Jax stood and walked over to her. He lifted a hand and wiped a crumb from her face with his thumb. The sensation of his caring touch sent a tingle through her, like a tiny electric shock. "Sachi, your father was an extremely respected man in the supernatural community. He was no drunk and he wasn't into black magic, except where the portal was concerned. If that story is what everyone around here believes, then I can understand why you worked so hard to change the image here." His words were full of empathy, and it made her heart squeeze. "No wonder I got such odd looks and dismissive replies whenever I asked about him. Everyone probably assumed the worst about me just for asking. You must have thought I was after something nefarious and that's why you sent me to werewolf territory."

She didn't know what to say, it was a nice story and she wanted to believe him, well, except for the whole portal to Hell thing. She definitely did *not* want a portal to Hell in her basement, would that be some kind of health code violation? Would she lose her license to sell to humans? Her father had never had one, the bar had been for supes only, was that why? She shook her head, because that was the least of her worries at the moment and although she should be focusing on the fact that there was a portal to Hell in her basement she was stuck on the fact that her father wasn't what she thought she remembered.

She looked up into Jax's kind, dark eyes and saw a truth there that tugged at something deep within her. "Truly?" She wanted more than anything to believe him, needed it so much it hurt. "My father was a good man in charge of something important?"

Something angry flashed in his eyes so fast she wasn't sure she actually saw it. "It's the story I was told. I never met him, but I have to believe that my predecessor was telling the truth when he spoke of the great man who guards the South Texas portal."

She looked at him pleadingly and felt a little sting in her eyes. "Well fuck," Sachi whispered and cleared the emotion from her throat. "What do we do now?"

Jax smiled and touched her chin gently. For a moment she thought he was going to lean down and kiss her. The space between them was intense and they were alone in the quiet of the evening. It would have been a perfect opportunity and she wouldn't have stopped him. He dropped his hand and stepped away, leaving her disappointed and cold.

"I'm going to make some calls and look around the district tonight. We'll talk tomorrow and figure this out."

He handed her a card with his cell number on it, then left without another word, leaving her confused and overwhelmed. She stared at the door to the basement and shivered. A portal to Hell… in her basement.

"What is going on?" she whispered, wishing her father was here more than she ever had in the last ten years.

CHAPTER 4

Sachi changed quickly into white jeans and a pink tank top, deciding she would attend Val's birthday party after all. She had a present ready for him but hadn't planned to attend, and face Stavros. She didn't want to be alone in the shop right now though, not after Jax's revelations. She locked up, giving an extra careful look at the shadows inside as she did so. Was there something creeping in there, or was it her overactive imagination? She stared harder and double checked the lock, as if that would stop a demon, and did she want to lock it in or out, she wasn't sure.

"What are you looking at?"

She jumped and screamed at the voice, twirling around so fast she nearly fell over. "What the fuck is wrong with you?" she hissed at Lance.

The vampire just laughed. "Sorry, I was coming to grab Fern, but it seems she's already gone for the night." He was dressed in typical vamp style; black leather pants and a black t-shirt, motorcycle boots and two belts with far too many buckles. He looked like he belonged to a motorcycle gang with his tattooed neck and arms, lots of silver jewelry and big strong hands. Sachi knew he was actually a very intelligent, very kind and gentle, respected scientist in the district despite what he looked like.

"Oh, yeah, she was helping Seraphina with something." She didn't want to tell him that they were currently trying to give Seraphina's ex a bad case of indigestion. "She's probably back at the home tree by now though. I'm heading over to Miranda's for Val's party."

"Cool, I'll go see if she's home then. Tell Val I said happy birthday."

"I will."

Lance walked off toward the eastside and Sachi headed south. The South Texas district was laid out with mini pockets of neighborhoods harboring each species. It had been designed by a human, despite the lie she'd told Jax earlier about the gnomes, and not originally intended to keep the species separate, but they preferred to be mostly surrounded by their own kind. The main strip was in the middle of town, with the road that led from the river, where a nice park ran the length of the bank. The road ran all the way east through a mostly empty mile of desert area to the district line. This kept the flow of tourist traffic safest. To the north was Witch's Row and farther north was a wooded area where most of the fae creatures took up habitation, also a few nymphs, elves, and a troll. South of the main strip was the vampire quarters and below that were the werewolf dens. To the north-east, between the witches and the nymphs were small neighborhoods for other shifters or those who didn't quite fit elsewhere, this is where Sachi and Fern had grown up.

Compartmentalized, that's how she would describe it. It made keeping order easy since each subset of the district policed their own for the most part. Though there was a local law enforcement of course, they mostly only stepped in when a tourist became involved in an incident or if one species had a problem with another.

Overall it was a safe place to be, especially if you were a supe, and she'd never felt like her life was in danger, had never hesitated to walk around at night or be alone. She didn't intend to start now.

As she walked through the streets toward Miranda's house she started to relax, everything looked as it always had. Jax was probably insane and there was really no proof that he was here for the reason he said he was.

The image of the floor opening up to a gaping glowing hole floated into her mind and she shook it off. That could have been an illusion, a good warlock could spin a great one and she *was* caught off guard. She could have just missed the telltale signs due to her overactive libido wanting him to not be insane and wanting to believe that her father wasn't just a drunk warlock who got bashed on the back of the head.

Never in her life had she been ruled by her libido or distracted by a male to that extent though, and she doubted that was the case now. But what about the gaps that appeared in her memories any time she tried to think about her father? It was hard to explain those away as libido-induced.

By the time she reached Miranda's house she had swung back to thinking it had to all be true and they were all truly fucked because she had no idea how to stop a Hell portal from opening up. That seemed like something a professional should be in charge of. She was barely a witch.

"Sachi!" Val screamed from the front porch. He was adorable, dressed in a Dracula costume with cookie crumbs all over his face. "Your cookies are the best! But Mom says I have to share them with everyone," he grumbled.

She laughed and crouched down to get on eye level with the boy. He threw his arms around her neck and breathed hot cookie breath in her face.

"I brought you a present, sorry it's not wrapped."

"Cool!" He jumped back and snatched the present then ran away to show it off, or maybe sneak more cookies.

She watched him go with a knot in her stomach. He was just a child, and if demons escaped from Hell, they could do horrible things to him and all the kids in this district, maybe even beyond. What would stop them from moving into human territory and other districts? They could take over the world! Panic overwhelmed her. She thought of Penelope's triplets and her gut twisted even more. Innocents that had no way to protect themselves were at risk.

"Fuck," she whispered and pulled out her phone. She shot off a text to Jax.

> Finding anything? This is Sachi.

"Are you going in?" Val asked, reappearing on the front porch.

She tucked the phone away. She would join the celebration and hopefully forget the possibilities of doomsday for a little while.

The party was loud, kids swirled around her, playing some sort of game that involved half of them pretending to be dead and spasming on the floor dramatically. Most were vampire children, but a few werewolves were there too. It didn't look like any of the witches had been invited, but that didn't surprise Sachi, they'd never come to her birthday parties either.

"I'm glad you could make it," Miranda said, coming up and giving her a quick hug. "Can I get you a drink? Randy's making bloody marys in the kitchen." She looked exhausted but she sounded happy and Sachi hugged her back.

"That would be great." Sachi weaved through the rushing kids and to the kitchen where the adults had mostly congregated.

"Sachi," Randy called as she came in. "Your cookies were a hit, as always."

"There are so many kids," she said with a laugh.

He nodded and handed her a drink. "This will help."

She took a sip, the real blood in it had her fangs tingling. It wasn't fresh, but it was still delicious mixed like this. "It's great." There was a legal blood supply that came into the district from human donors; it was bagged, and it was cold. No bloodsucking creature really enjoyed it as an alternative to hot from the source, but it was decent for this sort of thing, and it would keep you alive. The illusion of it kept the humans feeling safe and that's what it was really about.

"Thanks. Stavros is around here somewhere," he said excitedly. "He was hoping to see you."

"Mmm," she said noncommittally and took another sip, then changed the subject quickly to how Val was doing on the nighttime soccer team.

Randy happily launched into detail about how Val performed in his last game and Sachi listened with half attention. Stavros joined them after a few minutes with a warm smile and a too-friendly hug of greeting. She pulled away quickly and gave him nothing to misinterpret. A quick look of disappointment crossed his face, but he seemed to accept that she wasn't interested and kept things friendly from there, asking her about the bakery. She replied briefly and reciprocated the question, remembering he was some kind of salesman. He started talking about his job with enthusiasm, he sold mattresses over in the Mid Californian District.

She couldn't stop worrying about everyone's happy little existence being destroyed, so she excused herself from the group when he paused and she walked to a quiet part of the kitchen where she could pull out her cell. Nothing.

"You waiting for a boy to get back to you?"

She startled a bit and looked up to find the dark eyes of a werewolf. Tate was grinning at her and cocking an eyebrow.

"No, just worried about a friend." She'd known Tate all her life, they'd gone to school together, run in the same circles since she'd dated his packmate, Cash. He'd even tried to date her when her and Cash were on the outs, but she'd never been interested.

"No boyfriend?" He said with a wide smile and reached out to touch her waist suggestively.

"You'd know if I was dating anyone, this district is small as shit," Sachi said with a flirty smile. The alcohol in the bloody mary might be getting to her head. She took another sip anyway, letting the familiar taste of blood and vodka roll around her mouth. She needed to feed for real, soon. Tate was tall and broad, his shirt tonight was a flannel left unbuttoned halfway down and showing off a lot of tan skin.

"True. So," he said stepping closer so his body heat started to brush against her, "wanna get out of here?"

It was tempting, she could forget her worries and bite into him ferociously, no attachment, just let him satisfy all of her physical needs for a moment. Cash's face flitted through her mind, and she knew she'd never go through with it. She may not still be dating Cash but the thought of him finding out she'd slept with one of his packmates made her uncomfortable. A buzzing in her pocket gave her the excuse she needed to step away and put distance between herself and Tate. He looked disappointed as she pulled her phone out and frowned at the message.

Is that your boyfriend?

"What the fuck," she hissed and darted her eyes around, spotting Jax on the other side of the kitchen with a beer in his hand.

She bared her teeth at him and stalked across the room. Luckily a group of werewolf kids pretending to be vampires and groaning for *blood, blood!* Kept her from shouting at the idiot. She was at a kid's birthday party, no place for a yelling match. She was calm by the time she reached Jax.

"What are you doing here?" she demanded.

"I was walking by, and someone invited me in."

"Someone?"

He shrugged and sipped the beer.

"You know this guy, Sachi?" Tate asked, coming up behind her and putting a hand on her waist again.

"Tate, this is Jax, Jax, this is Tate."

They eyeballed each other the way men do when trying to size each other up and shook hands briefly.

Sachi rolled her eyes at the macho display of quiet aggression.

"I didn't think the witches were entertaining this month, or are you here for Penelope's boy?" Tate asked. Sachi didn't miss the hint of annoyance in Tate's tone, and she wondered if he had a thing for the witch.

"No, I'm here for Sachi," he said with a grin.

Tate growled low and Sachi elbowed him in the stomach as she glared at Jax.

"He's an old friend in town for a visit. Why don't you go away before Cash shows up and kicks your ass," she snapped at Tate.

He huffed. "Cash is still in trouble; he can't show up." But he walked away anyway.

Sachi hated to use the threat, but Cash was a strong werewolf and he still felt possessive enough over Sachi to keep the other wolves away most of the time. She didn't think he'd actually step between her and someone she wanted to date or mess around with, but she had never pressed the issue either, she just couldn't do that to him.

"Cash?" Jax asked when Tate was gone.

"Don't worry about it. Did you figure out anything while you skulked around the district, or were you too distracted by the lure of kids' birthday parties?"

Jax laughed and the sound surprised Sachi, it was so light and free, such a contrast to the seriousness of the situation he said they were in. It lit up his face in a delightful way too, and she found herself wishing she could make him laugh more.

"Sachi, who's your friend?" Miranda asked, sweeping into the room with an armful of crumpled wrapping paper.

"This is Jax, an old family friend."

"Welcome, Jax, I hope you don't mind a little noise," Miranda said.

"Not at all, this is great, reminds me of growing up. I had a large family."

Miranda smiled and hurried off to throw away the wrapping paper carnage and Sachi smiled at Jax. "That was sweet of you to lie."

He shrugged. "I may have been an only child, but I always wanted lots of siblings. The noise of happy children is definitely not a bother."

Most witches weren't from large families, especially the males because once a father took on a young one, they rarely went back to another witch to try for more.

Sachi met Stavros' questioning eyes across the room, and he looked like he was about to come over and ask if Jax was her boyfriend. She didn't want another delusional male interaction, so she grabbed Jax's arm and started to lead him out of the room. "Let's go outside and talk." The feel of his arm in hers was surprisingly easy and nice, like they fit together, and it was so disconcerting she dropped it as soon as she got him out the door. She led Jax to a fence and leaned against it, watching the kids run in circles. The vampire children pretended to be wolves and the werewolf children pretended to be bats, it was all great fun by the sounds of it.

It made Sachi's stomach clench. "If what you say is true, these children are in danger," she whispered.

"Serious danger," he agreed quietly.

"Look, Miss Sachi, I got it to fly!" Val said as he threw the toy plane she'd brought him in the air and it swirled and swooped as it floated to the ground.

"That's great," she said, her voice thick with emotion.

"We can stop it; I just need your help." Jax's voice was reassuring and urgent.

She looked at him pleadingly, knowing she'd do anything he

asked if it meant these kids were allowed to grow up safe and happy. "How?"

"I need you to remember. I am sure your father was teaching you to take over. He had no other children and a Portal Keeper's duty is to teach their child how to perform the spell."

"But how do I remember it? How did I even forget?" It felt impossible.

He reached out and touched her face gently. "If I knew that, we'd already be doing it," he laughed.

"Maybe we need a spell? Some kind of memory unlocking spell?" She would bet Penelope's coven could come up with something like that.

"If it's a demon curse that is blocking the memories, a witch's spell isn't going to bring them back. We need to kill the demon to break his spell."

"Kill a demon?" she gasped. "How the hell do we do that? Where would we even find the demon?"

He shrugged as if it weren't an enormous task he'd just laid out. "We find it. A demon can't be living out in the open without leaving signs, a trail of bodies most likely and I bet it's still in the area. Then we kill it."

"Just like that," she mumbled. That didn't comfort her at all. She stepped away from the warmth of his body, it clouded her judgement to be so close to him. Her body found him way too attractive, and her mind didn't fight very hard to deny the fact that it agreed entirely.

She cleared her throat awkwardly, hoping he didn't notice the flush of her cheeks or the hitch in her breathing when he accidentally brushed up against her while lifting his beer to his lips. Lips that she wanted to reach out and touch, they looked so soft and kissable.

She forced her eyes away, back to the kids playing. "So why aren't you out there looking for it?"

"I was, but then I spotted you in there." He pointed to the kitchen window where he must have seen her.

"You're stalking me?"

"Like I said, I was just strolling by. Figured it was easier to talk than text."

She didn't think she believed that. "Why don't you get back to your search. Let me know in the morning if you find anything."

He hopped over the fence and leaned back over it so that his face was close to hers. "Sachi, if you really want to help keep these innocents safe, your head has to be in it. I need you to work to remember. Search that pretty little brain of yours. The demon can hide your memories, he can't erase them. I don't know how much you may have forgotten, but it's probably only what relates to what the demon wanted to hide."

"The portal," she said.

"Yeah, so your father, the existence of the portal, any training he might have given you, and whatever else might have related to those things are likely skewed in your memory now. If you can remember on your own, we don't have to hunt and kill a demon." He winked at her and turned.

She frowned at his back as he walked away. How was she supposed to work on remembering? Where did she even start? The possibilities of her entire lifetime of memories being skewed by a demon curse made her head spin.

"Is that your boyfriend?" Val asked.

"No, just a friend."

"My mom always gets mad when my dad walks away," he said calmly then ran off.

Sachi barely held back a laugh, kids were so innocent, so truthful.

Her mood was thoroughly shot. She finished her drink, thanked Miranda for the invite, avoided Stavros *and* Tate, then headed back to her apartment over the bakery ready to sleep and hope she woke up with this all having been a bad dream.

She stood on the dark street, and supes passing by to go about their nightly routines greeted her. She stared into the *Butterfly Kisses Bakery* and frowned at the darkness. She didn't want to go in there alone and that pissed her off. She'd always felt safe in there, had felt close to her father in there. Now it was full of dark corners and questionable shadows.

Hating that she felt so chickenshit, she got into her car and drove to her mother's house.

CHAPTER 5

"Why are you out here so late?" her mother, Helen, asked as Sachi walked into the familiar living room. She loved being in her mother's house. It was so light and airy with its large windows and so many plants. Her mother had always had a lot of plants in the house. Butterfly shifters were partial to plant life and whenever Sachi shifted, she always took time to wander through a few flowers drinking nectar and gathering sweet pollen onto her body. As a child she had often spent nights sleeping in an open flower in the summertime and with Fern being so small, she'd been able to share a petal from time to time as well.

Sachi felt the weight of her day start to slide off as she was welcomed into her mother's warm embrace. "Just too hot above the bakery. So I thought I'd sleep here tonight if that's okay?"

Her mother gave her a doubtful look but nodded. "Of course, you know you're welcome any time, I keep your room fresh just in case."

Helen hadn't changed a thing in the last ten years actually, and Sachi welcomed the familiarity more than usual. Though now it was tainted by a touch of doubt. Was the memory of her child-hood just a fabrication of some demon curse? If she had forgotten about a portal and her father's real job, what else had she forgotten? How much of her life was a lie?

Sachi looked at her mother and tried to remember anything about the portal or demons, but how do you press yourself to remember something that you have no idea if you really knew in the past or not? She didn't want to freak her mother out, so she didn't say anything, didn't ask if she knew there was a portal to Hell in the bakery basement, or if she knew her father had been some kind of guardian of that portal.

"You look nice," Sachi said instead, noticing her mother was dressed for a night out. Despite the lateness of the evening, the district didn't really close down. Vampires and werewolves did a lot of business at night, they were less involved with the tourist trade and more into running the town for the other supes.

"I have a date," she said with a slight flush. Helen was beautiful in her old age, long grey hair that still held a hint of the dark purple it had once been. Her skin still glowed with a sparkle that indicated her butterfly shifter status and since she worked out consistently, she was still in decent shape too.

"Oh, anyone I know?" Sachi asked with a touch of sarcasm, she knew everyone in this town.

"Victor Marlen."

Sachi recognized the name, he was a vampire, had taught biology to the night classes at the high school. A nice man, older than her mother, but only slightly, and handsome in a silver fox sort of way.

"I thought you were seeing Brandon."

"Oh, yeah, I saw him last night," her mother said as if it didn't matter in the slightest that she was currently dating more than one gentleman. Sachi wondered if the gentlemen knew about it, but she didn't want to ask. Her mother's love life was definitely none of her business. And she tried not to be jealous that her mother had twice as much action as herself, currently.

It had always surprised Sachi that her mother hadn't ever

married. Her parents had never been married, which was typical for a warlock, but butterfly shifters were a little more settled, usually. Her mother had dated constantly, never too seriously though, and Sachi realized a long time ago that her mother's time spent in various dalliances with suitors often overlapped each other.

It was a small town and there had definitely been talk, but since no lover had ever been left feeling scorned and she'd never traipsed over the relationship of anyone else, no one judged her harshly, she was just a woman who liked men.

Maybe that was why Sachi had such a hard time with entering into casual relationships though, as if the entire town was waiting for her to follow in her mother's footsteps and take a turn with every eligible bachelor around.

"Well, I'm going to bed, I had a long day," Sachi whined and kissed her mother's cheek. "I probably won't see you in the morning."

"Probably not," her mother agreed. She'd be out late with her vampire date and Sachi would be up relatively early to bake for the tourists.

Sachi walked up to her old bedroom and stood in the middle of it, looking around at the remnants of her past. These solid things were undoubtedly real, but her memory of them might be skewed. She picked up a teddy that she'd had since she could remember. It was bare in spots from being her favorite nighttime cuddle object and one eye was completely missing. "Or are you just a dumb stuffed bear that I have and my love for you is a fabrication for some unknown reason relating to portals and demons?" she grumbled and set the thing back in its place of honor above her dresser.

She ran a finger over the other items there, a hairbrush, old makeup from when she thought she needed to look more witchy, even a butterfly shifter goes through a goth phase in middle school apparently. Pictures. These were probably the closest to evidence of the past that she could get and trust. She picked up the stack and flipped through them. Mostly just her and Fern, a few with Cash and Lance. One with Penelope. They had been a tight group. Nothing looked out of place or went against a current memory, so Sachi put the stack back down.

She felt a headache start and decided sleep was the best thing.

She slipped into some old pajamas that were still in a drawer, oddly fresh smelling. No doubt her mother came in regularly and washed everything. Sachi knew her mother dusted because the place was spotless despite ten years of time passing, but she couldn't comprehend what would possess her mother to wash the items in Sachi's dresser. Then she crawled into fresh sheets and inhaled the familiar detergent smell, her mother probably hadn't used anything new in fifteen years or more, it smelled like lemon and sunshine. Her mother was a creature of habit for sure and she'd never appreciated it more.

Sachi lay awake and listened to the noise of her mother downstairs. Soon she heard a knock on the downstairs door and the murmur of voices as her mother headed out on her date.

When the house was once again silent, Sachi couldn't stop thoughts of what Jax had told her. She couldn't deny what she'd seen in the basement. If it *was* what he claimed, then she couldn't deny the need to keep everyone in the district safe. But her part in it, that is what she struggled with the most. Jax said that the person who was in charge of the portal was trained on how to do it. He'd made it sound like years of training went into it and she didn't have any of that. She knew nothing of demons except in theory. She was no expert at magic, wasn't even a good fighter, and most of all, she didn't know if she wanted to be any of that. She was a baker; she was happy being a baker.

She thought of the children at Val's birthday party and groaned because she knew she would do anything to protect them.

"Ugh!" she grunted and flipped around on her bed. What the

hell could her father have possibly told her that she'd forgotten? Jax had basically ordered her to *try* and remember, as if it were just that easy. With a determined sigh, she stilled her body and closed her eyes, bringing up every memory of her father that she could. There weren't many to choose from, and none felt very significant.

Eating ice cream together. Walking by the river on warm days, her father liked the water, always put his hand in it no matter how cold it was. He said they had a connection to the life in the water, he'd even taken her to the ocean once.

Her mind perked, she had a sudden tingling inspiration. Jumping out of bed she pulled a box from the top shelf in her closet. It held all kinds of memories from childhood. She pulled out a journal from when she was ten.

She remembered that year, it was when she'd first shifted, when she had first started liking boys, and most importantly, when her father had taken her to see the ocean. It was on one of his business trips to the Florida District. Sachi paused for a moment and frowned. Why was a bar owner going on business trips? She bit her lip and shook her head, it didn't make sense, but he had, and often. She knew it for a fact in that moment even though she hadn't recalled it in years.

"Fuck, this is weird," she hissed as she took the journal to her bed. For her birthday that year he'd taken her with him so she could see the ocean. They'd stayed in a hotel right on the beach. She could hear the waves crashing in her sleep and it had been wonderful. One night she'd woken to find herself alone in the hotel room. She'd stepped out on the balcony and looked out at the beach lit by moonlight.

She'd recognized her father immediately; broad shoulders, long black hair blowing in the wind and the long leather duster he always seemed to wear. He was talking to someone, and it had frightened her.

Sachi found the entry in her journal, scribbled as soon as

she'd gotten home from the trip. *The woman was glowing with an internal light as if her heart was made of fire and her skin of glass. I could see her black eyes and white teeth, but no other features seemed to hold on her shimmering face. It was as if her particles were in constant movement and although there was a sound coming from her, I couldn't make out the words. My father spoke back, his voice deep and sure. "I will continue." Was all he'd said, then the figure had turned and walked into the ocean, the water steaming as it hit her glowing body.*

Sachi dropped the book and tugged at a loose curl in thought. She'd completely forgotten about that weird encounter before today. She still had no idea what that woman was or what her dad was supposedly going to continue doing for her, but he'd visited the Florida district many times after that, never taking her again though. She remembered now that she'd assumed he had a girlfriend there, perhaps even other children. But could it have actually had something to do with the portal there or that thing he'd talked to? There was no doubt in her mind now, that thing had to have been a demon.

How had she forgotten all of that? Why had she been left with memories of his bad reputation but not that happy memory of vacation together, that mystery woman, or the possibility that he'd had a lover in another district? What was even real? Who had her father really been?

A tiny knock on her window drew her attention. Fern was floating at the second story window just like when they were kids. Sachi let her in, and Fern grew to her full four feet before settling on the bed. "So, what happened with dark and dreamy, and why are you hiding at your mom's house?"

Sachi wasn't sure she wanted to talk about any of that. "How did you know I was here?"

"Saw the light."

"How did the cupcake delivery go?" She frowned at her friend, still not happy that they'd cooked up poison cupcakes in her kitchen.

47

"Fine, and don't change the subject," Fern said with a playful pout. "I want all the dirty details. Did he ask you out? What did he want with your dad? Did he ask you for a black spell?" Her voice rose a couple octaves as she spoke and Sachi grimaced at the piercing sound of fairy excitement.

With a sigh, Sachi relayed all that had happened with Jax, leaving her friend speechless. If she was going to go down this rabbit hole of possibilities, it might make sense to have someone on the other side who knew what she was doing in case Jax really was a psycho and she'd been duped.

"Do you really think we've forgotten something that important?" she whispered.

Sachi looked down at her diary, "Yeah, I do. There's no denying the sucking hole I saw in the basement," Sachi sighed. "And my memories, I know I can't remember things, like pieces are blank."

"And you want to believe your father was something good," Fern said gently.

"Yeah, I guess I do," Sachi said feeling like a complete idiot.

Fern just nodded. "Okay, what do we need to do?"

"We?" Sachi asked in surprise, but she shouldn't have been shocked by Fern's assumption that she would be a part of this thing. Fern always wanted to help, was usually the first one willing to jump into a fight that wasn't hers. It's what made her such a great friend and sister.

"Yeah, I'm not letting you do this alone." Fern shook her head. "Whatever it is, I'm going to help. Especially since we don't know if we can trust Jax. Handsome though he may be, lots of evil comes in a pretty package."

Sachi agreed, there was something about his story that wasn't sitting right with her, but she couldn't quite pinpoint what it was. Telling the truth wasn't the same as being completely honest and she was going to be watching him carefully.

"So, are we having a sleepover?" Fern asked excitedly. "Like in high school?"

"You aren't going out with Lance tonight? He was looking for you at the bakery when I closed up."

Fern shrugged. "I haven't heard from him."

Sachi smiled. "Well then, of course." She pulled the doll bed down from her closet that had served as a guest bed for her bestie all throughout their school years.

They made popcorn and watched late night television. Neither one brought up Jax or the possibilities of what he'd revealed as they enjoyed a familiar routine in their relationship. A few of Fern's siblings joined for a while, until their parents called them home for bed. It was so normal and comforting that Sachi could almost pretend she was seventeen again, safe in her mother's house, her father alive and... what, alive and keeping a portal to Hell closed? Or alive and drinking too much, possibly selling black magic charms? She didn't want to believe either was the truth, but one seemed more likely and the other would mean her father was a decent man.

She wasn't seventeen though and pretending that she didn't have a huge problem facing her wasn't going to help her solve anything. By the time they were shutting off the television to call it a night a few hours before sunrise, Sachi was anxious and scared.

Fern shrank down and tucked herself into the tiny bed.

"Do you really think there are demons walking around out there and we haven't noticed?" Fern asked quietly.

"Fuck, I hope not." But she did think so. All signs pointed to Jax *not* being a complete psychotic, and that was frightening.

Sachi turned off the lights and fell asleep to the familiar sounds of nighttime activity in the district. It was never really quiet except around dawn and dusk when most citizens were at home. It was all so normal, but a sinking feeling in her gut said it was about to change.

CHAPTER 6

When Sachi woke up to the sound of her phone ringing at seven, she was not happy. She'd tossed and turned well past sunrise and even on a good day she wasn't an early riser if she could help it.

"What?" she snapped without looking to see who it was.

"Meet me at the line."

"Jax?" she asked groggily, not sure she wasn't still dreaming. He'd starred in a few of her confusing dreams last night, some of them erotic enough to make her cheeks burn just hearing his voice.

Fern huffed and rolled over in her tiny bed, pulling her tiny pillow over her ears.

"Yes, you aren't home," he accused.

"No, I'm not," she snapped. She was definitely awake, and it was his fault.

Silence.

She sighed. "Which line?"

"Am I interrupting a date?" he asked.

"You're interrupting sleep, that's for damn sure," she hissed, and Fern grunted agreement. "I'm not an early morning creature."

"East entrance."

"Give me thirty minutes, and you'd better pick up coffee."

"Deal," he said, and hung up.

"Who the fuck was that?" Fern asked as Sachi got up.

"Jax, apparently, he wants me to meet him at the east line entrance. You sleep and I'll meet you at the shop later. It's still a mess by the way."

"I'll have Seraphina take the youngsters over and clean this morning," Fern assured her and covered her head with the blanket. Fairies tended to be early risers so hopefully it really would be clean before Sachi got there.

"Stay out of the basement," she reminded Fern. There was no reason to risk anyone finding a hole to Hell, if that's really what it was.

Fern just grunted.

Sachi showered and dressed in her clothes from yesterday because it was either that or her old cheerleader uniform or prom dress. No makeup, but she didn't use much most days anyway, then headed out of the house as quietly as possible. She didn't really want to face her mother this morning, so the early wake-up call was grudgingly appreciated. She couldn't imagine sitting across from her mother and not divulging everything she was worried about, but what good would it do to worry her? Her mother liked to gossip and would tell Fern's mother, then it would spread like wildfire through the whole district. She imagined panicking the entire district was not the best plan and even telling Fern had made her nervous, but she'd had to, Fern needed to know what was in the basement of their bakery and besides, Fern was her best friend and they shared everything.

The drive to the east line was peaceful. No tourists were bussed in until eleven and the locals were mostly still in their houses too. A few school-aged kids were making their way to the park and there was a werewolf loping down the sidewalk delivering papers. All was as it should be, and she wondered if there was really any harm in none of these people knowing that there was apparently a portal to Hell in their vicinity.

The lines that portioned off the district were very distinct. The river to the west, a freeway to the north past the forest, to the east and south was a wide stretch of desert. When tourists came, they came in groups, on busses usually, and although there weren't any guards at the entrances, it was an unwritten rule that humans were not coming and going when the sun was down, for their own safety.

Of course, there was a vampire bar close to the east line and humans were known to frequent it when they were feeling adventurous or suicidal. There was no way to keep stupid humans from thinking they could be something special to a creature who literally wanted to drink every drop of blood in their body and move on to the next one. Maybe every human was born with a natural savior complex that told them they could make this evil creature change, when in reality they just needed to accept that the vampires were something different from them. They didn't need saving from their instincts, they needed a regular food supply and to be left at a safe distance from anyone who wasn't able to protect themselves. Which is exactly what the districts were designed to do.

Sachi pulled up to the entrance at the east line where Jax stood beside a black truck that looked like it was made for going fast and attracting women. It made her feel a little bad about her own old car, but it was all she needed for getting around in the district where walking or flying was usually faster than driving and parking. Jax was wearing a pair of black jeans, black T-shirt, and sunglasses, looking far too fresh for so early in the morning, making her frown. She was sleep wrinkled and tired. He was holding a cup of coffee though, so she got out of the car and ignored the fact that he looked like he was posing for a movie poster, all rugged background and sleek truck, a guy that was somewhere in between.

She smiled and strode forward with confidence. "Good morning. You're an early bird, huh?" she accused.

"When I need to be," he said, taking a sip of coffee and handing it to her.

"Really?" she hissed as she took it, feeling that it was half full.

"You made me wait," he said with a shrug. "I already finished mine."

She glared as she sipped it, black coffee, not her favorite but she wasn't going to complain. She also wasn't going to admit the sweet taste of his saliva on the rim sent a shot of pleasure to her brain, and below. "So why are we here? There's nothing here. About twenty miles that way is a bar that caters to vamps and stupid humans," she said gesturing south. "North is empty all the way to the highway beyond the forest."

"I came out here to see how the wards were doing."

"Wards," she said carefully, feeling like this was one of those things she should know.

He sighed heavily, reminding her of an overworked teacher explaining the simplest math problem to an obstinate pupil. She was familiar with that sigh, had heard it a million times in school because she'd never been an attentive student. Even in elementary school, before boys had added to the sidetracking of her mind, she'd been far too concerned with her social life to bother with whatever the teacher was trying to get across.

"The wards that are supposed to keep anything nasty that crawls through that portal from going rampant in the more human parts of the country."

"Oh, I guess I forgot that?" she said, not sure if she had or not and it really bothered her.

"Apparently." He looked her up and down, obviously noticing her in the same clothes as yesterday at the birthday party.

She had to stop herself from smoothing out wrinkles, she didn't want to give a damn what he thought of her.

"Did you stay at Tate's last night because you were scared of the portal in your basement?"

"No," she said defensively. "I stayed at my mother's because I was scared of the portal in my basement." She lifted her chin slightly as she admitted her fear. It wasn't as if it were unfounded, unless he was lying to her.

A curious look crossed his face, but he quickly let it pass. "Well, you're safe for another three days. The actual date of opening is every ten years on the first full moon of July. If nothing else has crawled out in the last ten years, then I doubt anything will before then."

"You think so?" She'd love to feel safe in her own bedroom tonight but doubted that once the sun was down she was going to want anything to do with the place, especially not alone.

"I do, otherwise this place would already be destroyed. I'm betting one or two got out and have been playing it safe, probably biding their time for the next opening so they can get more of their friends out."

"That's not comforting," she grumbled.

"It wasn't supposed to be," he said seriously. "It means they are being careful, and discreet, which makes it harder to find them."

"You didn't come up with anything last night?" She hated that her voice sounded so hopeful, as if she expected him to swoop in and solve this whole problem. It wasn't the attitude she usually had about things, she was a problem solver, a doer, she had taken the lead on the bakery without hesitation. She'd made it into a thriving business in the first three years. She wasn't a sit back and let others do things for her type but she looked at him and saw something powerful and capable and she wanted him to make this bad thing go away.

"No, everything around the district seemed to be functioning completely normally and with the factions policing themselves individually, there's not even any record of events that could point toward unusual patterns of behavior that I could find, at least not in public records."

She pursed her lips and took another sip of the coffee. It was barely warm anymore, but at least it was something and the caffeine was needed, especially now. It seemed like their job was an impossible one. "So, are they up?"

"I can't check them by myself, I need a witch on the inside to share energy."

"Oh yeah," she grumbled, she had known that. A ward was invisible to the eye and if it wasn't meant to keep their kind in or out, but was up and keeping demons inside, they wouldn't be able to share energy of any kind through it. It ensured that no one could accidentally deactivate it.

They moved into position, one on each side of the arbitrary line in the sand that separated the district from the rest of the country.

"Ready?" Jax asked.

Sachi drank the last of the coffee and dropped the cup. "Ready."

They both lifted their hands, it was a simple thing, children learned this first, usually using it to annoy their siblings. A thought brought a tingle of harmless energy into the palm, and a simple flick of the wrist sent it out to the other person. It could feel like a small poke or a small shove, not much more than that unless you amped it up with a few Latin words, but then you were manipulating people from a distance and that was illegal territory. Not that she'd bothered learning the words, but she was willing to bet Jax knew them. He struck her as the type to walk just over the line into illegal, and why was that so fucking sexy? She shook her head and tried to concentrate on the task at hand.

"I'll go first," Jax said and Sachi waited.

"Nothing," she said with a smile. "I guess it's working."

"Okay, you try."

She brought energy into her hands, she always envisioned it

was lilac colored, like her hair, and flew from her in an imagined sparkle of energy. Super girly, she knew, but it was what she liked. "Feel that?"

"Nope, I think the wards are working. That's a good sign."

This was the first bit of good news he'd brought into her life. She picked up her empty cup and looked up and down the line. "Do we need to check it other places?"

"No, the whole thing works on a connected system. One goes down and the whole thing breaks. So there's no way whatever crawled out isn't still here, unless the west ward line is on the other side of the river, water would make a weakness in the line there that could allow something to get out or in." Jax frowned as he thought that over. "No, I'm sure whoever set these lines was smarter than that."

"Good and bad then," Sachi said with a frown.

"Exactly."

"What now?"

"Now we need to make a plan to find and catch a demon. We should check the west ward line later though, just in case."

"I need to get to work, and I need more coffee before I can even think the word demon," she grumbled. She needed more than coffee before she dealt with that, and she intended to get it since she was up so damn early.

"How about I grab coffee and meet you at the bakery then? We can discuss plans while you bake me breakfast."

"Deal, I like cream and honey," she threw over her shoulder as she hurried back to her car.

"Of course you do, butterfly shifter," he said with a laugh.

Butterfly shifters consumed a lot of sugar, luckily their high metabolism burned it off and they didn't end up with health problems because of it. Sugar wasn't what she needed now though, and last night had reminded her that it had been too long since she'd indulged her other needs. She made her way back to town, then went south, past the sleeping vampire homes and into werewolf territory. The vampire houses all looked like regular homes until you noticed the extra heavy curtains and inside, you'd see that all the bedrooms were in the basement. No vampire bothered with a house that was more than one story above ground, but their basements were always lavishly done and comfortable.

The werewolves however, their homes were large, tall, and wide to support huge families. They used every inch too and it was always noisy. Sachi had to drive extra carefully because even in the early hours of the day there were kids running around, making their way off to playgrounds and jobs.

The house she pulled up to was as familiar to her as her mother's. She'd spent enough time there to know every corner and every brick. When she got out of her car it was to waves and greetings from familiar neighbors, all of whom no doubt knew exactly what she was here for. She knocked on the bright red front door, smiling at the gargoyle knocker with its ruby red eyes and sharp teeth. As a kid she'd named the thing Fred, the name made it less scary.

"Hey Cash, let me in!" she yelled when no one responded to her knock.

A moment later the door swung open, and Cash stood there in nothing but a pair of boxer shorts and a growl. "What the fuck? It's fucking morning." He had bed head, shaggy brown hair sticking up all over the place, and the imprint of his pillow on his cheek. He was all muscles and tan skin, a very sexy male and she knew every inch of him too, maybe better than she knew the house.

"I know, but I need to eat," she said cheerfully.

He rolled his eyes and moved so she could go in. She had a momentary thought that he might not be alone, then dismissed it because he was always alone. She didn't let her mind go down the path as to why he was always alone, why she never worried he had a girlfriend.

"Why are you in trouble with your pack?" she asked, just as cheerfully as she tried to keep her eyes off of his morning chubby.

"How'd you know that?" he grumbled, his voice still raspy with sleep.

"Tate was at Miranda's last night for Val's birthday party."

"Tate's an asshole," Cash growled.

"But he's not on the outs with the pack."

Cash growled. "I'm in trouble for eating Cynthia's cat."

Sachi laughed, Cynthia was a bitch of a werewolf and eating her cat was probably not an accident, though Sachi did feel bad for the cat. She followed Cash into the living room and sat on the couch. This had been his parents' house and he'd inherited it when they'd passed years ago. He hadn't changed anything in that time. The same old furniture from the nineties and pictures of Cash as a kid hung on the walls. There was even an old prom photo of the two of them, she grimaced at the horrible two-piece bright orange dress she was wearing, how did she ever think that was a good choice with her purple hair? She stood up and looked closer, she had used a self-tanner too, the overall effect was something cartoonish and horrifying. Cash was looking away from the camera, but very dapper in a black suit and tie, timeless and classic. She frowned and picked up the photo, what had he been distracted by just then? The photographer really should have retaken the shot.

"Good memories," he whispered far too close behind her.

"Some of them," she agreed. "Didn't we get in a fight that night?" She struggled to remember.

"We were always fighting." He grabbed her hips and kissed her neck. "Then we always kissed and made up for hours."

Sachi pushed him away and walked back to the couch. "That was a long time ago."

"Ten years isn't that long," he said with a sigh and flopped onto the couch next to her. "Feels like yesterday to me."

"Ten years," she whispered. Apparently ten years was a very significant time frame. She looked around his time capsule of a house and wondered if there would be anything here to further prove what Jax had told her.

She doubted it. Cash's father wasn't a Portal Keeper.

"What's up, butterfly? You look worried," Cash asked with uncharacteristic seriousness. He ran a finger up over her hand, his dark eyes staring into hers questioningly.

Cash was one of her oldest friends and she was tempted to tell him everything, but she was afraid of letting too many people know what was, or might be, happening in their little paradise, so she kept her lips closed about it.

"Just late for work," she finally said with a tight smile.

"So why couldn't this wait until a decent hour?" he asked, sitting next to her.

"Because I'm stressed, and there's this warlock in town—"

"Oh, a date?" Cash said with a raised eyebrow and a jealous growl.

"Don't get all possessive," she snapped. "And no, not a date, he knew my father and he's visiting." It was almost the truth.

"Okay, so you don't want to accidentally bite him? That means you find him attractive," Cash accused. "You're never tempted to bite people you don't want to sleep with."

Sachi rolled her eyes, "I bite you all the time and I have no desire to sleep with you again."

"Lies," he said with a laugh.

He'd let her keep drinking his blood on a regular basis despite their platonic relationship and it kept her from having to go to the blood bar. She didn't like the idea of taking blood from a stranger, or worse yet, giving her blood to someone she'd have to see walk into her bakery the next day to buy cupcakes for his kid. So she kept coming back to Cash and he kept letting her. She supposed he'd eventually get a steady girlfriend and she would be shit out of luck, but until then, it was a mutually beneficial arrangement, she let him have free cookies.

"Where do you want it?" she asked, smiling wide to show her fangs.

He sighed heavily and narrowed his eyes at her. "Can't have you biting the warlock by accident," he said jealously.

She frowned; she might have to consider other options if he was going to get bent out of shape when she talked to other guys.

"Well," he said with a low rumble and ran his hand over the front of his shorts.

"Don't be gross," she snapped, and he laughed.

"I was mostly joking," he said, but she could see the growing bulge, she knew he would enthusiastically take her to his bed if she gave the go ahead. She also knew she'd enjoy it, but his possessiveness was just too much, and she didn't want to enter into a relationship with him again. "Dealer's choice, I guess," he added.

She grabbed his arm and bit into his wrist, it was the least intimate way to do it. He ran his free hand into her hair anyway and made a sound of contentment as she drew his thick, hot, blood from his body.

She took what she needed quickly and gave his wrist a lick. "Thanks, I appreciate it."

"The pleasure is all mine, love. Are you sure you don't want to stay and cuddle?" His voice was low and sultry and there was a neediness in his eyes that tugged at her. Guilt started to fill her for what she was doing to him, but she pushed it away. If he wanted her to stop, he'd tell her, and she never made him promises about where it would lead. They were both adults and knew what this was.

"I'm sure I have to get to work. Come in later and I'll give you a treat," she said with a wink and stood.

He growled in response, and she knew he hadn't missed the veiled dog joke.

He didn't get up to walk her out but slapped her ass as she turned. She really needed to find another donor. It was too bad she couldn't feed off fairies. Fern would be willing and easy, but their blood was so different, so thin. It would kill her; Fern didn't even let Lance bite her.

As Sachi got into her car and looked in her rearview to make sure she didn't have blood on her chin, she thought she saw a sleek black truck. She twisted around and searched the street behind her but there was nothing.

Frowning, she started the car and headed to the bakery hoping Fern and her siblings would already be done cleaning up. As she drove, she thought about the prom picture, trying to remember what the fight had been about. It was a big one, it had been the eventual final end of their relationship, though not that night. She remembered clearly that they'd stayed the night together and she'd been grounded for a week when her mom found out. It would have been longer, but she'd turned eighteen a week later and her mother couldn't tell her what to do, or so she'd decided.

But the taint of that night had stained the relationship. She struggled to remember the last few weeks of school after that, why couldn't she remember the last weeks of her senior year, and graduation? When *had* they finally decided to call it quits and not get back together?

She shook the thoughts away, it didn't matter, she needed to find a demon not the long-lost memories of her high school breakup.

CHAPTER 7

When Sachi parked behind the bakery she was thankful to hear the quiet buzz of fairies inside, they would have it cleaned up in no time. She would be able to settle in and make a mess of her own and clear her mind. Baking had always relaxed her, and she was wound tight right now despite the blood that usually calmed her. Guilt over Cash's reactions plagued her more than usual and she started to wonder what had suddenly changed. Why was she feeling like he couldn't handle their arrangement after all this time?

"Hey Sach," Fern called as she walked in through the back and grabbed an apron.

"Hey, you guys about done cleaning up?" It looked pretty good but there were still fairies everywhere.

"Yeah, I'll kick them out as soon as you want to start working. What happened this morning?"

"Jax wanted to check the wards around the district to make sure nothing could have escaped," Sachi whispered.

"Wards?" Fern pitched her voice low to avoid all the tiny ears in the room.

"Yeah, apparently the city is sealed off so no demons can get out if the portal fails."

"Oh, that's probably good." Fern's eyes lit up as she ran them down Sachi's body. "You guys got frisky too!" she gasped and there was an answering *ooohhh* from the surrounding fairies obviously eavesdropping.

"What?" she yelped and looked down. "No!" there was blood on her shirt. "Damn, no, I went to Cash's," she shrugged as Fern made a gag motion. "Girl's got to eat," she said.

"Yeah, but he's an asshole."

"True, which is why I stopped dating him like ten years ago."

"You need a new donor."

"I need a lot," she sighed. "I'm going up to change, get your siblings out and start the cinnamon, chocolate chip cookies. Tera is coming in for a dozen at noon. The nymphs are having a celebration tonight for a baby born last week and it's the naming ceremony, they'll want red velvet cupcakes. And I got fresh wolfsbane from Penelope yesterday so we should bake up cookies for the weres too."

"On it," Fern said as Sachi disappeared up the stairs.

The apartment above the shop was small, a studio with just enough space for herself, and she loved it. Even if it was rather hot in the summer. She pulled her clothes off and rummaged through a pile she knew was clean but hadn't made it to the dresser yet; if she was being honest, it never would. She pulled on a pair of black shorts and a pink tank top. She went into the bathroom and put on a touch of makeup, threw her hair in a ponytail, and went back downstairs telling herself she had not put on makeup for him, it was just what she wanted to do today.

She froze at the bottom of the staircase when she heard his voice.

"You make these! Delicious," he was saying in a tone that made Sachi roll her eyes. Why did guys think they had to talk down to fairies like that? Fern was no child despite her small stature.

"She's a whiz with all kinds of things, want a cupcake?" Sachi said, coming into the back room and picking up one of the laced cupcakes from the night before.

Fern giggled and Jax just ate another cookie. His eyes swept up and down her body and he lifted a questioning eyebrow which she ignored and grabbed her apron.

"Seraphina said Franklin was in the bathroom all night, so I guess they worked," Fern said and took the tray of leftover poison cupcakes to toss in the garbage.

"Where's my coffee?" Sachi asked Jax as she tied on her apron.

"Honey and cream for the butterfly. I wasn't sure if you needed anything to eat." He held up a bag that smelled like sausage.

"Just coffee," she said with a grin and took the cup.

"You changed," he said.

"I'm going to bake, if you want to try and pry information out of my head while I do that, fine, but if you want to talk about my wardrobe, leave."

Jax pulled the sausage sandwich out of the bag and hopped onto a stool. "How much do you eat?"

"Rude," she snapped and banged a bowl onto the table.

"You smell like blood," he accused.

Sachi slammed a drawer shut as she got a mixing spoon. Fern giggled and got to work on the cookies while Sachi started on the day's cupcakes with annoyed movements. What the hell was his problem? Why was he so interested in her personal life, first the accusation that she'd gone home with Tate, now this? If she didn't know better, she'd think he was attracted to her.

Jax didn't say anything else as he ate his breakfast, but he watched her carefully and she stole looks in his direction. She was attracted to him, that hadn't changed since she first saw him across the street yesterday.

He seemed to be seething in his quiet and it filled her with a kind of pleasure to think he might be reacting negatively to the smell of another man's blood on her.

She shouldn't care, she reminded herself. It would be a bad idea to get involved with him while all this craziness was going on, and then, she assumed, he'd be gone again. But his dark eyes on her mouth as he fingered his neck absently sent a thrill up her spine that resulted in her putting a double pour of vanilla in her batter.

She grunted and doubled everything else. Fern gave her a curious look she ignored. She was never so careless and Fern knew it, Fern was darting looks between her and Jax with a sly smile on her lips.

"I remembered something last night," Sachi finally said when she couldn't stand the silence any longer.

"What!" Fern yelled. "Why didn't you tell me?" she asked with a hurt expression.

Sachi just rolled her eyes at the fairy. "I don't know if it's anything. I was thinking about my dad and remembering how he used to take me to the riverbank and would always touch the water, he loved the water. Then I remembered writing in my journal about a trip my dad took me on when I was ten. It was late in the summer and the only time he'd ever taken me out of the district. We went to the Florida District and I saw him meeting with," she hesitated, not wanting to call it a demon when she wasn't sure that's what it was, "something, something I'd never seen before or since and I didn't really remember it until I read it in my journal."

"Didn't your dad take trips to Florida all the time? He had a girlfriend there, right?" Fern said helpfully.

"Well, that was what I assumed, but maybe not, maybe he was meeting with that thing regularly."

Jax looked thoughtful. "What did it look like?"

Sachi described the fiery being she'd seen. Fern freaked at every detail, but Jax just sat there with a blank expression, thoughtful. She appreciated that he wasn't immediately calling her a liar, it sounded so ridiculous when she said it out loud, but something in her gut told her it wasn't ridiculous, it was real, and it was scary as fuck.

"Your father was visiting a fire demon in Florida on a regular basis," Jax said calmly but there was a heat in his gaze that bordered on murderous.

"A fire demon," Sachi whispered, it sounded horrifying. "Maybe that's what it was. Like I said, I only went the one time, and I was just a kid."

"What else was in your journal?" he prompted.

"Nothing important."

"You're sure?"

"Yeah," she said, refusing to look at him as she pretended to take great care in putting the cupcakes in the oven. She'd have to do half vanilla and half lavender, since she'd doubled the base recipe. People loved the lavender, she always put a sprig of real lavender on top for decoration and it smelled up the whole shop.

"You don't remember the portal though, or the wards? You don't remember that the purpose of this district is to keep that portal closed and you don't remember that your father was teaching you to do just that?" he said angrily.

Sachi laughed at that and got a glare from Jax.

"One thing I can be *very* sure of, is that my father was not teaching me to do anything. I barely talked to him the last four years of his life."

"Impossible," Jax snapped.

Sachi faced him with fury, hands on hips and at the end of what she thought she could take. "Get out."

"What?" he looked genuinely surprised.

"I said get out! I have no idea what you think I'm going to do, without a lick of training. My father was not in my life, he was a drunk who owned a bar and yeah, maybe it was over a portal to

Hell, but damn if I know what to do about that. I have two dozen lemon cupcakes to make for a little girl's birthday party after this so get out!"

Jax hopped off the stool and crossed the distance, getting right in her face. "You are the Portal Keeper, you were trained, you will be again, and your little bakery is now sitting over a portal to Hell. Do you think that's just going to keep working out once it opens? Use your brain Sachi, this isn't a game, we have to find the demon, that thing has to close, and you and me are the only ones who can do it!"

He was so close, she was frozen. His hot breath was on her face, and she was gutted by his words, filled with fear, and all she wanted to do was run away. She seriously considered shifting and flying as far as she could.

"I—"

"Sach! Where's my cookie?"

All heads turned to the front of the store.

"Cash," Fern said quietly.

"The boyfriend," Jax said with a grimace. He stepped back though and Sachi was thankful for that. "I'll be back later. I'm going to check the water wards." He hurried out the back door, leaving Sachi staring with jaw dropped.

"What the hell is his problem?" Fern asked.

"He's worried about the portal I guess," Sachi said but she wondered why, if that were the case, would Cash walking in chase him away and what the hell made him think Cash was her boyfriend?

"Sachi, Fern, my girls," Cash said, waltzing into the back and grabbing a hot, chocolate chip cookie. He froze with the whole thing in his mouth and started sniffing. "Who was here?" he asked with a mouth full of cookie.

"A warlock," Fern said.

"No shit, I can smell that," he growled around a second

cookie. "That the guy visiting you?" he snarled in Sachi's direction.

"Do you want a cupcake?" she grabbed a laxative cupcake out of the garbage behind him without him seeing where it was coming from and held it out. "This one got a little messy so we can't sell it."

Cash grabbed it and ate it in two bites. Fern had to leave the room to keep from laughing. "This is great! New recipe?"

"Yeah, Seraphina was helping with that one, I'll tell her you approve."

"So, where's the guy?"

"Left."

"Why?"

"I told him to."

"Is he bothering you?" Cash puffed out his chest as if he were ready to take out anyone she asked him to, as if it were his right and duty to protect her from other males.

It was tempting, but she doubted it would solve any of her real problems. Sachi shrunk against the counter. "No, he's not bothering me."

Cash still looked ready to wolf out and bite someone, but the door in front dinged as a customer walked in and it wasn't long before more customers were coming in and the kitchen was stifling hot from the ovens. After about fifteen minutes Cash made a quick escape with a look that told her the cupcake was kicking in.

When things finally settled down in the afternoon, right before she knew they'd get a second run of supes who don't really wake up and get going until early evening, Sachi sat on a stool behind the counter and stared at the door that led to the basement.

"So, what do you think of all that?" Fern asked, waving a hand vaguely.

"I wish there was time to go to the Florida district and find the fire demon. See what she knows about my father and all this, but the full moon is in like two more days, and I guess I have to do something to keep that portal closed." She couldn't believe what she was saying.

"Maybe we need to tell someone, have them close the borders and keep the humans out until it's safe?"

"Maybe, but I doubt anyone would believe us and if they did it could cause a panic. That might be worse than them not knowing at all. It also might make the demon run or hide deeper. I think we need to sneak up on the damn thing."

"How do you sneak up on a demon?"

"Fucked if I know," Sachi grumbled, then pasted on her friendliest smile, careful to keep her fangs hidden as a group of human tourists came in.

The tourists snapped pictures as they bought cakes and cookies, gushing about how beautiful she and Fern were. If she wasn't so stressed, she'd have appreciated the compliments much more. It was like any other day for everyone around her, and that bothered her because she knew, nothing was the same as it had been yesterday or the day before and she was pretty sure it never would be again. Good or bad, her world was making a turn.

Jax came in as the last wave of tourists was about to head out of the district for the night and she was ready to demand a plan. She was ready to try and wrangle some kind of control over the whole situation. She wasn't ready for him coming close and whispering in her ear.

"There's a body being taken out of the river," he said quietly.

"A body?" She froze at the news and told herself that the tingle she felt was because of the shocking news and not because he had placed a hand on her shoulder and his skin was touching hers in a delightfully warm way, or because his breath fanned across her neck and ear as he spoke.

"Human," he whispered. It was so quiet Sachi barely caught it, but Fern still heard it even though she was across the store and she stiffened as she sold the last cupcake to an older lady who was just tickled to meet a real fairy.

"Shit," Sachi said on a breath, earning a chastising look from the lady as she took her bag and left. They'd never had a human casualty in their district, not officially anyway, the vampires were careful to cover their mistakes at the bar. No humans even visited some of the northern districts, because they were far too dangerous. They were mostly inhabited by vampires who overindulged, and dark magic witches. Their district was clean and safe and pretty. Even Witch's Row was a nice place to stroll, yeah, the houses were all black and grey, but there were flowers in the yard and the sidewalks were swept daily. She couldn't believe this had happened here. She felt violated and shivered, wrapping her arms around her body.

Fern ushered out the last customer with a strained look on her face then hurried to them as soon as the door shut. "What happened?"

"Apparently it was a tourist on an early bus. A young woman. She has marks on her neck, bruises, not bites and she... well she was drained of her soul," Jax explained.

"Drained of her soul? How can you tell something like that?" Sachi asked with a shudder. It sounded like a terrible way to die.

"It's in the eyes, they turn white when the soul is stripped from the body premortem," Jax explained.

"Demon?" Sachi had to ask, wanting any other answer.

"I don't know of anything else that can do that," he said.

"How do you know all this; did you talk to the police?" Fern asked.

"Not exactly," he said awkwardly.

"What do you mean not exactly?" Fern snapped, clearly impatient with the way he was telling the story.

"I was there when they discovered the body and then when the police arrived, I ran off."

"Why?" Sachi asked, taking a step away from him. Running from the scene of a crime was a suspicious act.

He sighed. "I'm a stranger here, who do you think they're going to suspect of the first murder of a human in the district in years?"

Sachi supposed he was right about that, but she wasn't so sure they were wrong to suspect him. First bus comes across the lines around eleven, if the victim was on it, and he'd headed to the river when he'd left the bakery this morning... She met his hardened brown eyes, knowing suspicion was in hers. "What district did you say you're from?"

His eyes narrowed and his lips hardened into a thin line. "Eastern Montana," he gritted out.

"Fuck," Fern hissed.

Sachi's mind spun around that, it was a northern district, it was overpopulated with witches who were known for communing with demons on a regular basis. She stepped back. "Why are you here? Why aren't you taking care of your own portal?"

"I left it to my uncle, he's the main warlock in charge since my father died."

That made sense and Sachi felt her heart ache for him. "I'm sorry, when did he pass?"

A pained expression passed over Jax's features but it was quickly contained, and he looked at Sachi with a stoic expression.

"My father and uncle shared the duties of our district's portal, training me to inherit, but ten years ago my father came here to help yours. He died here ten years ago, and my uncle continued my training alone."

Fern gasped loud enough for both of them. Sachi just let her jaw drop a little and stared at his blank face.

"Here! How?" She ached for him, the obvious hurt he was hiding made her want to reach out and comfort him, offer him all the consolations she hadn't felt she'd needed when her own father had died. She imagined what he felt is the type of loss she'd feel if she lost her mother and ten years wouldn't be enough to make that hurt go away.

He met her gaze with guarded eyes. "That's what I intended to find out when I came here."

Realization swept through Sachi, and she couldn't hold back her anger. "You thought my father killed him?"

Jax didn't answer but his chin notched up defiantly and he held her gaze without shame.

"Oh my God, you came here to seek revenge."

"When his body was returned to us, he had been torn apart. He died a horrible death at the hands of someone he trusted enough to get close to him while helping *your* father close this portal. He should have been home helping my uncle close ours, I don't know why he needed to be here, but I know it cost him his life. For ten years I've wanted answers, Sachi. I can't say what I would have done with them, I just needed them." His words were fierce and full of emotion, but not a hint of deception was there. He had come angry and seeking answers, she couldn't blame him for either of those things.

She'd felt the same way about her own father at times, had often wondered if someone walking around their district had been the one who had killed him and had run off, unpunished. She'd had to let it go though, there were no answers waiting for her anywhere and anger only made your life dark. As she looked into Jax's eyes she could see that darkness there. He hadn't let it go, hadn't wanted to. He was still seeking answers, they just weren't what he'd expected them to be.

"I'm sorry, Jax," Sachi said because she didn't know what else to say.

"Whoever did the wards for this district stretched them over the water, I noticed that much when I was there today. It means there's a big gap where anything could get through. Anything could have killed that woman today."

"Do you think it could be the fire demon I saw with my father?"

"I don't know, and I didn't have time to look closely at the woman's body that was pulled out of the river today, but if she's got burn marks on her then I would be willing to bet it is. Damnit, Sachi, I want your help. Whatever killed my father probably killed yours too, and maybe that woman today. We have to stop it and we have to get it back in the portal before we can seal it with the full moon."

"My father had his head bashed in, certainly could have been the same as what killed your father," she agreed, trying to be calm and analytical as she talked of death. "No white eyes like the human though. Oh god, what if there really is more than one demon out?" She met his gaze knowing hers showed all of her fear and she didn't care. She wanted him to tell her it was going to be okay, wanted him to make this nightmare stop.

"Oh snap," Fern said quietly.

Jax met her gaze with an intense determination that made her want to believe he could do what she wanted him to do. "Then we have more than one demon to find and shove back in that hole, and we have no time to waste," he said simply.

That wasn't what she wanted to hear but it was the truth and so she nodded.

The door dinged and Val raced in with his new toy airplane, Miranda rushed behind to keep up. "Miss Sachi look! I didn't break it yet."

"Oh, good," Sachi stuttered, feeling like she was going to pass out. She went behind the counter and Jax followed, at least he was offering some kind of support after dropping that demon bomb. Fern busied herself gathering what Miranda needed and sending them on their way as quickly as possible. But as soon as they were out, more were in and for the next twenty minutes they had a steady stream of nocturnal customers buzzing about the news of the body being found and buying their breakfast or treats for later in the day. Every one of them asked about who Jax was and why he was here, suspicion clear in every inquiry. Jax was right, he'd be at the top of the suspect list just because he was new in town. Part of her wanted to tell him to hide in the back but she knew that wouldn't stop the rumors, not in this town. Often keeping things out in the open was better, gave the rumors less of a thrill to share.

"Are you guys closing early and heading over to the meeting tonight?" Lance asked, poking his head in as the last customer scurried out.

"What meeting?" Fern asked, rushing over to give him a hello kiss.

"Chief Wilson called a meeting about the dead girl. You *did* hear about that, didn't you? It's all anyone can talk about. I got five calls before sundown."

"We heard. We'll head down," Sachi assured him. How could they not?

"Cool, meet you there." He gave Fern a quick kiss goodbye, shot Jax a curious look, then left. It struck Sachi as odd that he didn't try and introduce himself to the newcomer, but figured he'd already heard about her—apparently he was hers—guest in town anyway.

"Looks like we're closing up early," Fern said brightly.

"Let's pack up the extras and hand them out at the meeting." Sachi pulled out her phone to message her mom, but when she turned it on she saw that she had multiple texts from her mother already. The meeting was at ten and *everyone* was going to be there, so according to her mother she should wear something cute. The next message demanded to know who the warlock was she was seen with and why she hadn't mentioned him last night. "This should be fun." Sachi grumbled. And looked at the clock. "I'm going to go up and change."

CHAPTER 8

Sachi threw off her flour-covered clothes and changed into jeans and a white t-shirt and even though her mom was wrong, and she didn't need to impress anyone, she touched up her makeup and brushed her hair, letting the long lilac curls land around her shoulders. She knew she looked good; the shirt was cropped showing a hint of skin between it and her jeans and the pink boots she'd chosen gave her a little height that made her feel good.

When she reached the bottom step, she found the bakery empty except for Jax.

He was sitting behind the counter looking deep in thought, but he turned as she creaked on the stair and his eyes swept over her like a caress—slow and sensual from her head to her feet and back up again. When he was looking at her eyes once more, his lips curled into a sexy smile that made her stomach flutter.

"I don't know if I can protect you from demons as well as every male in the district, Sachi."

She took the last step down and raised an eyebrow. "Who said I need or want your protection from the males of this district?" she asked haughtily and flipped her hair back. She couldn't help herself; he made her stomach flutter, and she hadn't felt that in a long time. If he wanted to flirt, she'd respond, there was no harm in flirting with a near stranger, she hoped.

He crossed the space quickly and she held onto the thought that it was fine, this was just flirting. He touched her chin and held it, making her look up to meet his gaze. Even with the boots she had to bend her neck to do it.

"I say, because, butterfly girl, if I have to see you with someone else, I'm not sure I can do the job I need to do here." His words were quiet, but they sent a shock of delight straight to her core. He only touched her chin, but her entire body felt scorched by it, and she had to bite her lip to keep from leaning into him with a groan like a hussy.

He slipped a hand into her hair and dipped his head, pressing his lips to hers.

The kiss was soft and demanding, she had no choice but to answer. Her lips parted and he slipped his tongue along them before darting in to play against hers. His free hand rested on her back, his fingers teasing against the bare skin her shirt revealed.

She moaned as the fire in her was stoked by his gentleness and her long-denied needs raged. She pressed forward, letting her body meld to his, loving the feel of his sleek muscles against her soft curves. She didn't care in that moment if it was risky, didn't care if she knew almost nothing about this man, she wanted him to show her where these kisses could lead, and she wanted it badly.

His lips left hers and she mewed in disappointment. He chuckled as he kissed along her jaw and to her ear, his hand at her back slipped seductively to her belly, drifting along her waistband as if waiting for permission to dive in, ready to take this to the next logical step. Her hands went to his waist and gripped his belt. She wanted to tear it off and throw all caution out the window.

"Fern took the cookies with her, we can be late," he whispered in her ear.

The reminder of the meeting, the dead body, and the crisis of demonic proportions was a sobering one. She couldn't sleep with this man, she didn't *know* this man. More importantly, she had to make sure her district remained a safe place.

"Jax," she whispered as his teeth grazed her earlobe and her entire body vibrated.

"Yes, Sachi?" he breathed into her ear. She had to bite her lip so she wouldn't moan as another tremble rocked her body, her hips moved forward, and she heard him chuckle against her neck. "I love the way your body responds to my touch as if it's been starving for me. It's fucking amazing," he growled, and she almost couldn't go through with stopping him.

She pushed him away and he didn't fight it, but he didn't move far, and he didn't let go of her waistband, which she noticed was now unbuttoned. When the hell had that happened? "We need to go to the meeting."

"Why?"

"Because we need to figure out the demon thing," she almost didn't get the last word out, he was raking his teeth along her neck again and she was about to lose control of her body. She wanted to throw him down to the floor. She wanted to rip off his clothes and let him run those teeth of his over every sensitive part of her body while she licked his muscled chest and figured out what that delightful package looked like that was currently pressed against her hip.

He pulled back and ran his finger across her chin, kissed her sweetly and looked into her eyes with desire that rivaled her own. She almost changed her mind, but he stepped back, dropping his hands from her and the loss brought her a little more sanity.

"I suppose we do have a duty to fix this situation," he said gravely, then pulled her to him and smiled wickedly. "But I won't forget what your body was promising there, Sachi." He leaned to her ear and nipped her lobe. "And I don't share. The next time you want to drink blood you won't be going to the werewolf district."

She pushed him away and put her hands on her hips, giving him her best glare. "You *were* spying on me! You had no right; you *have* no right. We are not in a relationship, Jax," she hissed.

"Aren't we?" he said with a grin that made her want to smack him as much as pull him close and smash her lips to his again.

"A business arrangement, kind of. Not a romantic relationship, Jax. You don't get to tell me what to do."

"We'll see about that," he said, and moved to walk out of the bakery.

What the fuck? She wondered as she followed, feeling a bit lightheaded and far too confused by his sudden change in tactics. What had happened in the ten minutes she'd taken to change her clothes to make him so obvious and aggressive? Normally she'd be all about that kind of male attention, she liked a dominant in bed, but his sudden show was a bit confusing.

As she stood outside and locked the front door she smelled it. Cash. His scent was unmistakable. When had he been here, what had he seen? She glared at Jax who was looking far too innocent as he waited for her to lock up.

"You're an asshole," she hissed.

"I like you, Sachi, and I know how the mind of a werewolf works. If I didn't stake my claim while he watched. He'd never have stopped sniffing around."

That was not the right answer. Anger filled her and she decided she had no desire to take him anywhere. She shifted to butterfly, hearing the clatter of her keys as they hit the ground, but she didn't care. She flitted off in the direction of the school. If he found the place, fine, if he didn't, even better. She didn't belong to Cash and she sure as hell didn't belong to Jax.

"Sachi! Damnit!" Jax yelled after her, but she didn't stop. Up and over the bakery then southwest toward the high school.

She was soon flanked by two bats, vampires. She appreciated the support, it was dangerous for her to fly at night, owls were a real threat. She breathed in the cool air and enjoyed the feel of it as it slid around her wings and body. In this form she felt free and relaxed. Butterfly shifters and vampire bats were related in more than just their thirst for blood, their transformation was magic in a way that allowed them to reform with their clothes on. It was as if their body didn't completely change, it was an illusion that fooled the laws of nature and allowed them to take flight and move about as if small. Similar to the way fairies grew or shrunk along with their clothing, a magic no one questioned. Werewolves on the other hand were actual shifters, their body literally took on the other form, which made it impossible for them to retain clothing through the transformation. She was thankful she didn't have that problem. She wasn't sure, but the legends said that it was because butterfly shifters and vampires were a type of fae, like fairies, but werewolves were something else entirely, demon-made perhaps, but that didn't make them evil any more than the fact that vampires surviving on mostly blood made them evil. Evil was a choice, and so was assholery, and Jax was a big one.

The worst part was, she'd enjoyed the damn kiss, a lot! But he was just laying claim, he just didn't want Cash to have her. What the fuck was wrong with men, why did they think they had to own a woman in order to be in a relationship with her? Why couldn't they share? That thought sparked all kinds of images in her mind that made her wings stutter, and she lost a bit of altitude before she got herself back under control.

Their little group swooped and landed in the parking lot outside the high school. The high school gym was the only place big enough to hold the entire district for an important town meeting and she could tell by the parking lot that it was already packed with people. She was glad she hadn't decided to drive here.

Miranda and her husband, Randy, appeared on either side of her.

"Thanks for the safe passage," she said as brightly as she could, pushing her anger and hurt down.

"Of course. You shouldn't be flying alone at night, butterfly," Randy chastised.

She gritted her teeth a bit, annoyed that he was trying to tell her what to do, even if it was only out of concern.

"Oh Randy, Sachi's a big girl. She can handle herself," Miranda said quickly, obviously noticing the look of annoyance on Sachi's face. She grabbed her husband's arm and quickly led him inside.

"Where's your boyfriend?" Cash growled behind her.

Sachi twirled around, hands on hips and glare ready. "Fuck you, all of you!" she snapped and went inside, leaving a shocked werewolf behind her.

Sachi was pretty sure the entire town had shown up for this meeting, which wasn't surprising. Nothing this exciting had happened in a long time. The high ceiling was buzzing with fairies, and in the rafters sat gremlins and gargoyles. The werewolves lined the outside, arms crossed over their chests looking angry, as usual. The witches took the seats, avoiding the first three rows, always were back of the class sitters and that forced the vampires to take the front, because they were last to show up, as usual, but also, they liked to control everything and if you weren't in the front of the class how could you intimidate the instructors? So they didn't complain. Most of the fae in the woods didn't attend, willing to get the news secondhand from whoever did come. The extras, like Sachi and her mother, the lone butterfly shifters in the district, usually hovered in the back along with the couple of trolls that lived near the river, if they bothered to show up.

Sachi found her mother where expected, standing with Fern

in the back. She gave her mother a quick hug and glanced at Fern. "Why didn't you wait for me?"

Fern shrugged but her face was too blank to not be hiding something. "I just thought maybe you and Jax would like a moment alone," her eyes scanned the space between them to the door. "Where is tall, dark and hottie?"

"I don't care," Sachi hissed.

Her mother gave her a chastising look for her rudeness. "Is that the gentleman I've been hearing about, Sachi?"

Sachi rolled her eyes as a noise near the door drew her attention around. Jax barreled into the room looking pissed and worried until his eyes landed on Sachi, then he just looked pissed.

Sachi glared right back and crossed her arms over her chest. When he got to her, he handed her keys to her. "You dropped these."

"Thanks," she snapped, shoving them into her pocket.

"Who's your friend?" Her mother asked with an appreciative glance at Jax and completely ignoring their obvious hostility.

"Mom, this is Jax. Jax this is my mother, Helen."

"Nice to meet you, Mrs. Pearl."

"Call me Helen," she said with a grin. "You look so familiar," she said as she shook his hand. "Do I know your mother? Is she part of our local coven?" Her mother's face pinched a little, her nose scrunched as if she had a sudden headache.

"No, but I think you met my father maybe, his name was Edvin Lintel."

Helen gasped, "Oh my God, you're Ed's son."

"Who's this asshole?" Cash asked, sidling up just then and wrapping an arm around Sachi's shoulder as if he didn't know exactly who it was.

The distraction was enough to pull everyone's gaze away from Helen, but Sachi didn't miss the look of confusion and terror that passed over her mother's face before she pulled herself together. Sachi wanted to ask her about it but stopping an impending male dominance fight was more important at the moment.

"The ex-boyfriend?" Jax asked with a raised eyebrow, challenging.

Sachi could smell the testosterone rolling off the two men, so could others, they started to turn and stare, probably hoping to see a fight.

"Yes," Cash said at the same time Sachi pushed his arm off her shoulder.

"Key word being *ex*," she hissed.

"I smelled you in the shop earlier," Cash accused, taking a step toward Jax and three other werewolves were immediately behind him, ready for a fight without a care as to what it might be about. Werewolves backed each other up without question.

She was glad he didn't mention seeing them kissing in the bakery earlier, that would have raised a few eyebrows.

"And I smelled you on her this morning," Jax accused, not backing down an inch. "Yet, she doesn't seem to want you now."

Cash growled, his werewolf buddies growled, and the crowd around them was deadly silent.

"Police Chief Wilson," a voice boomed across the gymnasium, stopping the dick measuring and drawing everyone's attention to the front of the gym.

The police chief was a werecat, a rare breed and very dangerous, even the werewolves gave him respect and distance which made for a great chief of police in any district. Next to him was a woman Sachi didn't recognize, but she wore the uniform of a human police officer and that was unexpected. The districts policed their own.

"I guess since it wasn't a supe they dragged out of the water, the regs care," Cash said with a huff.

Regs was a slur for humans and there was a mumble of agreement around them at Cash's words.

"This could mean trouble for our district. We can't afford to become a no human zone." Sachi couldn't help but worry about her business, she'd never make it on local money alone. The North Idaho District was infamous for human murders, it wasn't the supes fault completely, they were located near a college town, and it had become quite thrilling for the young humans to visit the district at night and go to clubs; they had often not made it back out alive. The Feds shut it down and now it was closed to anyone who wasn't a supe. She'd heard from others who had family there that it was nearly deserted by supes now too, they couldn't make a living without tourist money. She'd always wondered why the whole town didn't just disperse, but now she knew, there were those who had to stay and watch the portal there.

"Hey, wanna replay old times, sneak into the locker room and make out?" Cash whispered in her ear loud enough to be sure Jax overheard. "I'll let you sip blood from all your favorite spots," he added darkly.

Sachi pushed his arm off of her again and glared at him. He was acting like an idiot and making a fool out of himself, and she was about to tell him that when the Chief started to speak.

"Welcome citizens." Chief Wilson spoke, loud and commanding. "This is Police Chief Rodriguez. I expect you to show her the same respect you show me." His words were for everyone, but his eyes focused on the werewolves who were known to not welcome newcomers. "She is here to assist in the investigation of a murder of one of her citizens." He motioned for the woman to step to the mic.

She did and she showed no fear as she faced down a gymnasium full of supes with no human backup. "Citizens, I am disturbed and saddened by the events of this day. We have lived harmoniously side by side for a long time and although I had to agree that shutting the roads down to travel was the best thing for now, I want to assure you that I do not intend to keep them closed permanently."

"She's no reg," Jax whispered in Sachi's ear, gaining a growl from Cash for getting close, and supporting growls from his nearby packmates.

"What the hell are you talking about?" Sachi whispered back, hoping no one around had heard his insane remark.

"Look at her, really look. You're half witch, right? She's touched with magic."

Sachi tried to focus on Chief Rodriguez as she spoke about curfews and deliveries, but there was nothing strange about her.

"Her aura, can you see it?" Jax pressed.

"No I—" then she froze. Chief Rodriguez stepped sideways, and a slice of moonlight filtered in through a high window. It was just enough to highlight what Jax had seen, a slight blue tint to her aura. Humans all had clear auras because their bodies held no magic. But supes all had colored auras depending on what they were. Blue indicated she had fae blood. She may not even know it, but she wasn't fully human.

"I wonder if she knows," Cash said, butting into the conversation.

"I doubt it," Fern said, showing she'd been listening the whole time too.

Sachi looked around the room, it seemed they weren't the only ones to notice. Witches, warlocks, and fairies could see auras, their groups were tinkling with the news, and it was leaking out into the other groups quickly.

"Where'd my mother go?" Sachi asked, noticing she wasn't standing with them anymore.

"She took off once Chief Wilson took the stage," Fern said with a shrug.

As Chief Wilson reiterated what the woman had said about keeping the roads closed, allowing for deliveries only at certain times and no one coming or going, the room filled with the buzz of realization.

Chief Wilson could probably hear the whispers and he looked

annoyed. Chief Rodriguez couldn't, she just looked confused by what would likely seem to her as the entire room not paying attention to what their police chief was reporting to them.

Chief Wilson was angry and done, he grabbed Rodriguez's arm and ushered her off the stage and out the back, obviously not wanting her to be confronted by what had just been discovered.

"There's a fae in trouble somewhere," Fern laughed.

It wouldn't take long to figure out who had slept with a human. The elves would probably be at the station demanding blood tests as soon as the news reached them in the forest, they were the self-appointed rulers of the fae and they took their job seriously. Of course, none of them had bothered to show up here to hear about what was going on, they also thought they were far above anyone else's matters.

"So what now?" Sachi asked Jax as everyone in the room started to move out. Deciding to put aside her annoyance in favor of saving the district.

"We need to see the body."

"Gross," she grumbled.

CHAPTER 9

Lance walked up to their group and put an arm around Fern, giving her a quick kiss then gave Jax a polite nod. Sachi was reminded of the idiotic way Jax and Cash were acting toward each other, about her. Neither male could claim her, and she wasn't a damsel who appreciated a fight for her virtue, not that virtue was what she was offering.

"It looks like you won't be leaving any time soon I suspect," Lance said grimly. "Where are you staying?" he asked Jax.

"Well last night I slept in my truck, actually," Jax said uncomfortably. "There aren't exactly any hotels in the area." He gave Sachi a pointed look.

"Hey, did you see Penelope? I wonder if she's out of the house yet," Fern asked, changing the subject. Sachi would have to remember to thank her later.

"No, she didn't seem to be in the crowd," Lance said, not taking his curious eye off Jax.

"Well, we'd better go." Fern grabbed Lance's arm and started to guide him toward the door. "I told my parents I'd come back with a full report, they didn't want to bring all the kids down."

"See you around," Lance called back as he let Fern lead him away.

"You are *not* letting this guy stay with you," Cash said suddenly, reminding her that he had still not left her side.

"Fuck you," she hissed.

He growled and bared his teeth at her and that was the signal his buddies had been waiting for. They grabbed his arms and led him out of the room. They wouldn't let him lose it on *her*, she was a helpless female in their eyes, sometimes being a delicate butterfly shifter had its advantages.

"Sachi," came a deep growling voice.

"Bernard," she said quietly.

Bernard was a huge werewolf, old enough to have grey hair and a couple wrinkles but still in extremely good shape and he terrified her. His eyes narrowed at her, and his lip curled to reveal sharp werewolf teeth. Behind him was the rest of the pack that hadn't left to contain Cash.

"You need to stop stringing that boy along. He won't settle until you do."

"What the hell did I do?" she snapped, exhausted by all this male bullshit. They had real problems to deal with.

He growled again and she felt Jax move close behind her. The rest of the room was clearing even quicker now, no one wanted to get in the middle of werewolf business. No one apparently, was going to try and save her ass either, except maybe Jax.

"You don't bleed him for nothing," Bernard accused.

She pursed her lips, she knew he was right, had known it for a long time, but she just couldn't stop, didn't want to admit it was causing a problem. She liked taking his blood, it was easy. Was it more than that? She shook her head, not the time to look for old feelings.

"We have an agreement," she finally said.

"If that is yours," he pointed a finger at Jax. "Then you leave

Cash alone, he needs to take a mate of his own kind and quit playing fang bang."

Jax grabbed her shoulders and she shook him off, pissed now. Her relationship with Cash was no one's business. "I don't belong to either of them, and they don't belong to me. We are all adults here, Bernard, so fuck off."

Bernard laughed and the sound surprised her, full of cheer out of a face that scared her shitless. "Cash is yours, has been for years, otherwise he wouldn't wear your marks. He won't take a mate until you set him free. He isn't an alpha, Sachi, he belongs to you because you take his blood." He shrugged.

Everything he said made sense and that pissed her off even more.

"It needs to end," Bernard demanded quietly.

"I'll talk to him," she hissed.

"Let him go," Bernard warned darkly, then turned and left. The rest of the pack followed, all giving her glares, the females growled, they wanted Cash, she could see it now and she was standing in their way. She supposed she was lucky they didn't try and fight her for him. Probably only because they knew Cash would kill them if they harmed her.

"Fuck," she said under her breath, how had she not seen it before. She'd known he didn't date others, she just assumed he was playing the field not ready to settle. She'd never considered that she was stopping him. He would have told her if he wanted her to stop, wouldn't he?

He isn't an alpha, Bernard's words echoed in her head. She'd been taking his blood and by that act she was dominating him, she'd been owning him. He wasn't strong enough to tell her no. Guilt clawed at her insides. "Fuck," she said again and even stomped a foot. She hated when alphaholes were right.

"You didn't know?" Jax asked with real surprise.

"No," she admitted, ashamed. "He was a big deal in high

school, captain of the football team, everyone respected him, his dad was alpha."

"Was?"

"Yeah, he died. His mother, too. He lost them both at the same time, it was rough, he wasn't handling it well."

"When they died, why didn't Cash take up as alpha of the pack? That's usually how those things work unless the kid's too young."

Sachi frowned, she'd never thought about that. Bernard had stepped into the role. She'd been at the double funeral with Cash and he had been so upset, she had comforted him. It had been one of the only times since high school that she'd slept with him, a little backtracking in their relationship born out of grief. Bernard had stepped up to the podium and declared himself alpha, no one had questioned it. She'd assumed it was because he was the strongest, or oldest or some shit she didn't understand. She assumed Cash would take over someday, he was strong and people liked him. Maybe he just wasn't ready for the responsibility?

He couldn't be waiting because of her, could he?

"Werewolves are born with a level of dominance, Sachi. Cash is probably just below Bernard and probably half the rest of the pack, nice guy though he may be. Your ability to take from him is dominating no matter how you look at it. His brain can't break that, *you* have to."

Where the hell was she going to eat now? She wondered selfishly. She wanted to change the subject, so she lashed out at Jax. "So why does Bernard think *you* belong to me? You're not a werewolf with an ingrained sense of place in a pack and I'm certainly not your drooling bitch."

"Because any species that takes blood from another is more dominant than ones that don't." He shrugged as if it didn't matter.

That took her a second to wrap her head around. She certainly hadn't felt dominant when Jax had kissed her, had controlled her head, had touched her gently and sent thrills through her body. She'd felt anything but dominant and damn it had felt good. She packed that away as something to think about later. Cash had been dominant in high school, she was nearly certain of it, and she'd been all over his dick. But now, she had no interest. She dominated him with taking his blood and offered nothing in return. Jax acted a bit like an asshole, and she was drooling for what he had in his pants. What the fuck was wrong with her?

She cleared her throat and got back to his main point. "I'm a dominant species, that doesn't bother you?"

His eyes lit up and his smile turned wicked. "Not at all, because I know that a dominant woman often appreciates a male who is willing to dominate her in the bedroom."

His answer made her skin heat up and her breath catch. She needed to change the subject, fast. "You have to know you're going to be questioned, right? New guy in town, murder to solve."

He chuckled, not missing her quick redirection. "Yeah, but if I can avoid it, I will."

She wasn't sure she liked the sound of that. Innocent people didn't avoid answering police questions and she was once again reminded that she didn't really know anything about this man.

He seemed to sense her doubt. "We don't have time to sit in a police interrogation room, Sachi, do you realize night after next, the full moon will rise and that portal to hell is going to open up."

She frowned because he was right. Or at least she was pretty sure she believed he was. "So how are we going to get in to see the body?" she asked with resignation.

"I was hoping you'd have a connection," he said with a laugh.

She gave him a dumbstruck look. "A connection to the morgue? Who do you think I am?"

"I thought you were the Portal Keeper's daughter, but apparently you're just a baker," he challenged and raised an eyebrow that shouldn't have looked so damn sexy.

"Yeah," she snapped, "just a goddamn baker who dominates werewolves. But I do know everyone in town."

He smiled triumphantly and it annoyed the hell out of her.

"And who do we need to talk to in order to get in to see that body?"

"Brad, but first we need to go bake some cookies."

He just raised that damn eyebrow at her again and she hated that she liked his arrogance.

"Brad loves gingersnaps."

Jax laughed.

CHAPTER 10

Not talking about the kiss they'd shared earlier made every movement around the kitchen strained. Sachi hesitated to get too close and kept apologizing every time she accidently touched him. But she was in her element as she cooked, it's where she felt the most capable and currently, life felt out of control everywhere else. Jax quickly realized he was in the way and sat back, watching her as she flowed from step to step like a familiar dance.

She measured and mixed, making them extra spicy because she knew that's what Brad liked. The smells of ginger and molasses filled the air making her mouth water.

"Mind if I make us some dinner?" Jax asked, hopping off the stool he'd been sitting on and walking to the fridge, not waiting for permission. "You *do* need to eat regular food, right?"

She shrugged. "I like to, yes. I don't take in enough blood and nectar to sustain my body completely without it."

He smiled wistfully. "Nectar, what a delicate being you are."

She narrowed her eyes at him. "Yeah, and blood, don't forget that and apparently a demon killer too," she snapped. Not appreciating the reminder that she wasn't up for the job that she was needed for.

"No, not demon killer, Portal Keeper. Most Portal Keepers never even see a demon." He looked embarrassed. "They are too good at what they do, those portals don't get a chance to open."

Sachi huffed and turned back to the dough in front of her. His not-so-subtle dig at her father made her angry. She bit her lip to keep from pointing out that his father had been here too, apparently. She was certain their fathers had done everything they could to keep the portal closed and the district safe. No one would unleash demons on the world purposefully. Which means something very powerful had been working against them, something very big had gone wrong, and that scared the crap out of her.

Sachi straightened her shoulders and concentrated on her baking, because that was something she could control. When she formed the cookies on the tray, she made them into small bite sized rounds so they would look best displayed on a plate to carry into the morgue. Baking was an art for her, and she loved it.

When she shut the oven door and turned, Jax was holding out a plate with a sandwich and small salad. "Eat while they bake, then I'll help with the cleanup."

Sachi took the plate appreciatively and they both moved to sit on stools near the counter.

"Tell me something interesting about yourself, Jax," she prodded as she picked up the sandwich. It looked like he'd found some lunchmeat and cheese, simple but it would do the trick, her stomach was suddenly growling, and she couldn't stop flicking her eyes to his skin, wondering what he tasted like. Probably a bit of a spark, because of his magic. Cash tasted musky, very male and powerful. Jax would be lighter and full of energy.

As if noticing where her attention was, Jax reached up and rubbed his neck before talking. "Well, I have traveled a lot. I wasn't satisfied to stay put where I was born and my uncle didn't need me at the portal, he's capable on his own there and has a young son he's also training up."

"Oh, I'm a little jealous, I'd love to see all the southern districts."

He nodded and took a bite, chewing slowly, thoughtful. "The northern districts are nice too in their own way, more… raw. More like what the supes would make if they didn't have human constraints put on them and it's very cool to experience. I suggest you do it someday, in the summer of course. A butterfly must stay warm," he said with a wink.

She covered her smile with a bite of the sandwich. He could be quite charming when he wanted to be. They ate in silence and the smell of baking gingersnaps filled the kitchen.

"Oh my god, I think I'm drooling," Jax said as he took her empty plate and walked to the sink.

Sachi quite enjoyed being taken care of. She'd been on her own since she moved in here when she was eighteen and although her mother had doted on her when she was young, it had been a long run of doing everything for herself.

"I'll let you sample them before we go, they should be just about ready." She hopped off the stool and checked the oven, they looked close but not quite there yet. She joined Jax at the sink and they washed the dishes together in companionable silence. If it wasn't for the impending end of the world as she knew it, she'd say this was the best date she'd had in a long time, how sad was that? She'd really like a chance to date, maybe stop seeing Cash and really date around. Her eyes darted to Jax, maybe he'd stick around after the full moon if they survived.

"Do you think we can do it?" she asked quietly.

He turned to her with a serious look. "I do. It only takes one strong keeper to close a portal that's functioning correctly, this one, obviously isn't, but with both of us, I think we can do it. I wonder if it was malfunctioning before, if that's why my father came down. My uncle said he had no idea why my father left to help, just said he was needed in Texas and left, came back dead. He traveled a lot, too. All growing up he'd take off, usually I didn't know where he was going and he'd be gone for weeks at a time. He was good at what he did so I assumed he was just checking in on other portals, helping where needed." Jax shrugged. "I expected the same thing the last time, that he'd just show up again in a week or two."

"I'm sorry, Jax. Losing your father must have been hard, especially since you were close."

Jax looked at her with a deep sadness in his eyes. "I was too mad to grieve properly I think. Maybe when this is all over I finally will. I think when you remember your father, Sachi, you'll be needing the time to grieve properly too."

Sachi wasn't sure if he was right or not, she'd grieved, but she'd grieved for a man she barely knew, what if she suddenly remembered she knew him, would it be a new hurt all over again?

It was more than she could worry about now so she shook it off and focused on what they needed to do right then. "Even if we get the portal properly closed, that doesn't account for the escaped demon," she grumbled and turned to the beeping oven.

"Demons, plural, more likely," he pointed out.

She didn't want to think of that, how many could be out, what if they were already overrun and they just didn't know it? "Can a demon look like a normal supe or human?"

"Unfortunately, yes. Some can vary their shape. They could also hide inside of another living thing."

"Like possession?" she gasped and spun to him with a hot tray in her hands.

"Yes."

Sachi set the tray down before she accidently dumped the whole damn thing as her nerves began to vibrate with fear. "How would we know?"

"It should be obvious, there should be signs that the person isn't acting normal."

"Sure, unless we completely forgot what they were like before the possession," she pointed out and aggressively scraped at the cookies on the sheet, moving them to the cooling rack.

"It's why we have to prepare for anything and be watchful."

There was no time to waste and right now their lead was lying on a table in the morgue. She grabbed out a plate and piled it with hot cookies.

"May I?" Jax asked and grabbed one before she could stop him and popped the bite sized piece of lava into his mouth. "Fuck!" he yelped and waved frantically at his mouth.

"Yeah, they're still hot," she chastised, but she didn't hold back her smile. "Greedy boys get burnt," she teased.

"It's good," he choked out as he ran his tongue under the faucet. "When I regrow my taste buds, I'll have to try them again."

"Luckily supes heal quickly," she said and used a second plate to fan the steaming pile, she didn't have the patience to wait for them to cool naturally.

Jax glared at her and grabbed another cookie, this time he broke it open and blew on it. Sachi's eyes glued to his lips as they pursed, and she remembered exactly how they'd felt on her. Then he popped the cookie in his mouth and moaned in a way that made her knees weak and her stomach flutter.

"Good?" she asked, a little breathless.

"Heavenly," he said and met her gaze with his own dark and sultry eyes. She knew he was sensing her arousal at just watching him enjoy her food. It shouldn't have been so erotic, but damn, apparently this is what did it for her.

"We'd better go," she whispered as he stepped forward, closing the distance between them. He grabbed her waist and kissed her, soft and sweet, just once, then stepped back.

"Yes, we'd better," he said and licked his lips.

Her tongue dipped out and ran over her lips, tasting the sweet cookie from his mouth and the even sweeter taste that was all him. If he'd tried to take her right there on the kitchen counter she wouldn't have objected, but he reached for the plate of cookies and gave her a wicked grin.

"Do you want to drive?"

"Sure," she said, trying to chastise herself into not reacting to him so much. They had a serious mission, but then again what else would two attractive people want to do with the last days before the end of it all, but fuck?

The city was quiet as they drove to the morgue. Usually this time of night would be bustling with nighttime supes going about their lives, but it seemed everyone was inside, on edge no doubt because of the murder. It was nearly two in the morning, and she was exhausted but it was prime time for all the vamps, many werewolves, trolls and gargoyles. Even a lot of witches stayed to the nocturnal time schedule rather than the touristy daytime one.

But tonight it was just them on the road and many of the usual businesses had open signs but no patrons from the looks of things.

When they pulled up to the morgue it looked like Brad was the only one in the building. He was a ghoul, which made him perfect for the job. He communed with the dead and he never slept. He had red eyes and black hair, greenish skin, and sharp teeth. But if you discounted all that, he looked like a skinny nerdy man with glasses and a lab coat.

"Sachi," he said with surprise when they walked in. "What the hell are you doing here?"

"I thought maybe you'd like some gingersnaps. I made too many today and they just didn't sell well," she lied.

Brad grinned wide, his sharp teeth shining in the light. His eyes flicked curiously to Jax. "Who's the stranger?"

"Um, this is Jax and he's investigating the murder," she said carefully. "A family friend, so I told him I'd bring him by to take a look at the body."

Brad pursed his lips and crossed his arms over his chest. "Why does he want to look at the body? Does he know her?"

Jax stuck his hand out and forced a handshake. "I'm investigating privately. I didn't know her, but I have seen similar murders and want to make some connections."

Sachi held out the cookie plate. "Can we take a look at the body? Please?" She gave him a big smile, batted her lashes a little and because she was feeling desperate, used the movement of holding out the plate as an excuse to squeeze her breasts together with her arms.

"She's not talking," Brad said as he grabbed the plate, his eyes locking briefly on her cleavage. He must have already tried getting answers out of the girl. Usually the soul stuck around long enough for him to find out how a corpse really died, to deliver last loving messages to family, that sort of thing.

"That's because her soul isn't there," Jax said.

Brad gave him a surprised look as he unwrapped the plate and shoved a cookie in his mouth. "Oh my god! These are better than usual, what did you do?" he gushed.

Sachi blushed and smiled. "Oh, you know, just a little secret ingredient, I'm glad you noticed."

"You're amazing, Sachi," he said with a smile that revealed cookie mixed with sharp teeth and Sachi had to hold her smile in place with force.

"So, can we take a little peek, please?" Sachi asked.

"I don't know what you think you're going to see that the cops and I didn't." That comment was directed at Jax along with a narrowing of his eyes. He didn't trust the newcomer which didn't surprise Sachi at all.

For a moment Sachi thought he was going to deny their request, but he looked back at Sachi, and she grinned a little wider, letting her fangs show. She had it on good authority that he was into biting. It worked, Brad set the plate down and led them through a door and down some stairs. The air was cold down there and the smell was a mix of death and bleach. Sachi felt bile rise up in her throat, but she managed to hold it back.

"Were you at the town meeting?" Brad asked as he pulled back a curtain to reveal a table covered in a white cloth, an obvious body outline under it.

"Yeah," she said with a groan. This was not something she wanted to be doing. Jax put a hand on her lower back, preventing her from turning and running.

"Rumor is the *human* chief isn't so much. I think the elves are preparing to ambush her tomorrow," Brad said conspiratorially.

"Fae of some kind I think," she said with a nod. "I doubt she knows, otherwise she wouldn't have risked coming here."

"Interbreeding with humans is a big offense," Brad said with a whisper. He was a fae so he could speak to the possible severity. Fae were the only supernaturals that could successfully breed with humans, it didn't usually turn out well for the humans or their offspring.

Since supes lived so long, even though it was obvious that the chief was only at most a quarter fae, her grandfather who is fae would likely still be very much alive and up for punishment when found.

Brad pulled the sheet back off the body without preamble.

Sachi stepped back, bumping into Jax. He grabbed her shoulders and kept her from turning and running. Not only did she not want to be next to a dead body, but the smell of blood hit her, and she felt her fangs start to ache.

The woman was young, maybe thirty with short blonde hair and tan skin. She was naked now and Sachi could see the burn marks on her chest, black and blistered skin, they looked like handprints. Radiating out from the handprints were veins of black that covered nearly her entire upper body.

"I wish I could have helped solve this one, she's a hottie," Brad said with a shrug. "But…" he reached out and lifted an eyelid revealing a completely white eye. "No soul."

"What does that?" Sachi gasped, wanting any answer other than demon.

"The fae have legends of this," Brad said conspiratorially. "They say demons steal souls."

"Why?" Sachi whispered back as Jax slipped around her and approached the body.

Brad watched him carefully but didn't stop him.

"Demons can't survive above ground. Legend says that the demons and fae both lived in the underworld, but the fae stole souls from the sun and were able to come above and stay above. The demons were destined to stay below until they discovered they could steal souls from humans and then walk among them for a time. The fae locked the door though and saved the earth, it's why we are so powerful and loved," he said with a puffed chest.

Sachi had to try very hard not to roll her eyes. She was pretty sure she heard Jax snort. Brad caught it too, snapping his head around to glare at Jax's back.

"Demons, wow, I hope not," Sachi said, trying to keep him distracted.

"Well, it's the legend," Brad said. "This is likely just bad witchcraft."

"Witches don't steal souls," Jax said as he slipped the sheet the rest of the way off the body.

"Witchcraft done well doesn't need this sort of sacrifice," Brad agreed. "But powerful spells done sloppy need shortcuts."

Sachi couldn't argue with that. Spells were a lot of work and intricate in their casting. If you wanted to cut corners you had to bleed, or someone else did. She shuddered at the thought of one of their witches doing this to an innocent.

Sachi wasn't sure what Jax was looking for at this point, but it made her very uncomfortable to see the naked dead woman on the table and she turned away as he continued to stare.

"What does her back look like?" Jax asked suddenly.

Brad smiled brightly as if he were impressed. "You do know a little something, don't you?" Together the two men flipped the body carefully and she couldn't stop her curiosity, she turned back to look. There on the woman's back, burned into her skin, were runes.

"What the fuck," Sachi gasped.

"Have you ever seen anything like it?" Brad asked.

She wanted to say no, but something pricked the back of her mind, some kind of memory trying to push through. "I forgot," she whispered and Jax met her eyes knowingly.

Jax pulled out a notepad and quickly scribbled down the runes.

They left then, Sachi couldn't wait to breathe the fresh air outside. She promised Brad that she'd visit again soon and hoped that was a lie.

"I hope you learned something valuable there other than confirming we have more than one demon to search for." Sachi gulped in fresh air in the parking lot.

"You did," he said with a grin.

"Me?"

"You recognized the runes."

She pursed her lips, unwilling to admit anything.

"We just need to push your mind to open up enough to release the memory."

"Why does it matter, don't you know what they are?"

"Yes, but I need to know where you've seen them before." His tone was serious, and his eyes were worried.

Sachi's anxiety amped up, she didn't want to know that she'd seen that kind of death before. Maybe it was better to live in this demon induced happy place.

She knew that wasn't true, whatever the demons planned, it

wasn't to keep them all happy and healthy going about their daily lives. "Why?" she asked, resigned to discover more horror.

"Because they are demon runes, not witch runes. Something similar is on the knife that will kill the fire demon. Perhaps you know where that weapon is, perhaps your father had it and it's buried in the basement boxes?"

She bit her lip, the image of that woman, or thing, she'd seen her father talking to filled her thoughts. It was nothing she wanted to get close to, and why the hell had her father been dealing with it, what had he promised to do for it?

"I don't know, but I feel like at this point anything is possible."

"If it's there, I'll find it. It could be the only thing that tips the scales in our favor."

Sachi didn't like the sound of that.

They went back to the bakery, she didn't want to stay with her mother another night, and honestly, with Jax sleeping on a cot in the kitchen, she decided she felt safe enough. Anything that crawled out of the basement would eat him first and she could fly out the window as he screamed.

"Hey, I'm sorry about that kiss earlier," he said as she started to leave him with his sleeping bag and fold out cot.

"Sorry? Gee, that's what every little girl dreams of hearing," she said sarcastically.

"I wanted to assert my dominance over Cash. I didn't realize the relationship you two had was so deep."

"Neither did I," she said with a sigh as she headed upstairs.

"Do you love him?" Jax asked, standing at the bottom of the stairs now. She was almost to the top, she turned and looked down the narrow hallway at him.

"I care for him, he's my friend and when we were kids, yeah, I loved him."

"He still loves you."

"I guess I knew that," she sighed and waved a hand vaguely. "Somewhere in my messed-up head, I knew what we had going wasn't right. I guess when a demon messes with your memories, lots of things get twisted up. Not to mention it was easy feeding and I was selfish enough to take it."

Jax nodded thoughtfully. "If you let him go, there are other ways to feed."

"I know, I just don't like taking blood from strangers, or giving up mine in some kind of exchange."

Jax walked up the stairs two at a time, stopping just below her so their eyes were on level. "I'm not sorry I kissed you, Sachi, I'm just sorry that I did it for the wrong reason."

Her breath was coming in pants now, her body heated by his closeness and his reminders of the kiss. He reached out and grabbed her hips, his thumbs played along the skin at her waist.

"What's the right reason?" she asked, breathless.

"Because I want to," he said quietly. He leaned forward until his lips were almost touching hers. "And because you want me to." He pressed his lips gently to hers then. The kiss was soft and sweet, not deep and passionate like before, but it set her body on fire all the same and she groaned slightly, leaning into him. "I would give you my blood, Sachi, it would be an honor, but..." he trailed off as his hands moved to capture her wrists behind her back and his knee moved to force its way between her thighs.

She was trapped, by him and the stairwell door behind her. A flicker of panic went through her mixing with the passion he'd ignited and confusing her. She wasn't sure if she wanted to lean into him or run and it excited her.

"I *won't* be dominated or used," he whispered in her ear. "I give, you take." His teeth scraped over her earlobe and sent a shiver to her core. "I take, you give."

She melted into his body, "Yes," she groaned as his tongue flicked out and into her ear.

His answering groan was animalistic, and he picked her up. She wrapped her legs around his waist as he finished going up the steps and through her door. She pointed to the bedroom and he made his way with his mouth on her neck the entire time, tasting and teasing. She ran her hands up into his hair, holding him closer, encouraging him to feast at her neck. She pushed her breasts against his chest, his hands gripped her ass, and it felt wonderful.

He flung her onto the bed and stepped back to undress. She watched his quick movements, pulling his shirt off to reveal a muscled chest and pierced nipple that she couldn't wait to get her teeth on. His hands moved to his pants and she was frozen watching, leaning up on her elbows on the bed. He was male perfection and it had been too long since she'd had a body like that to play with.

"Are you going to undress too?" he teased as he bent to take off his shoes.

"Fuck yes," she said and started to remove her boots. Why did they have so many damn laces? She struggled with them, eager to be naked with this man. He stood from pushing his pants and underwear down and came to her with a smile. He was completely nude now and she locked her gaze on his erection. He had a tattoo on his lower abdomen that said *Relic*.

"Relic?" she asked with a laugh as he tugged off one of her boots and started to work on the other.

He looked a little embarrassed. "Yeah, drunk decisions."

"What does it mean?"

He didn't answer just pulled her other boot off and went to her waistband, his fingers were like fire where they brushed her skin and he worked quickly to undo buttons and zipper, pulling her pants down her legs, revealing her lacy pink thong.

She slipped her fingers under the delicate fabric and lifted her ass, slowly pushing her panties down her legs as his eyes devoured her. He still had her pants in his grip and she delighted in the way his hands were fisted in the fabric as if he were barely holding himself back.

"Purple," he groaned as she revealed her soft curls, matching the lilac of the hair on her head.

She bit her lip as he gazed down at her appreciatively then he dropped the pants and took over sliding the panties down her body. He pressed a kiss to each knee as he passed and when he slipped them over her feet he kissed the top of each. His slow pace and careful movements were surprising and left her aching for so much more.

He trailed kisses back up her legs, going from one to the other laying, first chaste simple pecks but progressively hotter, wetter and when he reached her mound of purple curls covering her now very wet and needy core she was unable to stop from arching her back and her hands gripped his hair.

"Yes," she groaned as his tongue snaked out of his mouth and ran the length of her slit. When he expertly found her aching clit and flicked it she cried out and shoved his head down hard, demanding more.

He gave it to her, with lips, teeth and tongue he had her spiraling in no time. His hands went under her to grip her ass and he lifted her hips off the bed as he feasted between her thighs. She could no longer hold on to his head, her hands above her gripped the blanket, trying to stay grounded, not wanting things to end too soon.

"Don't hold back, Butterfly, we're just getting started," he said and one thumb moved between her cheeks, pressing against her ass.

That was all she could take, the orgasm rocked through her and she screamed his name as her body stiffened and shivered and gushed. He laughed deep and satisfied as he lapped at her until she was still.

He crawled up her body, pushing her shirt up as he went, again laying chaste kisses on her. Belly, ribs, breastbone. She moved up just enough for him to slip the shirt off of her and she lay there with half closed eyes, feeling like jello after that orgasm. She watched him as he traced a finger around the edges of her pink lace bra. Her nipples were hard and obvious under the thin fabric and he bent his head, taking one in his mouth. The sensation of hot, wet mouth and the scratch of lace sent a jolt through her and she squirmed under him, her hands once again in his hair, holding him to her. He moved to the other and gave it the same attention then his hands slid behind her and he unhooked the bra. He sat up and pulled the last bit of clothing from her then stared down at her, his eyes roaming slowly up and down her body.

"Perfect," he said and leaned down to capture her mouth, dominating it with his tongue. Soon she was arching under him, desperate for more and loving that he was controlling the pace of the night.

"You will bite me here," he said indicating his chest. "Nowhere else."

"Jax, I—" she wanted to say she didn't need it, that she'd fed just that morning, but the look on his face said it wasn't up for debate. "Okay," she quickly agreed.

He flipped them and she was straddling him then. She knew what he wanted, and was excited to taste him. Her hips straddled his and she gently rubbed her wet sex against his cock as she leaned down to bite where he'd indicated. She was looking forward to mixing the pleasure of sex with the pleasure of feeding, it had been so long since she'd let herself have this. His hands ran up her legs and ass to her lower back and her entire body shuddered with anticipation. She locked eyes with him just before she dipped the final inch. She saw a possessive eagerness there that spurred her on. She licked the spot she was about to bite and his groaned answer made her smile. His hands moved to position his cock at her entrance and she adjusted her hips to give him better access.

"Good girl," he said and she thought she could orgasm just from that if he said it a few more times.

She opened her mouth and as her fangs entered him, he entered her. Thick and hot he pushed in easily because of how wet she was. His hands went to her hips, guiding the motions as he pushed all the way in. He was controlling every part of the interaction and she lost herself to it, taking and taking at his chest, his hot spicy blood filling her mouth and rushing down her throat as he took from her. His cock pounding in and out of her, his grip on her hips bruising as he moved her where he wanted. It wasn't long before she couldn't handle it anymore. She reared back, blood dripping from her mouth as she screamed. Her body shuddered on his with a second orgasm, clenching him deep inside of her as if her body didn't want to ever let go. His hands held her tight, still controlling the movement. He flipped them, never losing his deep position and loomed over her with his hands gripping the headboard as he thrust wildly, losing his own control until finally his body shuddered and shook his release, his head thrown back, groaning and hissing in pleasure. He was buried so deep she wondered if she'd feel bruised in the morning.

He gathered her in his arms and pulled her up, holding her tight against his body as they both shivered with aftershocks of pleasure. He pressed gentle kisses to her neck and shoulder and she wrapped her arms around his body, holding him close. She couldn't remember the last time she'd felt so satisfied.

When he stilled and pulled back slightly to look at her with half lidded eyes she became nervous, suddenly wanting to hide. But he just smiled and laid her back down then rolled so that they were laying on their sides, still joined.

"That was amazing," he whispered as he kissed her nose, then licked her lips, tasting his own blood. "You are amazing, Sachi."

And in that moment, she felt amazing. She kissed him and cuddled into his arms.

She moved one hand to the pierced nipple, disappointed she'd missed her chance to tug it gently with her teeth. Of course that just meant they had new things still to explore and the idea of doing this again made her very happy. Her finger ran around it until he grabbed her hand and held it away.

"You ready for more, Butterfly?"

She laughed and shook her head. "Just realizing I forgot I was going to play with that, you were far too demanding and distracting," she said, looking up into his face.

"I am," he admitted. "Demanding and possessive, however I would not deny you a pleasure, all you have to do is ask," he said, leaning down and kissing her sweetly. "You'll break up with the wolf in the morning," he whispered against her lips, his hands running up and down her back. "A submissive werewolf who thinks you own him is a dangerous thing, for both of us."

"Don't tell me what to do," she said carefully, a heavy worry slipping through the cocoon of pleasure they'd created.

He grabbed her chin and forced her to meet his eyes. "I thought we went over this. I'm the dominant in this relationship whether or not you're a blood sucker."

"What relationship?" she hissed and pulled her chin away. She would have gotten out of the bed but his other arm was holding her tightly to him. No matter that she'd just been thinking about how she wanted to do this again and again, he didn't own her or her actions with others, not this fast.

"Don't make me prove it to you."

"Prove what?" she demanded.

"That you like me, that you like this, and that I am indeed the dominant one."

She frowned at him and bared her fangs. She did like him, had loved the sex and partially both of those things because of his obvious dominance, but that didn't change the fact that one good fuck didn't equate to a relationship.

"Those don't scare me." He flipped her under him and caged her in with his arms. "I win," he said as he leaned down and kissed her.

She shifted to butterfly and was out from under him in an

instant flying away. She shifted back to human form standing at the bedroom door. "No, you don't. Now get out."

He leaned up on an elbow and looked at her with a grin. "That was cool."

She put her hands on her hips and tried to look serious even though she was naked; his blood dripping down her chin and his semen dripping down her leg, fuck she should have used a condom, she didn't even know this guy. How had that not occurred to her, how had she been so stupid?

"How about we call it a truce for now," he patted the bed. "It's late, let me take care of you and we can sleep."

She dropped her arms at his words. Take care of her? Why did that pull at her heart? She gave in, she didn't want to argue, she wanted to sleep and the thought of sleeping in his arms thrilled her a little too much.

"Fine, but this conversation isn't over," she said as she crawled into his waiting arms.

He spooned her perfectly and she almost wanted to cry at the feeling of rightness. His hands trailed over her body gently, soothing, and he kissed the top of her head.

"Bathroom?" he asked and she pointed. He hurried off the bed and into the bathroom, coming back quickly with a damp rag which he used to clean her thighs and sex gently.

She'd never been cared for like that and it did something to her, made her stomach flip as she watched him do something that was entirely about her care and keeping after he'd taken so demandingly from her. She thought she finally understood why this was an important part of sex, this was the unspoken thank you, the respect after the giving and taking.

When he was done and back in the bed, she cuddled into his chest feeling a kind of satisfaction she'd never experienced.

"So... relic?" she asked.

He huffed a laugh. "Yeah, I was on the football team in high school and it was my nickname."

"Why?"

"Because my dick is so amazing it belongs in a museum."

Sachi laughed, hard!

He popped up and glared down at her. "You disagree?" he challenged.

"I mean it's great but, museum relic worthy? I don't know about that."

"I guess I'll have to prove it to you."

"Not tonight," she said sleepily, an ache between her thighs told her she needed a rest even if her brain was questioning whether or not it would be worthwhile to power through another session of wickedly good sex with this warlock.

"No, not tonight my delicate butterfly," he agreed and continued to gently stroke her back.

She mentally made a list of ingredients for a birth control tonic spell as her eyes drifted closed.

CHAPTER 11

Sachi woke up slow and satisfied. Stretching out, she was surprised when her hand smacked against skin.

Then all the memories of last night came rushing back and she wasn't sure how she felt about it.

Jax groaned sleepily and pulled her body against him. He buried his face in her hair and nuzzled her neck. "Good morning my sweet little butterfly." He ran his hands up the front of her body and caressed her nipples. "There's a lot we didn't get to do last night." He pushed his body against her and she could tell he was ready to show her what he meant.

She bit her lip, her body already starting to react to him. Excited by his touch and the images his words brought up, her nipples hardened and her core began to warm. "Like capture a demon?" she said with a little gasp as he pinched one nipple playfully.

"Roll over and I'll show you," he demanded.

She did and as soon as her back was to the mattress, he moved above her, grinning triumphantly. "Good girl," he whispered against her lips.

"I want coffee," she said with a frown even as her hips pressed up against his hard cock, she couldn't help teasing him a bit, he already had an ego bigger than the district.

He pulled back and smiled. "Coffee, huh, can I convince you to wait fifteen minutes?"

"Fifteen, that's all it takes?" she teased, earning a hiss.

He pushed his hips against her, and she stopped thinking about coffee almost instantly as his cock pressed against her clit. She reached up and grasped his shoulders, arching her back.

He moved against her, sliding up and down her wet lips and clit. His hands braced on the bed, holding his upper body off of her so he could watch her face intensely as she shivered and gasped with each slide. Her eyes locked with his and she didn't even care that he looked so triumphant, that he looked so sure of himself. He moved masterfully against her body and she was desperate for it.

She slid her hands along his chest until she reached his nipples. His piercing was cool under her fingers and she gave it a light tug, watching as his eyes half closed at the sensation. She wanted more of that, more making him squirm. She kissed his chin and scooted her body down, instantly missing the feel of his hardness sliding over her clit, but she was on a mission to get what she missed last night. She laid a kiss to the almost invisible scar on his chest where she'd bitten him last night and she felt him stiffen slightly as if he expected her to bite again. But that wasn't her goal right now. She moved to his piercing and sucked it into her mouth.

The noise that emitted from his throat was half groan, half whine and she flicked her tongue over the sensitive spot a few times until his hips were thrusting against her belly and she felt the slick slide of precum relieve the friction.

Satisfied that she had him on the edge of control, she pushed him over onto his back. His eyes were tightly closed and he was breathing heavy now. She straddled his thighs and moved lower, dragging her tongue over the tattoo. With a gasp he grabbed her hair and she let him guide her head where he most wanted her. Licking at his head and down his shaft before gripping him at the base and taking him deep. His hips bucked and his hands pulled almost painfully in her hair as she worked carefully to avoid her fangs.

He didn't let her play long, she could taste him leaking out and his body was shaking with his effort to keep control. The temptation to pull back and sink her fangs into his thigh was nearly unbearable and when he pulled her head back, leaning up and gasping, eyes wide she met his gaze with triumph. He liked to be in control but she had him falling apart.

"I want to bite you here," she said, licking along his inner thigh. She looked up at him and whispered. "Please."

His eyes half closed and he grinned. "Such a good girl," he whispered and ran a hand from her hair down to her chin and gripped it firmly. "I think if you bite me now, I will be coming in your hair instead of your sweet cunt."

Sachi laughed and crawled up his body because she wasn't ready for this morning delight to end just yet, but another time, she'd take advantage of his weakened state to make him lose control like that and delight in her own feminine power.

He flipped them and pushed her thighs wide. His cock pressed at her entrance and he looked into her eyes like a predator. She shivered as he moved excruciatingly slowly.

"Do you need to feed?" he asked, his cock halfway in and her body desperate for more.

She could barely comprehend his words and his mouth quirked up in a cocky grin as he slid a little further in.

"No," she gasped out finally, her hands gripped his ass, her fingernails digging in trying to control what he was doing, trying to force him to go deep and fast.

His hand gripped her jaw and he leaned down, kissing her deeply. As his tongue swept into her mouth his hips bucked forward, finally giving her all of him.

She screamed into his mouth and his chest rumbled with laughter. He pulled all the way out and she thought she might cry with need but he flipped her to her stomach, lifted her hips high and slammed into her again. She could only hold onto the pillow and gasp against the fabric as he held her tight and slammed in over and over, touching her deep and then sliding out to hit that spot that had her rushing toward release.

He started to grunt and groan, his movements became more erratic and she knew he was close too. She slipped a hand down her body and started to rub her clit as he moved.

"Fuck, Sachi," he said and slapped her ass, hard, making her jerk and that was it, she was over the edge to orgasm, screaming his name into the pillow and he fell over the top of her, his blunt teeth biting into her shoulder as he groaned and shivered his own intense orgasm.

They collapsed together on their sides with him still buried deep, both shivering and sweaty. His hand ran up and down her front in a lazy pet. She reached behind him and swirled her fingers around one of his ass cheeks.

She barely knew him, but she couldn't remember ever feeling this good with another person and she knew she was going to miss him when he inevitably left.

He kissed her shoulder where he'd bitten her. It wasn't hard, she knew he hadn't even broken skin but she appreciated the care as he inspected the spot.

"I didn't hurt you?" he asked.

"No, not at all," she said with a smile she was glad he couldn't see.

"We may have to discuss more of what we like, Sachi, if we are going to keep doing this. It's hard to hold back in the middle of things and I don't want to cross any of your boundaries."

Her stomach clenched at his words. He was so caring and soft, even as he demanded from her and it was a balance she didn't know she wanted.

"You think we are going to keep doing this?" she asked.

He nipped at her ear. "Definitely."

"We have at least another day until the portal is closed, right?" she said, her voice hitching slightly and she wasn't sure if it was because his tongue was slipping into her ear or if it was at the thought of him leaving after they finished their job.

He sighed, "Which means we have no time to spare," he agreed. "Mind if I join you in the shower?"

Thirty minutes later they were out of the shower, and he was downstairs making coffee. She couldn't stop thinking about the way he made her feel, how he commanded her body and played it perfectly. She'd made him lose it in the shower, on her knees and hands gripping his thighs. He'd gripped her hair, pulled her head back and cum all over her chest. Then he'd pushed her against the wall and fallen to his own knees. He was all at the same time commanding and demanding and giving, she'd never been with anyone like that and it was addicting.

She dug around in the back of her closet and found an old tonic to prevent pregnancy and, hoping it was still good, she drank the whole thing, scowling at the bitter taste.

She couldn't stop herself from comparing Jax to Cash and she realized Cash definitely hadn't been submissive when they'd been together in high school. She remembered their sexual explorations clearly and even as young and inexperienced as they were, they had been satisfying. Cash had been almost as dominating as Jax, she was sure. He'd been in charge everywhere, the football field, classrooms, with friends and the pack. Had something changed when the memory spell took the town?

She supposed it didn't really matter because, either way, she had an embarrassing phone call to make and Fern to face too. Fern was going to know something happened between her and Jax as soon as she fluttered in the door, and Fern was not good at keeping her mouth shut about this sort of thing. She'd tell Lance and Lance would tell someone and soon the whole town would know she was sleeping with the new warlock in town who may be a murderer.

Once dressed, Sachi headed downstairs and found Jax sitting at the counter while Fern was starting on the day's cupcakes. He jumped up right away and poured her a cup of coffee, kissing her gently, making her blush as she took it to add her cream and honey.

Fern giggled.

"Thanks, um, Fern what are you starting?" she asked, distracted, and flustered. Apparently, he wasn't into keeping their tryst a secret.

"Chocolate cupcakes, next are snickerdoodles. You should make lemon glaze for scones," Fern suggested, barely containing her glee at the situation.

"Yum, I love lemon scones," Jax said brightly.

Sachi stirred her coffee longer than necessary to get her head straight, then turned to face Fern. "I slept with Jax."

"Duh," Fern said with a laugh.

"And I need to tell Cash," she added, flicking a worried glance in Jax's direction. He just sipped his coffee and watched with a smile.

"Why does he care? It's not like you two are a thing," Fern pointed out.

Sachi bit her lip and sipped coffee. "No, I didn't think so either but, Bernard last night, after you left, he pointed out something I think I'd been ignoring."

"And..." Fern prodded, impatient.

"I've been dominating Cash with my blood taking, especially since I haven't been giving him anything in return," she said in a rush. "Technically, he's my blood whore," she said the last like a whisper. A dirty secret she'd realized this morning and hated herself for.

"Oh," Fern frowned. "Yeah, I guess I can see that. But he's so strong, so big and virile. Isn't he supposed to be alpha?" Fern looked thoughtful and scratched at the back of her head. "He was supposed to be alpha," she said confused. "And he was captain of the football team, he was a big deal in high school."

"Yeah, I think so too," Sachi agreed. Something had gone on with the memory curse, it had changed Cash and when his father died... when was that? What had happened, why had Bernard taken over?

Jax finally spoke up, and obviously loved every second of it. "Oh no, the guy is super docile in the wolf pack, a real submissive wolf and she's been bleeding him for years, keeping her claim and owning his soul in the eyes of him and his pack."

"Damn! Sach, that's cruel," Fern said with a frown, angry for their friend.

Sachi wanted to stamp her foot. She glared at Jax. "It was an accident! And it has to be the demon's fault, not mine," she whined. She never would have intentionally hurt Cash or anyone else. She wasn't a cruel person. She cared for Cash, as a friend now and as so much more in high school, first love and all that.

"Sure, maybe you forgot that's what you've been doing for the last ten years," Fern agreed with an eye roll.

"We stopped dating ten years ago," she hissed. "I just forgot that it might be a problem, I was doing it because it was easy, I forgot..." she trailed off knowing it was bullshit. Best case scenario, she had been manipulated by a demon into stringing him along, worst case scenario, she'd been subconsciously dominating him for years. "He forgot he was dominant," she assured Jax. "And I forgot that taking his blood would keep him from moving on," she admitted to Fern.

Jax's eyes narrowed at the word *dominant*, and he got a thoughtful set to his lips. She wanted to ask what he was thinking about, but a knock at the front of the shop distracted her.

They weren't open for another couple of hours so she could have just ignored it, but she needed to get away from the conversation. Sachi hurried out of the kitchen and away from Jax and

Fern's gazes. She opened the door, still wound up in her head about how to talk to Cash. She was shocked out of it by the site of a werewolf police officer, most of the police force was werewolves.

"Zeb, can I help you?"

"I'm on duty, it's Officer Calin," he chastised.

"Okay," she drawled, annoyed. They'd known each other since kindergarten and she felt no need to be professional with him when she'd seen him eat his boogers and his glue stick. "Officer Calin, what do you want, we aren't open yet."

"You have an out-of-town visitor," it wasn't a question.

"She does," Jax said from behind her, startling her. She hadn't realized he'd followed her out here. "I'm Jax Lintel."

"Mr. Lintel, we'd like you to come down to the station and answer some questions."

"Of course," Jax said calmly. "Would tomorrow work? I promised Sachi that I would help deal with the mess in her basement today."

"Now," Officer Calin said, his eyes flashing and leaving no doubt that he would drag Jax in himself if necessary and probably enjoy it.

"I'll bring him down," Sachi said quickly.

"Of course you will," he huffed and gave her a dark look before turning. "Cash deserves better," Officer Calin threw over his shoulder as he walked off.

"How the hell is it that everyone is suddenly all up in my business about Cash," she hissed as she slammed the door. She faced Jax with hands on hips and a deep frown. Was it just because of him, because she'd shown up in public with a new guy?

Jax looked thoughtful. "When did you get your first memory back?"

"I guess it was thinking about my dad, it was when I was home in my old room. I pulled out my diary and read about the fire demon."

Jax nodded. "And the next day, you went to see Cash?"

Sachi rolled her eyes, "You know I did, you fucking followed me like a stalker."

He didn't deny it. "Did you remember anything there?"

"I... well yeah, I picked up a picture of us at prom and I remembered that we had been fighting that night and I remembered that we broke up soon after, but I couldn't remember what exactly it had all been about."

"Did Cash act weird?"

She thought about that. "Yeah, I think so, he was more possessive than usual. I actually started thinking I was going to need to find a new donor because he was starting to act like we were in some kind of relationship instead of just friends with a blood agreement."

Jax nodded. "I think you're not just unlocking your own memories, Sachi. I think maybe when you remember something, it triggers others to remember, but they don't realize they are remembering. It's like you unlocked group memories and they go back as if they knew all along without even realizing it. When you went to Cash's place and remembered your relationship, the breakup, and fights, it triggered the relationship in everyone else's minds. No one noticed or cared before, but now, they all remember and see why you two shouldn't be together. He's submissive to you and that's out of character for him." His face got that thoughtful look again. "Him not being a submissive werewolf could be a different issue," Jax said quietly.

"Shit. Did I bring the fire demon here by remembering it?" Sachi stepped back and leaned against the closed door, panic filling her. "Fuck, it's my fault that girl's dead." Tears stung Sachi's eyes and the picture of the girl's burned skin and soulless white eyes filled her mind.

Jax stepped forward and gathered her into his arms. He kissed the top of her head and rubbed her back gently. "No, Sachi. Demons destroy, that's what they do. You didn't bring it here.

You didn't make it choose to kill that girl." He pulled away and forced her to meet his eyes. "But you're going to help me destroy it and send it back to Hell."

She nodded. "I'm afraid to remember anything else," she whispered honestly.

"I know, sweet butterfly, I know." He pulled her in again and she buried her face in his chest. She had no business being this comforted by him, but she felt so at home in his arms she never wanted to leave his embrace.

After a few minutes she pulled away and wiped her face clean. "I'll grab my purse."

"You don't have to come with me if you don't want to. They don't have any real evidence otherwise it wouldn't have been a request to come in for questioning, it would have been handcuffs and the back of a squad car."

"I know those guys; I won't let them push you around. Fern can call in her siblings to help bake and we should be back about opening time, I hope." She frowned. "Not that we'll have much business today with the tourists locked out."

He smiled appreciatively.

When they arrived at the police station there was a group of elves standing around outside looking angry, which was their usual facial expression actually. They were all tall with long hair, but their similarities ended there, their skin and hair colors were varied to everything under the rainbow, their eyes too. They all had an essence about them that made them easy to identify as elf, but it wasn't like carbon copied. They all had pointed ears and dressed in muted colors, that helped give them a unified look which is something they strived for. Sachi noticed Chief Rodriguez on the other side of the glass glaring out at them from the waiting room.

"I guess someone told her the good news," Sachi commented.

"She refuses to give up her blood," one of the elves said casually. "But it doesn't matter, we'll get it."

"That sounds like threatening an officer," a police officer standing outside the doors snarled. Apparently posted there to keep the elves out so they couldn't harass the human.

"She's the threat. Her and whoever bred with her ancestor," an elf snapped back. "We don't even know if her parents and grandparents are alive. There could be more partials out there somewhere!"

"Not our problem," Jax whispered in her ear as he pushed her gently on past the officer standing guard and into the police station. "Elves breeding outside their kind is not a demon issue," he added.

"Sachi," the witch behind the front desk said cheerily as she walked in. Sachi wasn't sure if the witch was glad to see her, or if she was hoping to see her arrested. They hadn't ever been exactly friends.

"Hey, Beatrice. Have you seen Penelope's babies?"

"Oh yes," she gushed, "I can't believe how cute they are." Her face lit up with joy. Witches loved babies. "Who's this?" she asked darkly, her sharp blue eyes glancing up and down Jax, putting him directly into the warlock box and a stranger too. She didn't like him on sight and frowned. "You shouldn't be entertaining, this moon."

Sachi's cheeks flared. "No, I'm not. He's just a family friend."

Beatrice's eyes darted down to where Jax was possessively gripping her waist. "Sure. You smell like honeysuckle, at least you're being smart."

Sachi's cheeks flared even more and Jax raised an eyebrow at her. Honeysuckle was a main ingredient in the contraceptive tonic she'd taken that morning. "He's here to answer some questions. Zeb told us to come down, well told him to come down. I'm just here to make sure he doesn't get locked up for being my, uh, my out-of-town visitor."

Beatrice huffed, she wasn't buying it and honestly Sachi wasn't sure why she cared what the witch thought. Except that it wasn't as if she was planning to have a relationship with the guy. They were on a mission, and he'd probably be gone when it was done anyway, despite the great sex. Her stomach twisted a bit at the thought of him just walking away like it was nothing, she pushed it aside and bit her bottom lip, meeting Beatrice's unconvinced stare.

"I'll tell him you guys are here, wait over there," Beatrice said.

They took seats in the waiting area. Chief Rodriguez was still standing there, glaring out at the elves.

"What are you?" Chief Rodriguez asked, nonchalant. It was rude but seeing as she was the only human in a town full of supes, Sachi didn't hold it against her.

"I'm a butterfly shifter, though my dad was a warlock so technically I'm half witch."

She harumphed. "And your boyfriend?"

"He's not my boyfriend," Sachi said quickly.

"No, she wouldn't make that kind of commitment. She likes to dominate werewolves," Zeb said, coming into the room just then.

"You know what—" Sachi started but Jax cut her off with a pinch to her arm. Sachi rubbed it furiously as Jax got up and followed Zeb out of the room.

Zeb gave her a glare that clearly indicated she wasn't welcome to follow.

"I won't let you jail him just because he's staying at my bakery," she yelled as the door closed between them.

Chief Rodriguez looked at her with an eyebrow up.

"It's complicated," Sachi mumbled. "He's a warlock by the way."

"You own the bakery?"

"Yeah."

Rodriguez looked thoughtful. "You're a half something."

"Yeah," Sachi said carefully.

"So how often does that happen? I thought you all stuck with your own kind."

"We do, mostly."

After a minute of silence Chief Rodriguez asked, "Do you see it?"

"See what?" As if she didn't know.

"Whatever the hell has gotten the elves all fired up."

"Your aura, yeah, it's like just slightly blue. Witches can see auras. Now that I see it in the sun, it's got a bit of red in it too... that's an unusual color."

Rodriguez stiffened.

"Must be because you're mostly human," Sachi said quickly, not wanting to offend the officer.

"Why do they care so much?"

"They want to know because it means someone broke their laws, they are vicious about keeping order." Sachi looked the woman up and down. She looked worried under her tough act. "You might wish to know where you came from." Sachi sighed heavily. "It's good to know the truth of your past." *Like how your father is not a drunk criminal and there's a hole to Hell in your basement. Also good to know that you've been calmly dominating a werewolf for years, keeping him from being able to live a normal life.*

"Do you think they'll give up?"

"No," Sachi said honestly.

"They want some blood."

"Don't we all," she mumbled.

Chief Rodriguez didn't laugh.

"Would you do it?"

"Yeah, what if it's demon and not elf!" Sachi said with real terror as a new realization kicked in looking at that slight bit of red to her aura.

The woman looked at her with an inscrutable expression and walked outside.

"That was pretty good," Beatrice said from behind her desk. "I was getting annoyed sitting here staring out at them glaring at her."

"It could be true; demons can breed with humans like the fae and did you see that bit of red?"

"That's because they *are* fae," Beatrice said with a frown as if she knew it but wasn't sure why she knew it.

"Fuck," Sachi hissed and looked down at her feet, she was affecting people's memories again and she wasn't sure that was a good thing. Panic right now would really not be a good idea. If the demons got wind of their search they would disappear, or kill everyone, or who knows what. The only thing keeping her safe might be the fact that the demon probably thought she still didn't know anything.

Demons can breed with humans, demons are fae. As soon as Sachi had formed the thought she'd known it was true, like a fact she'd learned once and remembered just now. So what did that mean?

She thought of her father and the fire demon, could they have been lovers? She shook herself. No, that was too much to think about.

Sachi settled back and thought about her next move. She needed to unlock some more memories and she decided the best place to do that was the first place a memory had unlocked. She needed to go to her childhood bedroom.

When Jax walked out from the back, he looked annoyed but unharmed and free to go. Zeb came out behind him and glared at Sachi. "He's not to leave town. I expect I can find him at your place if I need to ask him anything else?" he said accusingly.

"Sure, he'll be staying on a cot in my kitchen."

Zeb huffed, disbelieving.

Jax gave her a wink and grabbed her arm, leading her outside.

Beatrice snickered as they went. "Kitchen," she huffed. "Bad moon, Sachi. Wrap that thing up. You can't trust honeysuckle in July."

Sachi looked over her shoulder and glared, but Beatrice

wasn't paying attention, she had her cellphone out and Sachi had a feeling she was telling all her coven sisters about this little interaction.

"Witches avoid making babies in July. I am guessing it has to do with the portal," Sachi said as they exited the building.

"Um, well babe, I think you're great and all, but I wasn't planning to have kids any time soon," Jax said smoothly.

"Very funny, I'm no idiot. I took a honeysuckle tonic this morning, but we'll wrap it up next time," she snapped.

He stopped and pulled her into an embrace, kissing her sweetly. "So you admit there will be a next time? I thought I was going to be sleeping on the cot in the kitchen tonight."

She glared at him and the very public display he was making. "Still might be." She pushed on his chest, but he didn't let go, just leaned down and kissed her nose.

She was annoyed enough to shift to butterfly, and he almost fell over at the sudden change. She reappeared behind him and walked on to the car with her head held high. The group of elves were gone, and so was Chief Rodriguez so maybe no one had seen that intimate exchange.

Jax caught up to her quickly with a grin and they climbed into Sachi's car. Once inside, she demanded to know what Zeb had asked.

"Standard stuff, where I'm from and why I'm here. How long I plan to stay, that sort of thing. Apparently, I'm not allowed to leave until the investigation is over, so it really didn't matter what my plan was."

"Took long enough."

"Yeah, he left me in there to sweat for a while, then came back and let me out after asking me the same questions over again."

He leaned across the car and captured her chin with his hand and her lips with his. His kiss was deep and left her lightheaded and warm in her center. When he pulled back, he looked deep into her eyes, and she melted. "I'm not sleeping in the kitchen, and I have zero problem with wrapping it up. I just assumed since you didn't say anything last night that you were on something."

Sachi's cheeks flared and her hand trembled as she started the car. "Um, yeah, it's been a while, so I guess I just kind of forgot the routine."

He nodded and sat back, clearly satisfied with her answer. "Where to now? Back to baking?"

Sachi groaned and looked at the clock. It was about time to open. "A couple hours at the bakery, then we can head to my mom's place. I think I might remember something more if I can be around my old things from ten or more years ago."

"Good plan, love."

She bit her lip and drove, ignoring the stab of delight that one little word sent into her.

CHAPTER 12

"I'm going to search boxes downstairs for the knife that has those runes drawn on it like the body. If you recognized them, it could mean your father had it and you saw it when you packed. There also might be other helpful things down there in that mess. If you remember anything, come get me," Jax said as they walked back into the bakery.

Fern was busy in the kitchen already and Seraphina was there helping. They both eyed Jax as he walked through and down the stairs.

Sachi pulled on an apron. "So far he's not under arrest, but he can't leave town," she said to the silent questions. "How did the revenge cupcakes go over?" she asked Seraphina, changing the subject.

"Well, I called Franklin the next night, you know just to see how he was doing. No big deal, we are broken up but we can still be friends," she said with teenage attitude as she stuck the knife she'd been frosting cupcakes with into her mouth. "He said that he hadn't been feeling well the night before and he thinks he'd just been coming down with something the night before that and that's why he was so angry and broke up with me." She said it like it made perfect sense, and to her teenage brain, Sachi figured it probably did. The poor girl was doomed to heartache by that boy's pretty face and shiny fangs.

"Don't!" Sachi hissed as Seraphina moved to stick the licked knife back into the frosting. "Give me that," she snapped and took the bowl. "Go out front and flip the sign, we can open at the regular time, even though I doubt we'll see anyone."

"Jeez, sorry, Sach, I thought you'd be less cranky, Fern said you got laid."

Sachi turned an accusing glare to Fern who just beamed a happy smile. "Truth, but she's still cranky, so go do your job," Fern ordered.

Seraphina shrugged and hopped off the counter, dropping the knife in the bowl of frosting on her way to the front.

Sachi had to take a breath, that girl was flighty as hell. "Fern, maybe one of your other siblings would be a better helper." She scraped the contaminated frosting into the garbage.

"Yeah, but none of them like to bake, Seraphina thinks it's fun because she can sample the sweets."

"Obviously," Sachi grumped as she started a new batch of the lemon frosting to go atop the vanilla cupcakes.

"So…" Fern hinted and nodded toward the basement door.

"So what?"

"What's the deal with you two?"

"No deal. He's here to help and I'm… enjoying his company while he is."

Fern giggled and then the front door dinged with a customer and Sachi grabbed the freshly frosted cupcakes, which honestly were probably full of fairy spit, and carried them out to the front to avoid any further questions.

"Cynthia, nice to see you. Are you looking for some wolfsbane cookies for the kids?" Cynthia was a werewolf Sachi had known since high school. Although she was a year younger than Sachi, she already had two kids at home and one more on the way. Werewolves really were all about big families.

"Can't get them anywhere else," she said with a tight smile. "And I'm too tired to bake right now." She rubbed her large belly.

Sachi tried to keep her own smile in place as she packaged the usual order and handed it over the counter. "Seraphina will ring you up."

"Thanks," she said and hurried to pay and leave without her usual happy conversation.

"Wow, cranky wolf," Seraphina said as the door shut behind her.

"Yeah, what's that all about?" But she knew, it had to be about Cash. Probably the whole pack hated her now.

Her theory was further assured when the next three werewolves who came in for wolfsbane cookies treated her with the same grudging politeness. It had all changed, just like that.

"I'm going for a walk. We aren't getting many customers anyway," she decided.

"Okay," Seraphina said as she stuffed what had to be her third éclair into her mouth.

"Fern, I'll be right back!" she called toward the back then walked out the front of the bakery. The sun was warm on her skin, she closed her eyes for a moment and breathed in the fresh air. She listened to the sounds of the district, quieter than usual but she could hear voices around, kids playing at the nearby park, and someone had gotten roped into a conversation with Maureen. Sachi could hear the old fairy's voice droning on happily.

Sachi opened her eyes and looked up and down the street. It looked the same as always, minus the tourists. Maureen was indeed talking the ear off of a young werewolf mother who had a baby in the stroller rocking back and forth. Maureen was probably offering parenting advice. She had raised a large brood of fairy children in her day.

Sachi was surprised to see so many witches out, they didn't usually come through until after dark. She supposed it was because they weren't getting any business today either so why not do their shopping while they could also enjoy the sunshine.

They weren't avoiding her like the werewolves were, now that she thought about it, she'd gotten more than the usual witch customer today and none of them had been pissy, well no pissier than usual, and they'd all looked at her with secret smiles. No doubt they all knew she was sleeping with Jax, because no one in this town could keep a damn secret. She sat on the steps in front of her shop and pulled out her phone. She should call Penelope and check in, but even better would be stopping by with a treat.

Sachi went back inside the bakery and boxed up some fresh chocolate chip cookies then headed to Penelope's house. She waved at Maureen who was still telling her story about when one of hers was small. The werewolf she was talking to wouldn't even meet Sachi's eye.

Sachi barely resisted forcing a conversation with her, she knew her of course, Willow, she was quite a few years younger than Sachi and married to a werewolf just as young. What right did she have to judge Sachi's love life?

When she turned onto Witch's Row the looks changed from hostile to curious. "Oh hun," a crackly voice called from a garden.

Sachi walked over to the gate and peered into the thicket of green at the little old witch sitting cross legged on a stone. She was wearing black spandex leggings and a black lace tank top. She was covered in wrinkles and her tan skin showed all the years of sun she'd never hidden from. *Sunshine is life*, Dolly had told her a million times growing up. And apparently, she hadn't discarded that theory because she was soaking up the July sun like it was about to disappear. She had completely white hair piled on top of her head, and her eyes were still as bright and shrewd as ever.

"What can I do for you, Dolly?"

"You heading over to Pen's with those cookies?"

Sachi laughed, "I am, but would you like one?" Sachi opened the box and reached it over the gate.

Dolly took one and set it on her knee to save for later. Or maybe she was going to do a spell with it, you never knew what Dolly's motivations were. Sachi remembered one time as a kid, Dolly had helped her after she'd scraped her knee on the playground nearby and had then tucked the bloody rag into her pocket. Sachi hadn't thought anything of it until a month later when she had gotten chicken pox and Dolly had shown up on her mother's doorstep with a lotion that took them right away. Sachi was willing to bet money that she'd made it from the blood she'd taken from Sachi's knee.

"You shouldn't be entertaining this month, it's a bad moon. Didn't your father teach you that before he died?"

Sachi's cheeks flamed, as if she would ever discuss sex with her father. "I guess not, but don't worry, I'm being careful."

The old woman huffed. "Careful is the middle name of many a child."

"Noted," Sachi said and stepped back.

Dolly closed her eyes and Sachi took that as a dismissal. She continued on down to Penelope's house.

The announcement banners were gone but the sign still said closed.

The door swung open before Sachi could knock and Penelope stood there with a baby in each arm. "Thank god, I need a cookie," Penelope said and handed one of the babies to Sachi. "I knew you'd come; I sent a heavy thought out into the universe asking for a sweet, and here you are!"

Sachi held the baby like it was a bomb as Penelope easily

juggled the one in her arms and the box of cookies at the same time. When she turned to go back inside, Sachi noticed that there was a third baby strapped securely to her back. "Damn, you're like a professional baby handler already," Sachi said with awe.

"Have to be," Penelope laughed and led the way through the shop to the private part of the house.

They settled into the living room and Sachi tried not to look longingly at the bassinet as she sat on the edge of the couch with the baby in her arms. How long until it wouldn't be rude to set the baby down?

"You're the talk of the district with that handsome warlock in your house," Penelope said around a mouthful of cookie.

Sachi sat back and groaned. "I know, I know, bad moon and all that. Trust me, I don't plan to get pregnant, I'm just taking some fun where I can."

Penelope nodded. "I get it, trust me, no witch is looking down on you, we just don't want you to have a cursed baby. July conceptions are an open door to black magic practitioners."

Sachi nodded as memories formed. No one wanted to get pregnant in July and any babies born in April were known to be predominantly black magic users. They were often ostracized as soon as they reached the age of magic, usually puberty, and sent to a northern district. It had to be because of the portals, the energy that the portals displaced during the July full moon must influence a delicate early stage pregnancy.

"How are these three doing?" Sachi asked to change the subject.

They talked about the triplets for a while and whether or not Chief Rodriguez was part demon, then Sachi excused herself. She needed to be back at the bakery before sundown and she needed to talk to Cash. She really didn't want to talk to Cash but Jax was right, everyone was right, she needed to let him go.

As if on cue, her phone dinged with a message from Jax.

You left...

Had to visit Penelope, did you find something?

Next time tell me you're leaving.

Sachi huffed and put the phone away. "Are all warlocks possessive and dominant?" she asked Penelope.

"Only the good ones," Penelope said with a grin and a wink. "Are you sure he isn't trying to make you his baby mama?"

Sachi rolled her eyes. "Definitely. But I better go. I do need to talk to Cash today." She handed the baby to Penelope and kissed her cheek. "Call me if you need anything."

"I will."

Sachi hugged her friend tight then turned to leave, tears burning her eyes. Those babies needed a safe place to grow up and damnit, she was going to make sure they got it.

The walk back to the bakery in the fading light was peaceful.

Maureen stopped her as she walked by the tailoring shop.

"I see you kept that handsome stranger," Maureen said with a raised eyebrow.

"I guess I did," Sachi admitted.

"He's a catch, don't let him go. Let me tell you, when I met Randal I almost lost him to a twit in the Central California District who had breasts the size of cantaloupes!"

Sachi bit back a laugh and nodded. "Yes, I'll do my best, have a good night, Maureen." She hurried away before Maureen could continue her story. She knew she was being rude, but she really didn't want to get into it with her, or anyone else for that matter. "Christ, why is my sex life top of everyone's list today?" she grumbled as she stepped into the bakery. Fern was behind the counter now, rearranging cupcakes in the display. Seraphina was nowhere to be seen and Sachi hoped the girl had decided to leave for the day. Probably off to get ready for a date with Franklin.

Fern just shrugged. "This district doesn't usually have much excitement."

Sachi couldn't argue with that. She debated letting Jax know that she was back, but didn't want to encourage his attitude of ownership. She went into the kitchen and started a batch of chocolate chip cookies. When they were in the oven she was left staring at the door to the basement, annoyed that he hadn't come up and said anything to her. Did he even know she was here, did he care? He'd certainly cared when she was gone without telling him.

She bit her lip and stared until she grew too frustrated. She threw open the door with a little more aggression and yelled down into the basement. "Some fresh cookies are about ready." She decided that was the perfect solution. She wasn't telling him she was back as if he were her keeper, but she wasn't ignoring him like a sulking child either.

"Cool, I'll be up soon," he called back.

"He needs real food," Fern said from behind her, making her jump.

"I know that," Sachi snapped back and stomped over to the fridge. She pulled out some simple ingredients and whipped up a quick salad and threw some chicken into the oven when she pulled the cookies out.

"Is this for me?" Jax asked, coming up into the kitchen. He pulled Sachi close for a kiss.

"If you want," she whispered against his lips.

"I do want," Jax said with a grin that told her he wasn't talking about food.

"Woah, get a room," Fern laughed, grabbing the plate of cookies and taking them to the front.

"I think technically this is my bedroom," Jax said with a sly look at where the cot was currently folded up and leaning against a wall.

"Eat. I hear customers," Sachi said and pulled away with a grin on her face.

Jax ate the salad greedily and the chicken once it was out as well. She was going to have to remember that warlocks needed more actual food than her.

She couldn't help wondering what would happen once the portal was closed, once the demons were taken care of. If they survived all that, would he be moving on, going home? She didn't like the way that thought made her stomach hurt.

He finished his food, ate four cookies and went back into the basement.

When the sun set and the vamps started coming in, she was relieved that none of them seemed to have any new knowledge and it felt like business as usual until Jax came up the stairs with a leatherbound book.

"Oh, what's that?" Fern asked.

"Instruction manual for the portal," he said, dropping it onto the counter in front of Sachi.

"Does that help us?" Sachi asked with hope.

"It helps you. I already know all this stuff."

Sachi glared at him and picked up the book then huffed with annoyance. "I've seen this before."

Jax came close and kissed her cheek, "I figured you had. Maybe it'll get some of your memories back."

Fern giggled at the show of affection.

"No knife?" Sachi asked.

"No," Jax frowned. "I only got through about half of the boxes though. Did you throw anything out?"

"I couldn't," she admitted with a shrug. "It just felt wrong. Even with the memories gone, I knew that he loved me and sending his life to the landfill felt like a betrayal."

Jax wrapped his arms around her from behind and she leaned into it, loving the comfort. "You need to talk to Cash," he whispered in her ear.

"I know," she said, pulling out of his arms. "I want to do it in person and it's not like I've had time today."

Jax looked around the empty shop. Even Fern had gone in the back to clean up.

"Fine," she snapped and grabbed her purse, flinging her apron off. "I'll go talk to him."

He caught her arm before she could get out the door. When she turned to him his eyes were intense and his lips set in a hard line. "You won't be biting him." He ordered.

"Excuse me?"

He ran a finger over her lips. "As long as I'm here, you won't be getting your blood from any other source," he whispered. "I own these lips." He trailed his hand down her throat. "And this delicious body." His finger trailed lightly over her breasts and lower, hooking into her waistband and pulling her body against his. "I own all of your hunger and need."

"As long as you're here," she said and tried to ignore the tightness in her belly.

He grunted and then his mouth was on hers and her mind was melting along with her body. He was making her feel things that had been dormant for far too long. Made her feel special and beautiful, desired, and sexy. She moved her hands up into his hair and pulled gently, delighting in his moan. It was going to hurt when he left.

His tongue slipped across one of her fangs, cutting it enough to drip blood into her mouth but he didn't pull back, wasn't afraid and it drove her wild. She lifted one leg, wrapping around his and pressing her body forward.

"Woah, we aren't closed, guys, cool it!" Fern said as she came back into the shop.

Sachi untangled herself from Jax who was smiling smugly at her. He wiped the blood from her lips then kissed them softly. "Go on, I'll be here when you're done, and we'll head to your mother's to unlock more memories."

"Where are you going?" Fern called, clearly not reading the intimacy of the moment well.

"I have to go break up with Cash."

"Oh good, poor guy's been strung along long enough."

Sachi glowered as she turned to leave. It wasn't her fault, damnit. She wasn't responsible for the memory-erasing demon that triggered this shit.

CHAPTER 13

Sachi drove to Cash's house, not sure how she was going to explain it all to him. It really wasn't her fault, and she did care for him. She just wasn't interested in a relationship with him. How did she tell him that without hurting him?

Cash was sitting on his porch when she got there. Just a pair of faded low-slung jeans on and looking sexy as hell. She hadn't dated him in high school for his brains.

"Hey Sach," Cash said with an excitement that made her feel guilty.

"We need to talk," she said, keeping a distance. She stopped midway down the walkway.

"Talk or eat?"

Guilt spiked in her. When was the last time she'd visited him and *not* taken what she wanted and left. Fuck, she was brutal.

"Did you sleep with him?" He growled, not meeting her eyes. His hands were clenched in front of him and she wanted to take a step back but she stopped herself. She knew he wouldn't hurt her and she deserved his anger.

"Yes," she said quietly, there was no use lying. "And why shouldn't I? We aren't in a real relationship, Cash."

He stood then and glared at her. He was angry but she knew it was just covering his hurt and that killed her. She had a feeling he'd been expecting her, she was willing to bet Bernard had been by today to tell him that they were to break up. She doubted he would have done it, he would have let her keep taking from him. Why would he do that?

"You've been on my couch with your fangs in my body twice a week for ten years, Sachi! How the fuck do you explain that? Now some new guy sweeps into town for what, a couple days, and I'm nothing to you? What about when he leaves, are you going to expect me to just be sitting here waiting with my tail wagging?"

His words hurt her, and he knew it, could see a hint of satisfaction behind his own hurt. He wanted her to feel as bad as him, and she couldn't say he was wrong to do it.

Sachi took a breath, trying to remain calm. "My fangs, Cash. Only my fangs. Once in those ten years we fucked and that was —" she stopped, not wanting to hurt his feelings more.

"Was what? Just because you felt sorry for me after my parents died?" He growled. Anger was his only defense. He ran a hand through his hair in frustration, leaving the already shaggy mess even sexier. "Damn it, Sachi," he whispered.

Tears stung her eyes as her heart broke for her friend. "I love you. You're important to me. But I am not interested in dating you and I'm sorry. I shouldn't have been using you like that. I didn't realize it was keeping you from moving on with your life." She thought of the way he lived. Stuck in a time when his parents had been alive and they'd been dating. He hadn't even ever moved out of his childhood bedroom and into the master bedroom of the house. He was frozen, maybe the whole town was.

"I love you, too. My heart, my blood, it all belongs to you, Sachi," he was quiet now as he tried another tactic.

"I don't want it," she said firmly.

"Don't want it!" he yelled, throwing his hands up in the air. "Why the fuck not?"

"Because we aren't a good match, you know that. It was never supposed to be forever."

"Says who?"

"Everyone," she sighed. "Talk to your alpha, get back on track with your pack, Cash."

He turned his head, breaking eye contact. "Bernard already *talked*."

"And," she prodded.

"He says if I let you in my veins again he'll kick me out of the pack. Says I need to do my duty to the pack and pick a bitch, settle down and make pups."

"Oh." She didn't know what to say to that. It made sense and it had been what she'd expected Bernard to say. Every other werewolf they'd gone to school with already had at least one kid. She crossed the distance separating them and touched his shoulder. "I hope we can still be friends."

"I would have left it all for you." He turned back and looked pleadingly into her eyes. "Sachi, I want nothing more than to lay down at your feet and be everything you want me to be, just like old times."

She gave him a weak smile, that was exactly what she didn't want. "I think we remember the old times differently."

He turned without saying anything more and walked into the house, closing the familiar door between them. His memories hadn't returned the same as hers. She remembered the strong alpha jock in high school, but he thought she'd *always* been the one in charge of their relationship. Not that it mattered now, she knew it was best to cut off what they had. As she walked back to her car she heard a deep mournful howl come from his backyard and answering calls all throughout the werewolf neighborhood and it broke her heart.

She knew she'd done the right thing, but it didn't make it any less painful.

"Not my fault," she gritted out as she started the car. It was the demon, it had done this to them, set them onto this weird alternate path. But why had it messed with her and Cash like that? What was the benefit of keeping Cash submissive?

She sat in her running car, hands on the steering wheel and deep in thought. It didn't make sense. Making them forget the Hell portal made sense, making everyone think her father was nothing more than a drunk bar owner made sense. Forgetting that demons existed in reality made sense. But why make Cash submissive, what did that have to do with the portal and the demons?

She looked at his house and frowned, turning the car back off. His parents died almost ten years ago.

"Holy shit!" she squealed and jumped out of the car and ran up the steps. "Cash! I'm coming in! We need to talk."

She burst in to find him naked, having shifted to wolf and back again. His eyes lit up as if she were about to tell him she'd changed her mind. She rippled with guilt all over again.

"There's a portal to Hell in my basement and you are *not* submissive. I think I need you to know that, to remember that. I think it's important."

His expression changed into one of disbelief as she explained what had happened since Jax showed up. Then she grabbed the picture of them at prom.

"Do you remember what happened right before we went to the prom?"

He looked thoughtful and rubbed his temples as if his head hurt. "I picked you up at your mom's place."

"No, you picked me up at my dad's bar," she corrected as memories flooded back in to her own head. "Your dad was there."

"My dad didn't drink..." he trailed off and his eyes widened as memories started to surface. "Shit, they were having a meeting."

"Like they did every week," she added, giddy with excitement. "Yes! I think your dad was involved in the portal keeping. I think *you* should be too. That's why the demon didn't want anyone to remember you are an alpha. I need you, Cash. The whole fucking district needs you."

A grin broke out across his face and he crossed the space in a flash, grabbing her roughly and pulling her against him, then he smashed his lips to hers. She stiffened and put her hands against his chest to push him away but was met with hot familiar flesh and she didn't want to push it away. His lips assaulted her expertly and his tongue demanded entrance. She couldn't say no, didn't want to.

The smell of him filled her nose and her insides burst into heated desire. Before she could think better of it, her lower body was rubbing against his hardening cock. He growled and his hands moved to her ass, crushing her against him, grinding against her.

"I am *not* a submissive, Sachi. I won't lay at your feet, but I will take all the fucking pleasure from seeing you at mine," he growled into her ear and she trembled.

"Oh fuck, Cash," she whined as all thoughts of control and stopping him left her. He'd always been able to push her buttons expertly. Her nipples were hard, her skin prickled and her panties were damp. His words were like a stroke against her clit and she was shivering with need already.

He was already naked and she slid down his body, kneeling before him, she grasped his cock and licked it, base to tip. The familiar taste of him made her groan and she clamped her thighs tight, trying to relieve some of the desire that was spurring her to act fast. His hands were in her hair and his dark eyes were watching her every move. She loved the taste of him, musty and male. She took him fully into her mouth, careful to only play the edges of her fangs across his delicate skin the way she knew he liked.

His responding moans and the way his hands fisted in her hair spurred her on and she used every trick she knew to take him to the edge, worshiping him the way she knew he wanted and deserved. Ten years of teasing, she was lucky he hadn't thrown her out on her ass.

A low rumble in his chest was the only warning she got before he was pulling her up, turning her around, and bending her over the back of the couch. He ripped her shorts and panties down, kicked her legs apart and thrust into her. She bucked against him and threw her head back, crying out with the pleasure of it. She was so wet and ready, there was no resistance, only fullness and pleasure as he slid in and out at a punishing pace. One hand was on her hip and one was wrapped in her hair, both inhibited her movements as he possessed her.

"Mine," he growled as he pounded into her and her cunt clenched around him, her clit pulsing. He wrapped an arm around her front to pluck at her nipples through her thin shirt until she was screaming at the sensation, begging him to take her over the edge. His other hand slipped down to slide over her clit and that was all she could take. Her body clenched and shuddered as wave after wave of pleasure rocked through her. He thrust his arm over her mouth, not to silence her screams but to give her that one last piece she so desperately needed. She sank her fangs, drawing his blood and came again instantly.

He growled and howled and thrust into her again and again as his own orgasm took him. Then he collapsed over her, his head buried in her neck.

She was shaking, her knees wouldn't hold her, and she loved it. "That was something else," she whispered, and he chuckled against her neck.

He moved slowly, pulling back and then lifting her gently into his arms. He carried her to his bedroom as she rested her head against his chest.

She was so confused.

He laid her down gently on his bed, then went and got a cool towel. Without a word he cleaned her intimately then cuddled beside her, pulling her against his chest tightly. It felt so right she wanted to cry.

"It's okay," Cash whispered as if he could sense her dilemma.

"How is it okay?" she whispered through the tears.

"This feels right, doesn't it?"

"Yes," she admitted.

"Then it's okay."

She turned in his arms and looked up at his face full of male satisfaction. "How?" she demanded. "I think I'm in a relationship with Jax."

Cash chuckled and smoothed her hair away from her face. "I'm going to challenge Bernard for alpha."

"What?" she hissed, sitting up. That wasn't what she'd expected to hear in response to her admission.

"It's my place, I can feel it. I didn't before, but I do now. Maybe I was grieving for the last ten years, maybe I needed to feel your acceptance to realize I could move on."

"That's dangerous."

"So is chasing demons," he said with a frown. "You really believe this guy who showed up with stories of demons?"

She nodded. "I do, Cash. I saw the portal with my own eyes and then I started to remember things. There's no way to explain what was forgotten without a really bad curse, nothing a witch or warlock could do. Demons have to be to blame." She shivered. "And I saw the girl's body. Cash it was horrible, nothing but a demon could have made those marks and taken her soul."

"A warlock could have taken her soul for a powerful black magic spell," he reminded her.

"I know, and I also know that there's no reason for you to believe me, but Cash, please, can you at least try to see? At least take a chance that it could be true, think of all the kids who could die at the hands of demons if we don't figure this out in time. I think you're important to the whole thing, I think I need you."

That was the clincher for him, she could see it in his eyes, the fear for the innocent and the chance to be what she needed. He nodded and kissed her. "I think I believe you and that's scary as fuck."

"I'm glad. I really do think I need you, but it doesn't change the fact that this thing," she motioned between them. "Is probably a bad idea."

"The only thing that is a bad idea, is not taking pleasure in life where you find it. Nothing like impending doom to up the sex drive."

She wasn't sure she agreed with that, but it fit nicely with her recent sleeping around, so she settled back into his arms to think. Was Jax going to try and kill Cash before she could explain that they needed his help?

"Will you try *not* to kill Jax? I think I need him too."

"No promises, but I won't do anything to endanger the district so if you say he's important to the closing of the portal, I won't kill him before then."

She figured that was as good as it was going to get for now and she was an adult, she made this bed, she'd lie in it. With two fucking sexy men? A thrill ran through her at the thought.

"I'm going back to the shop to grab Jax, then heading to my mother's."

"We. We are going to grab Jax and go to your mother's," he corrected.

She rolled her eyes as she got up and found her shorts in the living room, her underwear were in two pieces now and she had to throw them in the trash. Cash came out dressed in shorts and a t-shirt, ready to go and looking sexy as hell. There was a new aura about him, it was strong and fierce and made her insides tingle. She was seeing him like she had in high school, and it felt right.

"I missed you," she said shyly.

He wrapped his hand in her hair and forced her eyes up. "I missed me, too," he said with a wink, then kissed her before she could complain about the missed compliment. When he pulled away, he grinned wide. "I really missed fucking you and I am going to tear apart the demon who did this to us. We were on a track, Sachi. Wolf or not, we were going to rule the pack together."

She remembered that being a vague plan at one point and the knowledge that he was going to have to go after Bernard sooner rather than later worried her.

She drove them back to her bakery and she was full of anxiety by the time they parked. "Maybe I should go in first and talk to him."

"Maybe *I* should go in first and get rid of him," Cash growled.

They glared at each other until the back door to the bakery opened and Jax walked out and leaned against the building, arms crossed and face unreadable, he stared at them as they sat in the car.

Sachi hurried out of the car, ready to beg and plead for understanding.

"He figured it out?" Jax said when Cash's door slammed.

"Umm, yes," she said, unsure and a little annoyed that there was a chance Jax had manipulated this situation in some way. Had he known all along that the demon had suppressed Cash's dominance?

His expression remained steady, his emotions controlled and unreadable. "Alpha wolves aren't good at sharing, so how is it that you got him to not run over here and rip my throat out?" Jax asked with little apparent concern. Sachi had a feeling he wasn't as relaxed as he looked though, probably already had a spell ready in case Cash did exactly that.

Sachi wasn't sure what to say about it all. What was with all that possessive shit and sending her to break up with Cash if Jax had figured this was the likely outcome? Did he even care, or was he glad that now he had an excuse to leave her behind when the job was done?

"What the fuck?" she yelled, frustration taking over.

Jax straightened away from the wall and crossed the distance to her. He grabbed her chin gently and kissed her lips, ignoring the possessive growl from Cash. "Babe, if I had told you everything right away, I don't think you'd have believed me. Not only that, but I might have missed my chance to prove that you need me too."

She frowned at him, but she didn't pull away. "I don't like being manipulated."

"Would it help if you knew that I really don't mind sharing if it means I get you too," he whispered in her ear, but she knew Cash had heard it too, he was close and glaring at the two of them.

"I mind!" Cash snarled.

"Well, get over it. Butterflies don't mate with just one male, why do you think her mother never married? I knew that going in, but I would have kept her to myself as long as possible, don't get me wrong, sharing isn't my first choice, I'd just rather have her sometimes than never."

Sachi opened her mouth to deny it, then shut it. Jax wasn't wrong.

"And witches don't mate for life," Jax added. "So either you let her have all that she needs, or you'll lose her." He was facing her, but his words were for Cash. "I'll be here either way."

She felt the weight of his declaration, the truth there and she wanted all of it. "I'm not sure I can deal with this right now," she admitted.

Jax smiled at her softly. "Let's go to your mother's house and see if you can trigger anything else that might be helpful to find the knife or any part of your training. The rest can wait," Jax said gently, taking control of the situation, which still felt a little volatile.

Jax was a rock, solid and cool. Cash was fire, heat, and emotion; she needed both, wanted both.

"I'll drive," she said weakly and walked back to the car. Cash rushed to get in the front seat and Jax calmly got in the back. He did lean forward to touch her shoulder as she drove though, making clear that he was there. Cash noticed and not to be outdone, put his hand on her thigh.

She wasn't sure she could handle what she'd just gotten herself into, so she focused on the most important thing at the moment. They needed to unlock enough memories to find and stop the demon.

CHAPTER 14

The drive was less than relaxing, both men's presence was loud and intense even though they didn't say a word. Heat raced through her body, radiating from where each one had placed a hand on her and pooling low in her belly. She adjusted herself in the seat multiple times but neither man took the hint and removed a hand. She didn't want to say anything, didn't want them to know how easily they were affecting her, how much she wanted to suggest they stop in a dark alley and really see how willing they were to share.

Damn, her mind was filthy, and her body loved it even as she reasoned with herself that the likelihood of them actually being able to work together and share her was slim. If they did, there would need to be some discussions, some boundaries and they certainly didn't have time to work it all out just to satisfy her recently raging hormones. So she drove the short distance to her mother's house, biting her lip and clamping her thighs, willing her body to take each breath.

She was eager to jump out of the car when they arrived, breaking contact with both of them and gulped some air that wasn't saturated with male pheromones.

"Are you alright, Sach?" Cash asked, coming around the car with a look of concern on his face.

"You look a little pale," Jax added, but his grin was sly and she had a feeling he knew what she was struggling with.

"Fine," she grumbled and hurried into the house, body still tingling.

"Mom!" Sachi called as she walked inside.

"Sachi?" her mother's voice questioned from the kitchen.

"Who else would it be?" she asked, striding in. "We're just here to grab a few things from my room." She took a deep breath. "Oh and maybe eat? Is that pot roast?"

When Sachi got to the kitchen she found her mother standing in front of the stove where a pot boiled. She had a pinched look to her face, and she was gripping her hands in front of her nervously.

"Mom?" Sachi asked carefully. She'd never seen her mother look so uncomfortable.

"Oh, yes, I am making dinner for Kyle."

The boyfriend, Sachi thought. "Okay, we'll be out of here in a minute." She didn't want to cramp her mother's style and figured she could grab a few key items and take them back to the bakery to look over.

"Hey, Helen," Cash said familiarly and gained a smile from her mother.

Her gaze flicked curiously back to Sachi as Jax walked in and greeted her as well. Sachi just shrugged and went up the stairs to her childhood bedroom, a little embarrassed that she hadn't made the bed the other morning. Jax and Cash were close behind.

"Very pink," Jax commented.

"Looks like it did the last time I saw it," Cash said as he stared at the bed.

Sachi rolled her eyes and went to the closet. "You have a problem with pink, Jax?"

"Nope, I should have expected nothing less from a butterfly

shifter. You really don't take after your father at all," he commented lightly.

The accusation struck her though and she bristled knowing he would think it a failure to not embrace her witchy half. Just to prove him wrong, or maybe to show off, she wasn't sure, she shifted to a small pink butterfly and flitted up to the shelf high in her closet. She envied Fern's ability to be a person this size, it wasn't much use being a butterfly up there, she couldn't exactly grab anything, but she was able to look. She knew where the journal was, but she was curious if there were any other treasures hidden among her old high school yearbooks and prom corsages. She landed on her senior prom corsage, it was the same color as her dress, or at least it had been when it was fresh. Now it was brown around the edges and a slightly deeper orange.

She could hear the two men talking in low tones and she wondered what they were saying. And also thankful they weren't killing each other. She wondered how long she could hide up there before they started tearing flesh apart in a macho display of dominance.

How the hell was she going to navigate a relationship with them both? And would it even be worth the hassle, she couldn't help wondering.

She flapped her wings, trying to keep her mind on the task at hand, and looked at the flower, wishing she could just go back to that time and know what the fuck was going on. Was that girl prepared to take this on? Something told her yes; she must have been. Her father must have prepared her, or at least had been starting to. He surely didn't think he was about to be murdered leaving her in charge of the portal so soon.

Her thoughts circled around prom night, her mind prickling like it had when she'd looked at the picture in Cash's house. They'd fought. Cash had flirted with a witch and she'd bitten a vampire in retaliation. Their tempers had run hot with hormones at that age and neither of them were very good at being faithful.

If she could have laughed in this form, she would have. She wasn't much better now, was she? Maybe Jax was right, she wasn't bred to have just one lover, one love. Maybe she didn't have to deny what she really wanted. At least with Cash there was never any pregnancy concern. Werewolves couldn't get fae pregnant.

She closed her eyes and went back to that night. Had she been trying to get with another guy when she'd bitten him, was it more than retaliation for hurt feelings? Her mouth watered slightly at the memory of the blood, and something flickered to life in her head. There was an incident that night, someone had ended up dead in the bathroom and the dance was called off early. A girl, it had been knife wounds.

"Shit!" Sachi cried out as she shifted back to human so fast she smacked her head on the doorway.

"Whoa!" Jax said, reaching out to balance her. "You alright?"

"No," she groaned and rubbed her head, "But I think I remembered something." She turned and pulled the corsage down and held it up as if it meant something. Jax and Cash both gave her a confused look.

"Prom night when I was a senior. Cash and I had a fight because he flirted with Drew and I bit Terrance. Then I was crying because he said he was going to break up with me," she paused and looked at him as the old hurt crawled through her. "You said I was a slut like my mother," she whispered, and tears sprang to her eyes.

"Sach," Cash breathed the word and grabbed her to him, ignoring the harumph from Jax as he was pushed aside. "Sachi no. We were just kids."

"I know but," she pulled away and looked at Jax. "This—"

"No," Cash said, cutting her off and grabbing her chin to force her to meet his eyes. "This is what it is, Sachi. I love you, always have and if it isn't in your nature to be with one man, I'd rather be one of them, than not." He kissed her sweetly and Jax came up behind her, putting his hands on her shoulders. "Sach, we've already lost so much time, you can't imagine the deep hole just being able to hold you fills. We were robbed of ten years of this and I don't care if you need more than me, just as long as you need me too."

She looked into his eyes and saw only truth there and her heart flipped for him. She pulled his head down for another kiss. She'd missed his familiar touch so much and hadn't even realized it. "I really hate that demon," she whispered against his lips. "This isn't fair." She wasn't sure what she meant, not fair that they had lost the time, that they were having to deal with the consequences of the demon or her wanting Jax, it all felt wound together right now and she wanted to yell at the world to just stop fucking with her life.

"Everything's just fine, Sachi. Life's too short to put limitations on who we love and when," Jax said.

Sandwiched between the two men, she couldn't imagine a place she'd rather be, and she let the comfort of it float her away for a moment. Breathing in their combined scents was intoxicating and she had to push them away before she decided to see how far this could really go right here in her childhood bedroom.

"Thank you, both of you," she said as she stepped away from them.

They were standing next to each other without arguing or posturing, both had their intense gaze fully on her and it felt like she had won the lottery with these two.

"That night," she continued, "I ran to the bathroom after we fought. There was a dead body in the bathroom. Torn apart, bitten, and sliced. I thought it was a werewolf who'd lost control but then I saw a knife on the floor, so it definitely wasn't." She started to shake as more of the memory flooded into her.

"Hey," Jax said softly and led her to sit on the bed. He wrapped his arms around her comfortingly. Cash kneeled in front of her and put his hands on her legs.

She breathed in the scent of them again, it was comforting and settled her trembling body. "There were runes written in her blood, all over the mirror."

"What did they look like?" Jax asked excitedly.

She grabbed a paper and pencil from her bedside table and tried her best to copy what was flashing in her mind. "Something like that? It's hard to remember exactly, it's a very fuzzy memory and I was quite upset." She paused for a moment, her mind traveling back to that night. "My father showed up, he went into the bathroom with the investigators. Cash, your dad too, they must have been working together."

"Was your father an officer?" Jax asked.

"No, he was alpha, that was pretty much his full time job," Cash said with a slight frown.

Sachi reached down and touched his cheek. "He was a great alpha. I remember that clearly and you are so much like him."

"Am I?" Cash asked and shook his head. "Doesn't matter right now, the pack... well I'll figure out the pack after we survive the demons," he said with a dry laugh.

Jax nodded. "Some Portal Keepers have others who help them and if he knew the portal was compromised it would make even more sense that he wasn't working alone. The keepers also would have been called in by the police to investigate anything possibly demon related. Who was the girl?"

"She was a sophomore, a witch. She was Penelope's sister," Sachi whispered meeting Cash's eyes.

"Who's Penelope?" Jax asked softly, not letting her dwell on the detail, needing her to keep going as far as the memory would take her.

"Friend of mine." She met Jax's eyes. "Oh my god, she's forgotten her own sister!"

Jax looked thoughtful. "If it was a demon attack, which I'm willing to bet it was," he pointed to the runes she'd crudely drawn, "then the spell for memory loss must be attached to anything demon related, any murder, any history, all of it erased from the districts inhabitants' minds." He took a deep breath. "Intricate and powerful," he whispered.

"I have to tell Penelope," Sachi said, meeting his eyes. "She deserves to know."

Jax nodded solemnly and Cash gripped her hands in her lap, offering support.

It took her a minute to compose herself enough to go back downstairs, she didn't want to freak out her mother. When they did arrive back in the kitchen, Helen was still standing over the stove and whatever she was cooking was smelling a bit done.

Sachi gave her mom a quick hug and told her to check the pot, "Might be burning," she said, wrinkling her nose then ushered the men out.

"Be careful out there," Helen called after them. "Watch out for each other."

When they were back in the car Sachi frowned. "Do you think she was acting odd?" she asked Cash.

Cash shrugged. "Maybe she's got some memories coming back to her that are telling her trouble is in the air. She could have known a lot about the portal too."

"Yeah," Sachi agreed. "Probably. I'm glad she won't be alone tonight."

Sachi wasn't going to go over to tell Penelope she had a dead sister empty handed, so they headed back to the bakery and boxed up some cupcakes left from the day and tied a black ribbon around it.

"She just gave birth," she warned Jax. Witches were not fond of warlocks visiting when infants were around, it could be seen as a threat, especially if one of the infants was male.

"I can stay here and finish looking through boxes," Jax offered.

"I'll go look through stuff at my place," Cash said. "If my dad was involved somehow then maybe there's something I never noticed before. It's not as if I've gotten rid of anything in ten years."

"We've all been sort of stuck, haven't we?" Sachi said.

"Not anymore," Cash said and pulled her to him for a deep kiss, his tongue sweeping through her and lighting a fire that flowed straight to her core and had her knees weak. She gripped his shoulders to keep from falling and a little moan escaped her mouth. He broke the kiss and she was happy to notice he was breathing just as heavy as her. "Now I can't think of anything except moving forward with you," he whispered against her lips.

"I hope we get that chance," she replied and pulled out of his arms. Her gaze darted to Jax who stood nearby with a blank expression. She'd give anything to read his thoughts at watching that kiss. Did it make him resent her, did it turn his growing feelings off? Would it make it easier for him to walk away when all was said and done?

"You can take my car, Cash. I'll walk to Pen's." Cash pulled her in for a last quick kiss then headed out the door. She turned to Jax. "Thank you for understanding about Penelope," she said.

"I understand witches," Jax said and pulled her in for a kiss that matched Cash's for expertise and passion. She was wobbly-kneed and smiling like an idiot as she hurried out the door. Maybe he didn't mind seeing her kiss Cash?

This couldn't be her life, could it? Two incredible men and they were okay with it, at least for now. She wasn't sure how long the we-might-all-die-anyway truce would last, or if Jax wouldn't just leave once the portal was sealed up, but she was living in this moment as much as possible and she loved it.

Sachi called Fern on the way to Penelope's and explained the situation. Fern was on a date with Lance but left quickly to join her for moral support.

"You slept with Cash!" Fern said, the instant she flitted to Sachi's side.

Sachi blushed but kept up her quick stride. "Yes."

"And you slept with Jax, so... what does that mean?"

"It means I'm seeing them both, currently."

Fern stopped walking and when Sachi turned to face her, the look of joy on Fern's face was a complete surprise. "I'm so happy for you!" she trilled and pulled Sachi in for a hug.

"Why?"

"Because you're my best friend and you deserve to have everything you've ever wanted, and you've always wanted that big dumb football player and oh my god the day we saw Jax across the street I could tell he was your kind of candy."

Sachi was embarrassed at how transparent she apparently was, but she pushed Fern on down the street with a smile. "I'm happy," she said firmly.

"Good, now about this whole mess," she pointed at the box of cupcakes. "Are you sure?"

"Positive, I remember it so clearly it's like it just happened." She looked at Fern, tears were stinging her eyes. "How the hell could I have forgotten something like that?" It scared the shit out of her.

They knocked on Penelope's door and waited. The cry of a baby from inside told them she was home, and likely indisposed so they risked a hex and opened the door. "It's me and Fern, bearing cupcakes!" Sachi called.

"Again? Come on in," Penelope called back. "I'm glad you're back, I forgot to give you honeysuckle earlier. I was going to bring it by tomorrow but you can take it now. I haven't had a chance to mix it up though so you'll have to pull out your old recipe."

Penelope's knowledge of Jax wasn't a surprise and her thoughtfulness wasn't unexpected. There was no privacy in a small district and soon they'd all know she was sleeping with Cash, too. His pack was going to be pissed.

They found Penelope in the living room with a baby on each boob and one in a basket at her feet where she was gently rocking it. That was the source of the crying. Fern immediately picked up the crying girl and started to rock and coo at her. She had plenty of baby experience, being the oldest of a fairy family.

"Cupcakes," Sachi said, setting the box on the table and taking a tentative seat across from her friend.

"I appreciate it, but why are you here? Your aura is vibrating with nerves," Penelope cocked her head. "And sex, more than earlier... don't forget the honeysuckle."

"She's got two men in her bed now," Fern pointed out helpfully.

"Good for you!" Penelope said with a laugh. "I hope one of them is Cash, such a hottie and he's utterly devoted to you." She wiggled in her seat and scrunched her nose. "He's such a strong alpha, it's a wonder he didn't take over for his father."

Sachi sucked in a breath, she'd just witnessed the switch, the universal knowledge change. The truth about Cash was spreading. She wondered how long it would take for the knowledge to reach Bernard and have him seeking Cash out for the challenge. Suddenly she was quite worried about Cash being alone at his place.

"I need to make a quick call." She hurried from the room and phoned Cash, no answer. She called Jax. "Go over to be with Cash," she said without explanation.

"Why?" he asked, curious in a way that told her he was going to follow her directive no matter what she said next and that made her like him all the more.

"It's spreading, knowledge of him being alpha material and I'm afraid Bernard is going to force a challenge. I'm afraid," her words caught and Jax's soothing voice was like a balm to her soul.

"Don't worry, love, I'll go over there. If he's important to you, he's important to me but you know I can't interfere in an alpha challenge. I can only make sure it stays fair."

Sachi swallowed a hard lump in her throat. "I know. Thank you,

Jax." She didn't know why he was so understanding, but she was beyond thankful for it. Did she dare hope he wouldn't walk away after the portal closed? It felt like the universe was giving her a glimpse of all the wonderful things her life could be, but with a black cloud of death and doom right behind it ready to sweep it all away.

She almost missed the happy unknowing mind she'd had a couple days ago, even if she had been going through a massive dry spell.

She hurried back into the other room. "I think there's something terrible happening in the district," she started, meeting Penelope's gaze. "Do you believe that a demon could curse an entire district to forget years of memories, years of training and purpose, death, and destruction?"

"Yes," Penelope said without hesitation. "Demons can do a hell of a lot and I wouldn't doubt their ability to do anything. Is this about the girl they pulled out of the river yesterday?"

"Kind of," Sachi said. "What do you remember about senior prom?"

A look of surprise flashed over Penelope's face at what she would interpret as a total change of subject. "I went with Paul from the north Florida district," she said. "We were casually dating; it was great fun." She paused and looked confused for a moment and Sachi waited, breath held.

"Something happened that night," Sachi encouraged.

"I can't—I can't remember," Penelope said in frustration. "Why can't I remember?" She looked at Sachi with fear on her face.

"You know that warlock in town? He came to find my father. He came to help my father close up the portal to Hell that opens every ten years, to keep the demons out." It was close enough to the truth, no one needed to know Jax had actually come to kill her father in vengeance for his own father's death. Sachi took a steadying breath. "We think my father failed ten years ago, something escaped and covered its tracks rather well. I should know how to help him close it, it's my job."

"No way, it can't—" Penelope shook her head and rearranged the babies, reaching for the one in Fern's arms, handing her another and putting one in the basket, now content and sleepy. "Sachi, if what you're saying is true, then we're fucked."

"There's more," Fern said, looking at Sachi.

"What?" Penelope demanded.

"Your sister was killed that night, at prom."

"Sister?" Penelope breathed the word and stared down at the baby in her arms. "June," she said, a tear slipping down her cheek. "My sister's name was June." She looked up at Sachi then. "Dear Goddess, Sachi, do you know what this means?"

"Yeah, unfortunately," she admitted.

"I have to talk to my mother. I have to warn the coven."

"I wanted you to know as soon as I found out. The memories seem to spread when triggered, you might find that suddenly everyone knows and don't even realize they forgot. It's kind of annoying actually."

"That doesn't make sense, if it's been this way for ten years, why haven't memories been triggered in others all along?" Penelope pointed out.

Sachi pursed her lips and thought about that. "Something's changed, it had to have. I know I've touched that damn corsage in the last ten years. Not only that, why haven't I remembered anything each time I walked by the school or spent time with Cash?"

"Jax," Fern said firmly. "Nothing happened until Jax showed up."

"The warlock?" Penelope asked.

"The warlock," Fern agreed.

"Where is he now?"

"Staying with Cash in case Bernard decides to show up and force a challenge." Sachi thought about everything that had occurred since she walked up to Jax on the street. "He's the trigger." She thought about the odd way her mom had acted when she met Jax at the meeting and when they'd just been at her place. She stood. "We gotta go. Do what you need, Penelope, keep your coven safe but we can't have a panic. I don't want the demon to know we're onto it, or them. Who knows how many might be slinking about?"

Penelope nodded, understanding. "Let me know if you need anything and don't trust that warlock more than you have to," she warned.

"Jax is a good guy," she assured Penelope. "I think my mother knows something more though, we should get back over there, something's not right with her." She suddenly knew it without a doubt and she was anxious.

"Go, but call me soon," Penelope ordered.

As soon as they were out of Penelope's house, they both shifted to a small flyable size and rushed to Sachi's mom's house, carefully avoiding any owls or non vampire bats along the way.

"Mom!" Sachi called as she rushed into the house, still a bit breathless from the fast flight.

She wasn't prepared for what she walked in on. The smell of blood and death mixed with burned pot roast, and her stomach churned, threatening to empty. She held it back with effort and ran for the smell, fear rippling through her. She found her mother sitting at the kitchen table with a map spread out, black candles lit, and blood dripping from a heart held in her hand. She was muttering as she stared at the map, laying drips all around what looked like the lines of their district. She didn't move or speak to indicate she knew Sachi and Fern were there.

Sachi approached slowly. "Mom," Sachi whispered, afraid to touch her.

Fern turned off the stove where whatever was in the pot was smoking.

"Mom, where's Kyle?" The boyfriend had been coming over. Sachi's stomach twisted, whose heart was in her mother's hand?

"We have to stop them," Helen said, not looking up. "We can't let them win. I almost forgot." A frown creased her mother's face.

"Who, Mom? Who can't win?" This is what she'd feared, panic as the citizens remembered the demons, the portal, and the danger they could all be in without her father here. She never would have foreseen this though, her mother performing a dark spell in her kitchen, her mother had always been so soft and sweet and... had that been a false memory? Was her mother a dark magic practitioner?

"The demons," Helen whispered, then she hissed a Latin word, and the map began to vibrate. "I need to stop them." She looked at Sachi then, her eyes glowing white and her lips black. "I forgot." There was pain in her face, this wasn't like the others, the ones who remembered and didn't realize they'd forgotten.

Sachi took a step back, gasping at the terrible sight of her mother. "We can still stop them."

"Demons," Helen said and turned back to the map where the blood was starting to pool at the river. "Demons are powerful and your father is gone."

"Um, Sachi," Fern called from the laundry room just off the kitchen. "I think I found Kyle."

Sachi hurried to the laundry room and gagged as she saw the ripped open body of a vampire she recognized. He'd come into her bakery in the past to buy lavender cupcakes, her mother's favorite. It looked like her mother had chewed a hole in his chest and taken his heart out. "Oh goddess," Sachi gagged and she couldn't hold back any longer, she turned to the nearby laundry basket and puked, and puked, until it was only acid and spit coming out. She'd never be able to erase the memory of this, of what her mother was capable of.

Fern rubbed her back gently until she stopped shaking. "His

hands are tied and there's a large bump on his head. At least she knocked him out first," Fern said lightly.

It wasn't a comfort.

"Go get Jax and Cash," Sachi said quietly.

"Shouldn't we call the police?"

Sachi shook her head and left the laundry room. "Not yet, not until we know what's going on."

"What's going on!" Fern snapped. "What's going on is your mom has gone off the deep end."

Maybe, but maybe she was trying to help them and that thought terrified Sachi. "Just go get them!" Sachi snapped back and hurried to her mother's side. She knew Fern would do it, she was a loyal friend. Whatever her mother was doing, it had to do with stopping the demons, and she didn't think interrupting her now would help anyone. Consequences of murder could come later.

"There's one at the river," her mother said, indicating the blood that had pooled there on the map. "And one at the school." A smaller pool of blood had started to form at the high school.

"Two demons," Sachi hissed.

"Five," her mother corrected.

"Where are the others?" Sachi demanded.

Her mother turned to her with a sad look in her eyes, then collapsed just as the front door flew open and police poured in.

Fern's siblings had seen the body and called it in. Sachi couldn't blame them, who wouldn't report a dead and mangled body in their neighbor's laundry room?

Five. The number reverberated around her mind as she held up her hands and stepped away from her mother's limp body and the map. How were they going to find and kill or capture five demons?

CHAPTER 15

Sachi found herself in an interview room across from officer Zeb. Chief Rodriguez was leaning against a wall behind him, arms crossed and glaring. Apparently, she'd made it back from her visit with the elves.

Sachi was worried about her mother, who had been taken to the hospital to be monitored until she woke up and was, no doubt, arrested. Sachi didn't know what had happened to her mother in the kitchen to make her pass out. Perhaps the magic had been draining, or maybe the shock of it all had overwhelmed her. She'd dropped so hard and Sachi hadn't even had a chance to check her for injuries before officers had dragged her out of the kitchen demanding answers.

"Can I call to check on my mother?" she asked the silent officers.

"She's stable, when she wakes, we'll be there to arrest her," Zeb said and Sachi thought maybe she saw a hint of regret in his eyes.

Sachi nodded, not nearly as relieved as if she'd heard it from the doctors, but she knew Zeb wouldn't lie to her. "Why are you here, the guy was a vampire," she asked Chief Rodriguez casually.

What she really wanted to ask was, what the fuck are you, but that would be rude.

"It could be related to the murder of my citizen," she said simply.

Detective Tyler walked in then, stopping her from probing into what had happened with the elves. Tyler was Cash's uncle and she watched him carefully as he took a seat and met her eyes with a calm face. What did he know? What did he think now? She was dying to ask, to see how the memories she'd unlocked with Cash had spread through his pack.

"Cash is in the lobby waiting for you."

"Oh, nice," she said carefully.

"So is some warlock."

Her cheeks heated a bit, but she lifted her chin defiantly. "Jax."

He nodded. "Everyone out," Detective Tyler demanded and although they grumbled about it, Zeb and Rodriguez obeyed.

When the door shut, she relaxed a bit, sitting back in her chair, she met his eyes straight on. In truth she'd done nothing wrong so she wasn't afraid of being arrested, she was more worried about being judged by this werewolf and delayed in what she needed to be doing.

"Is he going to continue denying his place so that he can be a part of your little harem?" Detective Tyler accused.

The question shocked her, and also told her that the pack was well aware of what Cash's place should be and were still blaming her for him not doing what he should.

"I don't own him," she said simply.

"No, he's an alpha, no one owns him, but he loves you and that has stood in the way for too long. Bernard is getting nervous and a nervous alpha isn't good for the pack."

This had her attention, she sat up straight and leaned forward. "Is he going to attack Cash?" Fear and worry ran through her, and Tyler's eyes softened at her caring.

"He will. It's the way of things. I don't know what he's been waiting so long for, it should have been handled ten years ago." He shook his head. "You love him, I can see that. That's what I needed to know." He stood as if he were about to leave.

"Am I done here?" she gasped, no one had asked about her mother or the dead guy.

"No, you're not." He opened the door. "All yours, Rodriguez."

Chief Rodriguez walked back in and sat across from her as the door shut behind Tyler.

"Tell me what happened tonight," she said simply.

Sachi told her how she'd walked into her mother's house and what she'd found, leaving out the fact that Fern had been there too and not mentioning the word demon. There was no saving her mother from consequences, no denying what she'd done. It was the why that mattered right now and she wasn't sure she should share that, especially with a human.

"What was she trying to do with the map?"

Sachi bit her lip, unsure what to reveal. "Why are you in here and not one of the District people?"

Chief Rodriguez shrugged. "Because I wanted to talk to you," she took a breath and flicked off the recorder.

This was interesting. Sachi sat forward conspiratorially. "What did the elves tell you?"

Her eyes darkened and her shoulders stiffened. "I know it was a demon that attacked the girl, but Chief Wilson doesn't. What do *you* know?"

Sachi was surprised, she didn't think humans knew anything about demons, but maybe it was just *most* humans didn't know. "There was a spell that was cast ten years ago by a demon that escaped the portal," she explained, assuming the Chief would know everything if she knew demons existed. "No one in the district remembered the portal or the demons or... lots of things."

There was a hint of surprise in her eyes, but not enough to indicate she hadn't known about the portal. "You do?"

"Now I do, or I'm starting to, anyway. Jax, my warlock friend, he is here to help, he started triggering memories in me and we are doing what we can to figure it out. We have to find the demons and we have to get them back in Hell. We have to keep the portal closed tomorrow night."

"Is that what your mother was doing? Locating demons with that dark spell? How many did she find?"

A sort of relief filled Sachi, here was an authority figure with knowledge of what was going on. Maybe she'd be able to help. "I think so, she was doing a spell to track where the demons were."

Rodriguez's eyes lit up. "And? Where are they? How many are there?"

"Five, she was able to identify two locations before she passed out. The river and the high school."

Rodriguez sat back looking satisfied with Sachi's answers. "Okay, so you plan to take care of them? How?"

"We are trying to figure it out. We need a knife my father had, and I don't know if we can do anything without it. I wasn't properly trained," she admitted shamefully.

Rodriguez nodded and stood up, then walked to the door. "Good luck," she said and walked out, leaving the door open.

Sachi watched the woman go with jaw hanging open, she was confused. What did Chief Rodriguez know, what did Sachi's information tell her that was satisfactory? She didn't have time to think on it, she hurried from the room and out to the lobby where Cash and Jax sat waiting for her. Time was running out and they were nowhere near ready for the portal to open.

She saw them before they saw her, and she smiled at the two beautiful men. Cash was all rugged sexy; work boots, khaki shorts and a white T-shirt stretched taught over his muscles. His hair shaggy and dark, messy. Jax was more smooth, sophisticated sexy. He was wearing crisp jeans, black boots, and a black button-up shirt unbuttoned at the top to reveal his tan skin underneath. His hair was slicked back from his face, giving him a dangerous look.

They both looked up at the same time, stood, and crossed the room to embrace her, no care that the other was there. They held her tight between them and she breathed in their combined scent. This was the only place she wanted to be.

"Are you alright?" Jax asked quietly, lifting her chin to meet his gaze.

"A little shook up," she said honestly. "Cash, your uncle said Bernard is nervous that you are going to challenge him, apparently they all remember that you're not a submissive." Her cheeks heated a bit as she remembered how he'd dominated her.

He growled, following her thoughts. "No, I'm not," he agreed. "I'll deal with that when the portal is closed."

"But they still blame me for you not doing your job and taking up the alpha position," she grumbled.

"I don't give a fuck what they think. I'll be alpha and you can be my queen," he whispered into her ear making her shiver. "But first we have to survive."

"Let's get out of here," Jax said, his gaze darting around the lobby where all eyes were on their loving display.

Sachi realized that Jax had moved as she'd spoken to Cash, standing between them and everyone else, protecting them.

"Yes, let's go," she agreed and allowed the two men to guide her out.

Behind the front desk Beatrice winked at her as they passed. "Bad moon," she reminded.

"What's that?" Cash asked when they got outside.

"Oh, it's a bad moon for witches to breed, apparently everyone needs to remind me not to let Jax get me pregnant," she laughed.

Both men grunted and shared a look that she didn't understand. She got into the passenger seat of her car. Cash got in the driver's seat and Jax slipped in behind her, touching her shoulder reassuringly.

"Are you alright?" Jax asked.

"Really alright?" Cash added, reaching out and stroking her hair.

Having their attention and touch did things to her. Made her heart stutter, her stomach clench with desire and happiness and, inexplicably, made her want to cry.

"I'm alright," she said, taking a shaky breath. "I'm really alright now that I'm here with you two. I don't have time to be anything except alright, not until we get through this thing alive."

Both men leaned in and kissed her. Jax on her shoulder and Cash on her cheek.

"What did your mother do?" Jax asked as they pulled back and Cash started to drive. "Fern was frantic and not making any sense. By the time we got to your mother's house it was all blocked off and they said you'd been taken in for questioning."

"Assholes wouldn't tell us a damn thing at the station," Cash snarled and she wondered if it was his alpha instincts grating against the werewolves not bowing to his wishes.

Sachi told them what she'd walked in on and what her mother had told her as they drove to the bakery. She sent off a text to Fern, telling her she was out of the police station and to meet them. Then she called the hospital to check on her mother. Helen was still not awake, but they assured her they'd call as soon as that changed. Her mother would be arrested as soon as she was awake though, and Sachi had a feeling she wouldn't be able to talk to her alone after that, and she had so many questions.

Sachi didn't understand why her mother had done it, or how she'd known how. Her mother wasn't a dark witch or a black magic practitioner of any kind. She was a sweet innocent butterfly shifter. But she'd been working that spell without hesitation, without a book open anywhere to tell her how. What else might she know about this situation? Sachi was kicking herself for not asking her mother about it all before, for not trusting that her mother was strong enough to know. She had a lot of questions for her mother, but she may not get answers before it was too late.

When they got to the bakery parking lot, Fern and Lance hurried out of the back door. Sachi was relieved to see her friend and embraced her.

"What did the police say?" Fern asked, pulling away and looking into Sachi's face with concern. "Let's go inside, this conversation deserves something sweet," Sachi said. Once they were all settled with cookies and coffee being made, Sachi told them what had happened after Fern left Helen's house.

"She said five?" Fern asked.

Sachi nodded and accepted a cup of coffee from Jax, made just the way she liked it. She dipped the cookie in and ate slowly, letting the sugar and caffeine give her comfort.

Sachi sat on a stool with Cash on the floor by her feet. He was constantly rubbing her somewhere, her back or arm or leg, whatever he could easily reach without getting in her way. She was pretty sure he needed the simple connection just as much, or maybe more, than her and so she let him. Jax handed Cash a cup of coffee, black the way he liked it, then stood on her other side, a firm warm hand on her shoulder. Once again she had the feeling of Jax protecting them both, standing guard while they comforted each other. This wasn't his district, these weren't his people in danger and she knew he wasn't feeling the betrayal and loss the same way she and Cash were.

"But the map only indicated the two demons?" Lance asked.

She nodded again, finishing off the cookie.

"So what do we do?" Fern asked.

"We start with what we know, we check the school, and we check the river. If we can get one, he might lead us to the others," Jax said.

"How did she even know to do that?" Sachi whispered into her coffee.

"I have a feeling your father bred with her for a reason. Is she originally from another district?" Jax asked.

"Yeah, she came from the North New Mexico District," Sachi said. "She moved here a year before she got pregnant with me."

Jax nodded as if his thoughts were clicking into place. "I don't think that was accidental. I bet she was the second child of a Portal Keeper in her district and moved here, willing to breed with your father and produce a guardian to train up with guidance from both parents. It would explain why she knew enough about demons to know how to track them."

Sachi didn't like the idea that her parents had created her for the sole purpose of guarding a portal to Hell, but she had always known they weren't deeply in love. She'd always assumed she had been the result of a one-night stand between a couple of drunk or lonely people.

"And here I am, really great at making cake, not so much reining in demons," she said with a laugh that bordered on hysterical.

"You just forgot," Fern said with a shrug. "Other memories are coming back, maybe you had some training you don't remember."

Sachi nodded, it was what Jax had told her too, and she hoped they were right.

"We need to trigger the memories." Jax pulled out the paper that had the runes drawn on it from the dead woman's back. "Where did you see these before?" he asked gently.

"On the bathroom mirror when I found the dead body at school," she whispered and pulled out the paper where she'd scribbled what she thought she'd remembered. They weren't a perfect match because no memories were ever exact, but close enough to assume and as she thought about it, she became even more certain. "Why would they be on the girl's body and the mirror?"

Jax looked confused as well and he frowned. "I think we need to see that body again."

Sachi's stomach clenched. "Not the morgue!"

"I think we have some gingersnaps leftover from today," Fern said helpfully.

Fifteen minutes later they were pulling into the parking lot of the morgue. "Kyle's probably in there, too," she said with a groan, she didn't want to be reminded of what her mother had done seemingly so easily.

"We don't have to look at that body, Sach. Just the girl. Do you want to wait here?" Jax offered.

"I know Brad too, I can ask to see the body and deliver the cookies," Cash said confidently.

"No," she said with determination. This was her job, she needed to see it all, and with her men by her side she felt confident.

Fern and Lance had stayed behind to search the last couple of boxes for the knife in the basement, so it was just the three of them walking into the morgue with bright smiles for Brad and a plate of cookies to bribe him with.

"Sachi!" Brad said, his red eyes going wide. "Are you here to see the vamp?" he asked carefully. Probably assuming she was going to bury evidence against her mother.

"No, we need to see the human again. Is she still here?" She handed him the plate of cookies. He smiled at it, showing all his sharp teeth. The men stayed back a step, letting her work her charms.

"Oh yes, she's on ice until the mystery is solved, then she'll get shipped across district lines to be buried with the regs."

"Can we see her?" she asked sweetly as the greenish ghoul took a bite of her cookies. His eyes slid to the men behind her.

"Why?"

"I think she might be holding a demon," Jax said casually.

"No shit?" Brad said excitedly. "Fuck yeah, follow me."

Why that would be exciting to the ghoul, she didn't even want to know.

Brad led them down to the cold basement and she tried not to look at the fresh corpse in the corner, that would be Kyle. Brad pulled out a drawer and there lay the human, perfectly frozen in time.

Jax stepped forward and pulled back an eyelid. Last time they'd been here the eyes were completely white, showing that her soul had been removed.

Not now, though, and Sachi screamed as the swirling red and black seemed to look right at her.

Cash embraced her from behind. Brad giggled like a school-girl and Jax hissed *fuck.*

"There's a goddamn demon in her!" Brad said with glee. "Can I have it?" Brad whispered stepping closer to the body, his mouth open and drooling.

"What?" Sachi gasped.

"Ghouls consume demon souls," Jax explained. "If they find one that's in between like this, that is. It hasn't managed to completely attach itself to the body yet, it's vulnerable as it tries to take over the body. If it was attached, the body would have gotten up and walked out of here, likely killing whoever was upstairs at the time."

"Do you think this is one of the five my mother was talking about?"

"I hope so, because I doubt the other four will be this easy to get rid of. Take it," Jax instructed Brad.

With a giggle, Brad jumped on top of the body and crouched. He grasped the woman's head and pulled it up, his mouth hovered over hers and he forced her lips to open. After a moment, a black haze started to flow from the lips of the corpse. The body started to twitch as if it were fighting to hold on to the demon, but Brad didn't stop and as he inhaled the demon, his skin turned black and the stench of brimstone filled the air.

When Brad stopped and hopped off the body, his skin slowly changed back to its usual greenish.

"That was disturbing," Sachi admitted.

"Don't worry, Sachi, I still like your cookies," Brad said with a grin.

She tried to give him an appreciative smile. "What would have happened?" Sachi asked, staring down at the body.

"She would have woken up and looked normal, but the demon would have been in control. Anyone who didn't know she'd died, wouldn't question her existence and she would have killed others. A demon can't keep a body healthy without sacrifice," Jax explained.

"Happy to help," Brad said with delight and pushed the drawer back in.

Sachi turned to the body of Kyle with a frown. "Did you talk to him?" she asked Brad.

"Didn't have a chance yet, they just brought him in and I was working on the paperwork," Brad said.

"Do you think we need to check him for runes?" Sachi asked.

"I think it would be prudent," Jax said and stepped over to Kyle.

Sachi stayed in Cash's arms as Jax and Brad looked over the body. "No burns, no runes, just a missing heart," Jax said when they finished.

Sachi knew it was more than a simple missing heart. Her mother had been savage, and Sachi wanted to puke again just thinking about it. At least there was no sign that would connect her mother to the other murders.

"Want me to ask him anything?" Brad offered.

Sachi thought for a moment, did she want to know what he knew, what he might have thought of her mother at the end?

"No," she said, deciding whatever Kyle had experienced at the end at her mother's hands, she didn't want to know. It wouldn't help them now.

Brad led them upstairs with an extra pep in his step, apparently energized by the demon soul he'd consumed. Jax led Sachi right on through to the parking lot for fresh air and Cash was just a step behind.

"What do we do now?" she asked as she took deep breaths of clean air.

"I think we need to check out the high school," Jax said.

"Let's go demon hunting," Cash said enthusiastically.

"With what?" Sachi asked, a little frantic. "Unless it's trying to attach itself to a body, Brad can't eat it," she huffed. "What the hell are we going to do?" She pulled out her cell, hoping for a message from Fern. "We don't have the knife."

Jax snapped his fingers and a black flame leapt from his palm. "I have my own weapons, we might not be able to kill it, but if we can get close enough, we can knock it out and tie it up, drag it back to the portal and throw its ass down the hole."

"Fuck yeah!" Cash agreed, always quick to physically solve a problem.

Sachi was sure it wouldn't be as easy as Jax made it sound but what other options did they have, they couldn't just not try.

CHAPTER 16

They headed to the high school, it was getting late and she was yawning but she had a feeling sleep was far off for all of them. Cash was driving, radiating heat and hormones, she could smell the musk that was uniquely his, wafting off of him stronger than usual. Jax was relaxed and touching her shoulders gently, his thumb running up and down the side of her neck. His scent filled her nostrils as well, it was a little bit magic and a lot male. The mix of the two men made her body respond delightfully and she wondered what it would be like to drag them both back to her place and try to forget everything else for a while. Her thighs clenched, her body liking that idea very much no matter that she was tired and stressed.

They pulled into the parking lot and her erotic thoughts fled her mind as they sat silently staring at the dark building.

"Prom was before July," Jax said, breaking the silence and making Sachi jump.

"Yeah."

"That means this demon's been out of the portal for twenty years or more."

"Do you think it's the one I saw with my father, the fire demon?" Sachi whispered.

"Do you remember seeing any burns on the girl's body that night?"

"I don't think so."

"Fire demons rarely go far from water, it's too risky. They'll burst into flames and there's no way to hide that. They rely on water to keep them cool enough to remain undetected outside of Hell," Jax explained. "If it had been a fire demon there would have been a fire in the building, definitely in the bathroom. It had to be something else."

"You're saying more than one demon has been out for at least twenty years and my father didn't do anything for at least ten years, then the next time the portal opened he was killed and more escaped?"

Jax shrugged, "It seems so. Doesn't mean your father was doing anything wrong, but it might be why my father was here ten years ago to help and he already had Cash's father helping. If he knew things were already going wrong, he'd call for backup."

Which meant they were going to be trying to succeed where the three of their fathers had failed. The demons had killed all three trained men and here they were, untrained aside from Jax, and they were supposed to contain and possibly kill them.

It felt impossible.

"How are we going to get in?" Cash asked with a snort, obviously not doubting their ability.

"A touch of magic," Jax said with a wink and hopped out of the truck.

They walked up to the main doors and Jax worked a little human magic, picking the lock expertly, and opened it for them. Sachi led the way through the halls, it was eerie and quiet. She turned the corner that led to the bathroom where the horrific thing had happened.

A memory welled up.

She'd been upset so she had run from the dance, Cash was flirting with Amanda again who was a huge slut, wearing a red dress showing off so much cleavage her nipples were about to pop out and a slit so high Sachi had caught a glimpse of no underwear underneath. She'd retaliated by biting a vamp, then Cash had called her a whore. That still hurt.

Lance had met her here in the hall, he'd caught her moments before she'd reached the bathroom and held her while she'd cried. When Cash had called her name and come around the corner and saw them embracing, Lance had backed off, rushing the other way to avoid a conflict... and leaving behind bloody footprints.

"Oh my god!" Sachi hissed as Cash and Jax both looked at her with worry.

"What is it, Sach?" Cash asked. "What did you remember?"

"Lance was here and he had blood on his shoes!"

Cash looked at her with confusion.

"What?" Jax pressed. "What exactly did you remember, Sachi?"

Sachi took a breath to steady herself. "Lance was here, comforting me after Cash and I fought, but Cash came around the corner yelling and Lance took off that way, away from the dance and he left bloody footprints. He'd been in the goddamn bathroom! Fuck, what if Lance killed her, what if Lance is one of them? Fern could be in danger!" Sachi was screaming now, frantic. She'd left her best friend with a possible killer, possible demon. Was there anyone she truly knew?

"On it," Cash said and kissed her quickly before he shifted into a huge blond wolf and bounded back down the way they'd come. He would get to the bakery faster than the car and she knew he would do anything to keep Fern safe, she'd always been like a sister to him.

Sachi grabbed her phone out and tried to call Fern. When she didn't get an answer, she started to tremble, her mind filling with the possibilities of Lance torturing or killing her. Sachi wasn't sure she could survive losing her best friend.

"Sachi," Jax whispered and pulled her in for a quick hug. "I need you to finish this, we need to go in there. Cash will get to the bakery and Fern will be okay. Lance hasn't hurt her in all these years, I'm sure she's fine. Even if he did kill that girl back then, even if he is a demon, he won't want to give up his cover."

She met his eyes with tears stinging her own. "You don't know that. If he knows we are here, if he knows we are digging up that night, he'll know we are onto him."

"You're right," he agreed with a heavy sigh. "But if we don't figure out what we can here, it could get a lot worse, Sachi. Trust Cash to do what he can, there's nothing we can do that he can't," Jax added the last quietly, and it wasn't comforting.

"She's my best friend," Sachi whispered. "If my mother goes to jail, she's all I have. I can't lose her too."

He didn't deny the risk or danger, just hugged her tighter and it made her feel so good to be comforted in his arms. "You have me," he reminded her gently.

His voice filled her with desire and the memory of the amazing sex was undeniable, but she still needed Fern, a man couldn't take the place of a best friend and a mom. Even two men couldn't. "And Cash," she reminded him. "You and Cash, but I still need Fern to make it through this with us."

"She will," he promised, but she knew it was a thin promise.

"You can't guarantee any of us are going to make it through. Is that why you're so willing to accept my and Cash's relationship? You don't really see a future where we all are above ground?" She truly wanted to understand, wanted to know if that was where his thoughts were because she couldn't understand his willingness, his acceptance.

"No," he said fiercely and grasped her chin, forcing her to look up at him. "Sachi, I didn't expect to find you, to fall for you." His lips curved up into a sexy half smile. "But I think I have, and I will do anything to make sure we have a future together." He leaned down and kissed her until her toes were curling and her breathing became labored. "I don't even mind the idea of sharing you with that wolf."

"Truly?" she hated how small and desperate her voice sounded. She wanted to be a strong, confident woman, the type who would take on the keeping of a portal to hell with an eager smile, but she wasn't. She was scared and she was desperate for an inkling of hope that her future was going to be happy.

He nodded. "I play well with others," he whispered in her ear, sending a shiver down her spine. He pulled back and his heated gaze softened. "But now is not the time for that. You need to face this memory, but I won't leave your side while you do it, I promise."

She nodded and took a steadying breath, checked her phone for a message, nothing, then opened the bathroom door and stepped into a memory.

She could practically smell the blood, there had been so much. It had spattered everywhere, touched every surface. The girl was mutilated to the point Sachi wondered if her organs hadn't been harvested. She heard screams and her throat felt sore. She'd screamed, terrified by the scene and Cash had come in behind her. Cash's hands had gripped her upper arms and as she turned to let him embrace her, she'd spotted the mirror.

"A face!" Sachi said, surprising Jax enough to make him jump. "There had been a face in the mirror, behind the runes."

"Your reflection?"

Sachi put her hands on her hips and gave her head a little shake. "I'm not an idiot, Jax. It wasn't mine and it wasn't Cash's. There was a strange face *in* the mirror, behind the runes, looking out at us."

"Are these the same mirrors?" Jax asked, suddenly excited.

Sachi looked closely, "They look the same, but it would be hard to know for sure." She reached out and ran a hand over one, a shiver went through her.

"Don't touch it," Jax snapped, pulling her away. "There could be a demon living in there."

"In the mirror?" she asked, doubtfully.

"Mirrors are often used as portals to another space. Not quite another dimension like the portal in your basement, more like an alternate here."

"Could the runes have kept it in, like the body in the morgue?"

"Yes, if someone knew what they were doing."

"Like Lance?"

Jax looked thoughtful. "The runes on the mirror, I wonder." He pulled out a flashlight, but when he turned it on it produced a green light unexpectedly and when he shined it on the mirror, runes appeared, lighting up black as if they had been etched into the glass. "There's no reason the demon would have trapped itself in there on purpose. Maybe Lance had a reason to want him locked away, but not dead."

"That doesn't sound good," Sachi whispered, staring at the mirror as if it was about to reveal all its secrets and she was sure she didn't want to know them. She was about to suggest they leave when something in the mirror caught her eye.

A shadowy figure took shape and had Sachi spinning around to see if it was in the room with them. It wasn't, but that didn't make her feel much better. She couldn't even see her own reflection in the mirror anymore. She looked closer at the image. It wasn't the bathroom they were in, it was the bathroom as she remembered it from high school. Now it was painted a plain white but when she was in school here it had been pink and white with old graffiti messages in black marker scribbled all over. The room in the mirror was empty of people except for the shadow taking shape, forming arms, legs, and a body. Then wings that filled the space and a head complete with horns. It had non-distinct facial features and no clothing, just a black blob shaped like a nightmare. Despite its unfinished form she could feel it looking at them, was sure it stared straight into her soul, hungrily.

"Shadow demon," Jax hissed. "It's definitely trapped there, or we'd already be dead. It won't get out unless the mirror breaks, destroying the runes etched into the glass with the witch's blood."

"So we're safe from it?"

"For now," Jax agreed.

"Do you think Lance trapped it in there to keep us safe?"

"If he did, why wouldn't he tell anyone?"

"Maybe he did and we forgot," Sachi pointed out, but she didn't believe the words. There was no way someone trying to save others would mutilate a witch to do it and then run away. Her mind went back to the horrifying scene in her mother's kitchen. Or maybe someone would... sacrifice one to save many? The big difference there would be the fact that her mother didn't run, of course she had passed out and had yet to wake up and tell anyone what the hell she'd been up to or why.

The demon in the mirror room lifted a blade, it was solid and real in his shadowy hand, blood dripped from it, seemingly fresh and in his other hand he held up a heart that looked just as fresh.

"What's happening," Sachi whispered.

"I think he's showing us what he took into the mirror with him," Jax hissed.

Sachi flicked her eyes to Jax and back to the mirror. Jax looked worried and that made terror tighten her throat. "What can he do with that?"

"Cast a spell to break the fucking glass," Jax whispered as the demon stabbed the knife into the heart and the glass began to crack.

"The time has come," it said with a deep crackling voice that sent shivers of fear straight to her bones.

"Fucking RUN!" Jax yelled and grabbed her arm.

Sachi panicked, she could have flown faster than she stumbled behind Jax, but she couldn't think straight as the sounds of breaking glass echoed in the empty halls. Jax didn't let go as he darted down the halls and out of the building and she was thankful. He practically dragged her along as he sprinted across the parking lot and shoved her into her car. He pushed her over to the passenger side and slid into the driver's seat.

As the engine roared to life, a horrific screech filled the air. The demon was loose.

"Why now?" Sachi gasped.

"I think they've decided it's time to make a play for the portal. If Lance is on their side, I'm guessing he locked the thing in there to keep the body count low enough to be without suspicion until it was time."

The image of the demon holding the heart was eerily reminiscent of her mother in the kitchen and she shuddered, pushing the thoughts away. Her mother was not a demon, just a dark magic-using, demon hunter... maybe. She pulled out her cell and called the hospital.

"Sorry, she hasn't made any changes. I assure you, Ms. Pearl, we will call you as soon as there's a change," the nurse said.

"Thank you," she said, despondent, and hung up. She pulled her feet up onto the seat and wrapped her arms around her knees.

"It's going to be okay," Jax tried to reassure her.

"You don't know that," she said and looked out the passenger window as they moved through the district. Jax laid a hand on her thigh and squeezed gently but he didn't try to argue. Neither of them knew if things would turn out okay. She sent up a silent prayer to whoever might be listening, that Fern would be at the bakery, and safe. She was losing her mother one way or another she couldn't lose Fern too.

"Why not stay and fight?" Sachi asked Jax when the reality of what was happening settled over her. She was worried about her friend, her mother, herself, and the whole district at this point. But she couldn't dwell, she had to concentrate on what she could control, what she could do now.

"I can't stun a shadow demon," he admitted grudgingly. "They aren't corporeal enough for what I can manage alone."

"So what the fuck are we supposed to do?" she asked, a little panicked.

"We need that knife, it's the only thing that will do it."

"Are you sure my father had it?"

"Every Portal Keeper had one," he assured her.

"I have an idea," she said and pulled out her phone, firing off a text to Fern's sister. There were more than enough fairy siblings to get through the rest of those boxes a second time and fast, they'd have the knife before sunrise if it was there.

Thinking of Fern made her hurt, she wanted so badly to find her friend alive and well. Could Lance really have hurt her? Was he a demon himself, or just helping them?

When they got to the bakery Cash was sniffing around the parking lot and a flood of fairies were hovering around him firing off a million questions that he was not going to answer in his current form.

"What's going on?" Seraphina asked, fluttering close to Sachi's face as soon as she got out of the car.

"Fern isn't here?" she asked, her eyes darting between Seraphina and Cash.

"No one is here except the dog and he won't stop sniffing long enough to talk," Seraphina huffed and crossed her arms over her chest, giving her best annoyed teen glare.

That could only mean one thing. "Lance kidnapped Fern. A shadow demon just escaped the high school, and I don't know what the fuck I'm doing even though I should. What I do know is there's likely a knife downstairs that should help and I need all of you down there searching." She rushed to explain, tears bursting out as the weight of it all pressed on her again.

"On it," Seraphina said without question. Sachi wasn't sure if Seraphina didn't fully understand the gravity of the situation or what, but she was stoic and ordering her siblings to help in the search as she flew away.

"Thank god," Sachi breathed, she needed others to be strong so she could try and be strong too.

"It will have runes on it, and it'll be made of silver with a bone handle," Jax explained. "If you don't find it there, check Cash's place."

"Find my sister," Seraphina demanded, then whistled and there was a whirlwind of fairies as they fell in line and followed her inside.

"We will," Jax called after the swarm.

"Should we warn them about the portal?"

"Fairies are pretty sensitive, I'm sure they'll notice something's not right there, and they'll avoid it," Jax reassured her. "Besides, you probably explained enough to unlock most of that knowledge for them."

Cash howled then and took off running.

"Do we follow?" Sachi asked, frozen with indecision.

"If you want to find Fern, I think we have to," Jax urged, grabbing her arm and pulling her back to the car.

They took off in the direction Cash had gone. Windows down, they listened to Cash's howls when they couldn't see him and made their way through the town.

"Do you think that's what he wants? Lance, I mean. Does he want us to go to him?" Were they just going to walk into some kind of trap?

"Yes," Jax said dryly.

Sachi gaped and he shrugged. She didn't like it, but she got it. They had very little choice. If they didn't go, they couldn't possibly save Fern and they would be no closer to knowing what the hell might be going on. Trap or not, they were doing what made the most sense.

"We aren't going in unprepared though," Jax said reassuringly. "I *was* taught the skills to protect a demon portal. I can put up a fight and I think you can too, if you remember."

That felt like a really big *if* and Sachi's stomach twisted with fear.

CHAPTER 17

They were headed toward the eastern district line. A row of district police cars came into view when they got close, no doubt monitoring to make sure the closure mandate was adhered to.

"Fuck. Do you think he got out of the district?" Sachi asked.

Before Jax could answer, a howl to the right had them turning and barreling off the road. Sachi had to grab onto the dash to keep from bouncing out of her seat and she hoped her little car made it through this adventure. It wasn't made for this kind of thing.

Sachi glanced back as they bounced along, no one was following. No doubt, the guards at the line assumed they were horny teens looking for a place to make out and wouldn't follow to investigate. The police had more important things to worry about tonight than teenage antics.

Soon they were out of sight of the police vehicles and still going. Chase flashed in and out of the headlights as he raced in a zigzag following the scent of Fern or Lance, Sachi wasn't sure. There was nothing out this way except the vampire bar where stupid humans walked on the wild side and mixed with vampires and blood needs could be exchanged. Sachi couldn't imagine why

Lance would have headed there, and at the same time hoped he had, because then they'd be almost caught up.

They came to a stop at the crest of a small hill and Cash stood there, naked and human, staring down at the vampire bar. She'd seen him naked a million times, but never got tired of it. The sight of his tanned ass with its paw print tattoos leading from cheek to mid back made her mouth water. She'd taken blood there before, when they were wild high school sweethearts, right where a heart circled a pink and purple butterfly on his left cheek. She could do it again now that they were sort of back together and the thought sent a little thrill up her spine.

She jumped out of the car and hurried to Cash's side. "Is she in there?"

"It's hard to tell for sure, the scent of vampire is strong here of course, but her scent definitely came this way. I'll circle and make sure I can't pick it up leaving the area." Cash kissed her swiftly then looked at Jax. "Keep her here until I know," he told Jax then shifted back to wolf and darted off to circle the building.

"The man has a butterfly on his ass," Jax said, giving her a curious look.

"Don't we all do stupid things in high school?"

"Like get a tattoo to represent our girlfriend? Do you have a little paw print on your ass that I missed last night?"

"Maybe you'll have to investigate later," she said with a smile and a wink.

His eyes narrowed and he smiled wickedly, pulling her in for a rough kiss. "I'd love to."

Cash was back quickly and shifting to his unashamed naked self. "She's in there, not a scent of her leaving anywhere around the area."

"It looks abandoned," Jax said.

"It always looks that way," she explained. Windows boarded up and paint peeling. Vamps didn't care what the outside looked like; they never saw it outside of moonlight anyway. Sachi knew that inside it was crisp and clean. She'd been in there a time or two and it was a proper dance club with a stage and bar. Below that was where the real action happened, blood rooms. Some went down there to give, some to take. It was impersonal and dangerous, but if you didn't have a regular source, there weren't many other easy options.

"What's the plan?" Cash asked. "He's expecting us I'm sure, he didn't do anything to hide his trail."

"Feels like a trap," Sachi grumbled.

"I think we walk in and see what he wants, trap or not, we are out of time and options," Jax said. "We make sure Fern is safe, then we kick ass," he said with a dark smile that surprised and delighted Sachi. "Don't let him bite you, they have venomous bites and depending on what kind of demon he is, he could throw some nasty shit so be on alert."

"I'm not really the kick ass type," Sachi said quietly, fear building.

"That's what I'm here for," Cash said, pulling her against his naked body. "We won't let anything happen to you, Sach."

"I hope you are more kick ass than you remember," Jax said quietly. "Stay behind us and if we can distract Lance, you grab Fern and run, or fly, as fast as you can."

It wasn't a good plan, but it was something and they didn't have time to come up with anything better. So they approached the building without worrying about sticking to shadows and when they got close, they could tell there were lights on inside, but it was quiet. Usually, the place was hopping by this time.

"I guess since the borders are closed and no dumb humans can risk their lives, they closed the club for the night," Cash said. "I'm wolfing. Stay close, Sach," he ordered then shifted back to wolf form.

Sachi had no problem staying behind the two men. She wasn't a fighter, and didn't believe she'd forgotten any kind of fight training either. She was a baker, a good baker, and although she was a vampiric species of shifter, she was no match for an angry vampire demon.

The door opened when they got close and light spilled out to reveal a blood-stained front porch—old blood, Sachi could smell it. She took a deep breath and sent up a silent thank you to the goddesses that there wasn't even a hint of fresh fairy blood on the air.

"It took you long enough," came a voice she didn't recognize, and a sharp pain stabbed at her head as if a memory was trying to surface. Cash shook his large wolf head as well and she wondered if he was feeling the same thing.

"Where's Fern?" Sachi demanded.

"Come and get her," the voice said, darkly

"Sachi!" Fern yelled. "This asshole! I'm going to fucking kill him!"

Sachi smiled, Fern was fine, she was mad and that meant she wasn't hurt. A huge weight lifted and with it came a new determination. This asshole wasn't going to terrorize *her* town, *her* friends. She knew a couple spells by heart, and one was a light ball, it couldn't do any damage, but it would tell them what they were walking into. She called it to her fingertips. Magic pooled in her palm and a bright orange ball developed. Jax flicked her a surprised look, then smiled approvingly. She flung the ball into the dark room to reveal Fern sitting on a bar stool wrapped in iron chains, they had to be iron, otherwise she'd have shifted tiny and flown away easily enough. Lance was beside her, looking smug and frustratingly normal.

"You see, unharmed and she'll stay that way, as long as you three don't try to stop the release."

Jax took a small step forward and Cash matched it. Sachi was a half-step behind, but she moved too, hoping that it wouldn't piss Lance off. He was holding a dangerous-looking knife.

"What are you, why are you doing this?" Sachi demanded.

"I am a demon with a talent for memories," he said with a too wide grin revealing many sharp teeth.

"You," she snapped. "You did this to us?"

She slid another step closer, they needed to be closer, or they would never be able to save Fern, but she didn't want to get closer to Lance. Still, she followed the men's lead and they were inching forward whenever they thought they could.

"I did, and if it weren't for the little twit warlock there, all our plans would have been quite successful, but I still don't think you have it in you to stop me," he said with a laugh and suddenly it wasn't Lance standing before them, it was a monster. His body bulged, his skin turned inky black, and his eyes were bright red. His teeth were huge and sharp, his hair stretched to reach nearly to his feet and turned a bright blue. His hand holding the knife was now a clawed thing of nightmares and when he spoke again, it was with a deep resonance that chilled her soul.

Behind him, Fern looked frozen in shock, this beast had been her boyfriend for years, they'd been intimate even.

"I escaped that place years ago and bided my time. I became one of you and no one suspected a thing. I fed my body with the blood of your kind and then, I took your memories, I took it all. No one was going to be able to stop us if they didn't know they needed to." His grin was fierce and chilled Sachi.

"My father," she whispered. "You killed my father and Cash and Jax's too."

"I needed them out of the way. Your father, Sachi, was beholden to Ainu, the fire demon, and she didn't see the same future as me." He shrugged as if their father's lives meant nothing.

It enraged her and she leapt forward, ready to attack the huge beast with her bare hands. She didn't make it far. Jax's hands clamped around her arms, stopping her, and Cash leaped in front of her, growling and snarling at the demon. They were on the threshold now though and as a group they moved into the building.

"It won't work," Jax said. "Even if demons pour out into this district, they won't be able to leave."

"Ah, but you're forgetting the river. It breaks the ward, and from there to the ocean and from the ocean... everywhere," he said with a darkness that spoke of mass destruction.

"We won't let you," Sachi whispered, not sure what they could possibly do.

"How will you stop us? You don't even know your greatest power," he laughed, and anger filled Sachi.

Power, did she have power? Was there training buried in her mind somewhere? "Fuck," she whispered as she tried to remember anything that might help them and came up with nothing.

Demon Lance reached up to the ball of light she'd thrown into the room and with his giant clawed hand he squelched it, plunging them into near darkness, the light of the nearly full moon filtered through clouds not enough to dispel the shadows.

Noise erupted around her as her eyes struggled to adjust. She felt fur brush her leg and heard the door slam, completing the darkness. Then a light filled the room again. This time it came from a red orb floating over the demon and revealed the damage that had been done in that short period. Cash was gone, apparently thrown out the door that shut behind him and Jax was lying on the floor passed out and bleeding from the head.

"Just you and me, darling," the demon said with a sneer.

"You asshole!" Fern snapped and struggled in her chains. "You didn't have to hurt anyone, Sachi isn't dangerous."

"Oh, but she is, she just doesn't know it."

Sachi stood still, trying not to quiver with the fear that was coursing through her. She was alone, alone with a demon. He circled her slowly, heat poured off of his body and she started to sweat. His scent was like rotting flesh and smoke hit the back of her throat, making her gag. It was that scent that triggered something, linked to another night, a night of terror and pain... she was crying, hunched over her father's body and *he* was there. He was casting a dark spell and her father had tried to stop him.

"You are remembering, that's good, it's not satisfying to squish a helpless bug." He gestured toward Fern who glared at him. "Here, let me help," he whispered, suddenly behind her. She swung around and stepped back. He reached out and pressed a finger to her temple. Pain coursed through her, she felt like she was going to explode, she screamed until darkness took the pain away.

"Sachi, my dear, you have to try harder."

Sachi grumped at her father's voice. "I need to get my dress from Maureen, she was adding some great detail to the hem!"

"Prom night doesn't outweigh training."

"Fine," she snapped and flung a fireball at the target. This time it was a plastic representation of what her mother assured her was a realistic demon. It looked like a terrifying nightmare and she hoped her mother was wrong. She hit it in the neck and decapitated it swiftly. "There, can I go now?"

Her father laughed and conceded. "Okay, go get ready."

Sachi flung her arms around her father and kissed his cheek. "Thanks Dad, love you."

"I love you too, be careful tonight, something feels off."

Sachi pulled back and looked at her father with concern. They were in the middle of the woods and she couldn't see the moon even though it was starting to get dark. "It's not July."

"No, it's too early for the portal, but there's an energy I don't like. I'm meeting with Cash's dad tonight to discuss it; the pack has been feeling antsy too. How's Cash been? He hasn't gotten violent with you, has he? His dad said some of the young guys seem to be having a harder time controlling their instincts lately, even Bernard."

"No," she assured him. "I'll come to the bar when I'm dressed. Cash can pick me up there so you can see for yourself that he's fine."

He smiled lovingly at her. "Thanks, now go, enjoy your youth," he teased, and she shifted to butterfly and took off toward town.

Another memory pushed to the front of Sachi's mind.

Sachi was about twelve when she stood with her father at the edge of the river.

"We have a deal, and if I'm not here, Sachi is going to take it over," he said to the fiery demon that stood on the water.

Sachi was frightened, she hid behind him and peeked around him at the being she recognized from their trip to the ocean a few years ago. How was she ever going to be able to do what he does, she just couldn't imagine not being terrified of these things, and supposedly there were scarier ones than this. But she was to be in charge, she was very important, according to her father.

"She stinks like her grandfather. How can she be trusted?"

Sachi stiffened and stepped away from her hiding place, offended. "I smell like pollen and blood! I am a butterfly shifter, but I know magic too," she hissed and held up a hand, throwing a spark of fire at the demon. In retrospect it wasn't the best thing to throw at a fire demon, she simply laughed and absorbed the small bit.

"Well, I see she's got a bit of fire in her gut, she'll need that." The fire demon turned to her father. "Make sure you train her well." She sunk into the water then and disappeared.

Her father turned to her and knelt down, she thought he was going to be angry, thought he was going to chastise her for using magic that failed, but he hugged her tight and whispered in her ear, "I am so proud of what a brave soul you are, Sachi. You are going to be a great keeper someday because of what you are, not in spite of it."

"What did she mean, about my grandfather?" Sachi pulled away from her father and looked up at his face.

"Your grandfather is a demon, Sachi. Your mother was born in Hell, the daughter of a butterfly shifter and a demon, but it never defined her and it doesn't define you." He poked a finger over her heart. *"You are what you want to be."*

"I want to be a keeper like you!" she assured him proudly and threw a ball of fire at the water. It sizzled out quickly, but it was the biggest one she'd ever been able to produce, and now she wondered if it was her demon heritage that gave her such a gift. She didn't know of any witch that could do anything like it.

"Yes, Sachi, I think you will. Come now, I need to get you back to your mother."

He took her hand and they started up the small hill to the road and district beyond. They were north, near the nymph and elf woods and as they passed, a troll child scampered out and growled, practicing his scare technique. Her father pretended at fright and the little boy ran away giggling happily.

Hands were shaking her, she opened her eyes ready to scream and fight. It was dark but she could see it wasn't the demon Lance that hovered above her, it was Jax. "Fuck," she hissed and sat up. "Are you okay?"

He sat back and touched the blood on his head. "Yeah, the bastard knocked me out in one shot." He looked embarrassed, so Sachi didn't comment.

"Where's Fern?"

"Gone, so is the demon. Cash is outside trying to pick up the scent."

"How long have I been out?"

"Not long, I think. What happened? Are you alright?"

Sachi rubbed at her temple and flinched, it was bruised where the demon had touched her. "He made me remember," she whispered, and tears stung her eyes as she looked at Jax. "He made me remember everything." She was part demon, her mother was half demon! She couldn't even speak the words, too horrified by the implications and terrified of how Jax and Cash would look at her if they knew. Was she partly responsible for all of this, was it her fault somehow because she had demon blood in her veins?

Then, a new horrible thought, what if her mother had helped somehow, she was half demon. The image of the vampire sacrificed in her mother's home filled her mind and she wanted to puke. It wasn't something even a dark magic practitioner would have done lightly and yet, her mother had been so calm, so practical about it all.

A smile spread across Jax's face, making him look so handsome she was almost distracted from all the new thoughts running through her head. She had to look away to continue on.

"My father was teaching me to guard the portal. He was training me in spells and fighting. He failed that night because Lance was there to stop him. My father thought he was there to help, but he revealed himself as a demon. It shocked us into not reacting fast enough, he killed my father. Your father ran, I think to try and get Cash's dad. I'm sorry I don't know what happened once he left the basement but apparently, he didn't get far." Sachi met his gaze and felt tears stinging her own. There was an old hurt in Jax's eyes but an acceptance too, now they knew. Now he had a new person to seek revenge against for his father's death, and she did too.

Jax stroked her face tenderly. "Okay... what else happened?"

"Lance was in his demon form, and he was casting a spell to forget. I—I was afraid," tears filled her eyes and spilled down her cheeks as shame enveloped her. "Oh god, I didn't even try to stop him, I was too scared, I couldn't."

"No, you couldn't have, he would have killed you too." Jax shook his head. "My father never should have left you there alone. What was he thinking?" Jax hissed.

"So many mistakes," Sachi whispered.

"The spell was to make us all forget, he said that he would be strong enough in ten years to do what *she* couldn't."

"She?"

Sachi shrugged. "The fire demon Ainu, he implied my father might have been involved with her. Then I woke up in my bed at my mother's house and knew nothing. Police were at the door telling my mother that my father had been murdered, probably a magic deal gone bad. I remembered nothing, no one did. I went about life as usual, new usual I guess. Lance was still one of my best friends." She was more than a little bitter about that last part.

Jax gathered her in his arms. She clutched his shirt and let the tears flow freely. Ten years of lies filled her soul with sorrow and she had to let it out.

"We have to kill him to stop the spell," Jax whispered. "We need the knife to kill him."

"No, we don't," she said with a grin, pulling out of his arms. "There's another way to kill a demon."

Jax looked at her doubtfully.

"My parents taught me well," she whispered and suddenly her hands were burning, a bright red light emitted from her fingertips. She threw the light at the bartop and it exploded. Cash yelped outside. "Don't worry," she said confidently. "I am *not* helpless." She strode from the burning vampire bar ready to kill some fucking demons.

"Cash, are you alright?" she asked him as he loped up to her.

He shifted and pulled her into his arms. "I'm fine," he assured her then pushed her away from him and inspected her carefully. "What about you, you were really out."

"I'm great actually," she assured him, pulling him in for a quick kiss. "I remember everything and I know how to kill them." She pulled away and started toward the car. She didn't want to waste any more time, ten years already gone was enough.

"I haven't picked up on the right scent yet," Cash called after her.

She let her fangs show as she sneered into the darkness. It didn't matter which way the demon had gone; she knew where he was headed.

"Where are you going?" Jax asked as he ran beside her. Cash followed, whining slightly.

"The bakery, I'm willing to bet that's where Lance has Fern now. He'll want to guard the portal and she's his insurance against me going in and throwing fireballs his way."

"We'll save her," Jax assured her.

Maybe, maybe not, but it wasn't the only problem they faced. "There's a fire demon in the river. Ainu, the same fucking fire demon that my father visited time and again in the Florida district and here at the river. I don't know what his deal was with her, but if he was trying to help her, I want to know why. There's a shadow demon that stalked the school and Lance must have fed it for years to keep it strong until now, which is on the loose again. We are looking at four demons all after one goal, opening the portal tomorrow night. My mother knows something more," Sachi took a calming breath, not saying the horrible demon thing. "She was training me too. Maybe you're right and she was a child of a Portal Keeper." Sachi bit her lip to hold back more of the truth, afraid of the look on their faces when they found out what she really was.

"Where's the fourth demon?"

When they reached her car there was a police cruiser parked by it.

"There," she said darkly, eyes locked with Chief Rodriguez. "Demons have a red aura."

"I thought you'd never figure it out," she said gruffly. "Too bad it's too late."

"You crossed the lines," Jax hissed. "How the hell did you manage that?"

"It's easy when you're dormant. I've laid in the belly of this bitch for years, waiting for the time to strike. Your demon mother recognized me when I stepped onto that stage in the gymnasium, I thought she would have told you everything right then. Curious that she didn't."

Sachi refused to look at the men as the words settled around them heavily. She notched up her chin and faced the demon in front of her. "My mother was born in Hell," she said as explanation to the men.

"Your mother is a demon?" Cash snarled beside her.

Hurt cramped her gut at his harsh tone. "Half. My grandmother was trapped in a cage by a demon who impregnated her. My mother escaped as a child and was raised by a Portal Keeper, but she has enough blood ties to demons to be able to track them. That's why she was able to twist that spell in her kitchen."

Rodriguez smiled at her obvious discomfort.

"But it's a dark magic spell and she had to sacrifice Kyle for it," Sachi whispered, ashamed at what her mother had willingly done. "She must have known as soon as she saw you that something truly horrible was going on in this district." Sachi knew, no matter what, that her mother had not, would not, act without reason. She must have felt as if she'd been left without options. She may have thought she was the only one left in the district with the knowledge to stop things from going the demon's way. She was backed into a corner and when you're talking about the lives of everyone in the district, one life lost is a reasonable sacrifice.

Or was that just her demon blood making excuses for death and destruction? Sachi wasn't sure and that scared her.

"A demon will sacrifice anything and anyone to save themselves," Rodriguez said and stepped closer, earning a growl from Cash. "And you're a little bit demon yourself, aren't you?"

Sachi narrowed her eyes at the demon and refused to look at the men. "I am," she said.

"It's why you never felt bad about using Cash and why you can't hate your mother, even for sacrificing an innocent vampire."

Cash growled beside her.

Sachi hated that this demon was speaking all of her fears aloud. She called power into her palm, felt the weight of the dark ball ready to blast this demon back to Hell. "Why are you here?" she demanded.

"I won't let you stop Ainu," the demon Rodriguez said darkly, a grin too wide, revealing black sharp teeth. Her eyes started to glow red and she leaped forward to attack.

Cash reacted first, jumping, and shifting in the air.

"No!" Sachi screamed as the demon turned mid leap and crashed into the wolf, taking him to the ground with a loud thud. Sachi couldn't throw the energy ball, it was too risky with Cash tangled with her. Jax was by her side, one hand on her shoulder, she wasn't sure if he was offering support or holding her back as if she'd willingly risk Cash's life in this moment if he didn't.

Sachi watched, horrified, as the demon wrestled with the wolf and looked to have the advantage, despite her small stature. Sachi wanted to jump into the fight and help, but Jax held her tightly now.

"There's nothing you can do. Just wait, Cash has got this," Jax assured her, but she didn't believe him, couldn't, and the words of the demon rang in her ears.

Cash finally got his mouth around the demon's throat and clamped down, she stilled immediately, and her body shriveled until it was an emaciated corpse, long dead and decayed.

"Get in the fucking car!" Sachi yelled and tore out of Jax's grip, rushing to her car. She hopped in the driver's seat and cranked the engine, no worry as to what the boys were doing. They just made it in as she peeled out and through the desert back to town. Fuck the roads, she had to get to the bakery. She had to try and save Fern first.

CHAPTER 18

Sachi was frantic and driving a little crazy she had to admit, but she wasn't going to let demons out of her portal and she wasn't going to let Lance use Fern as a shield.

"Are you okay, Cash?" Jax asked.

Cash shifted to human in the backseat and Sachi couldn't turn to look, she had to assume he was okay, he had to be okay. She couldn't handle any other option even if he no longer wanted her, even if he hated her for what she was, she needed him to be okay.

"Fine, a few cuts and bruises," he said with a groan that didn't make her think that it was as fine as all that.

"I know what happened to your parents," Sachi said quietly.

"Mine?" Cash said with a groan as he buckled his seatbelt.

"Yes. Your father was in charge of my mother that night. When the portal opens, the draw on her demon side is strong and your parents kept her locked up, kept her safe so she wouldn't be drawn into it. The alpha of the wolf pack has a cell in the basement for wolves who lose control, right? That's what they kept her in."

"Shit," Cash said, "That's crazy. Because she's demon?"

Sachi clenched her hands on the steering wheel and tried to ignore the fear that trickled into Cash's voice. "Half, yeah. That's why your father wasn't there that night, he was helping, just not at the portal. Lance, well... demon Lance, forced most of my memories to the surface in the vamp club and more bits are still coming. He killed your parents so they couldn't remember or help again," Sachi said quietly.

"They died protecting the district, it's honorable," Cash said, voice deep with emotion. "But what does it all mean for your mother now?" Cash asked.

"It means that she might be better off asleep in the hospital for the next twenty-four hours."

Both men put a hand on her, offering comfort and the simple act settled at least some of her doubts about how they would continue to feel about her. She didn't slow until she hit city streets, then she made her way as quickly and safely as she could to the bakery. It looked dark but she wasn't fooled, she could feel them in there. Jax had crawled into the backseat with Cash to check his wounds at Sachi's insistence so when she pulled into the parking lot. She was alone in the front seat, and nervous.

"I think you'll heal," Jax told Cash who just grunted in response.

Sachi wanted to jump in the back and inspect his wounds herself but wasn't sure he'd allow it, wasn't convinced her demon part was acceptable and so she just stared at the building and tried to concentrate on what they needed to do now. "Do you think they're all in there?" Sachi asked.

"No, the fire demon can't leave the water, but I bet Lance is in there with the shadow demon, waiting for us."

Her phone rang then and everyone in the car jumped. It was her mother's cell.

"Mom!" she answered frantically.

"Guess again," came a dark voice that sent a spike of fear

straight to her spine. The shadow demon, somehow she knew it without a doubt.

The men were at her side instantly, leaning close to listen and offer support with their hands on her shoulders. She drew strength from them, she accepted their touch and hoped it wouldn't go away.

"What do you want, demon? Where's my mother?"

"She's safe, for now," he said darkly, and she recognized the familiar sound of beeps from a hospital room. Her mother was still safe. Sachi breathed a sigh of relief.

"I want you to get in your car and drive away," the demon said, coming back on the line.

"I can't let you open the portal, I won't give you my district."

"Then your mother will die," he said simply and hung up.

"Fuck!" Sachi hissed as she slammed the phone back into her pocket.

"Sachi!" A flutter of wings drew her attention then Seraphina appeared at her door.

Sachi got out of the car and pulled the young fairy into her arms, "Seraphina! Oh my god, he's got Fern in there doesn't he?"

"Yeah," she said, pulling back. "We hid when they came down, he didn't know we were in there still searching for the knife."

"It's not safe. You have to get everyone out of there," Sachi panicked, she couldn't be the cause of so many fairy deaths.

"Don't worry about us, we hide well," she said with a wink. "And Lance isn't going to hurt Fern, not yet anyway. He's waiting for something that another demon is supposed to bring. Something that will tell them how to open the portal early."

"Did he say where they're looking?"

"No, but I know she's safe for now." Seraphina's eyes narrowed and she glared. "Don't let that asshole hurt my sister," she snapped, then shrunk back down and flitted away.

"Shit," Jax hissed. "If they find the spell, they could open the portal at any time with a sacrifice."

Sachi didn't need him to tell her how dangerous that would be, and they already had someone on hand to sacrifice.

Sirens in the distance brought them all to a standstill "I think they found Rodriguez's body," Cash offered.

"How many of them saw us drive by and knew she'd gone to check on us?" It wasn't as if Sachi's car wasn't recognizable.

"We'd better move," Cash said as the sirens sounded closer.

"We have to hide," Jax agreed.

They darted into the shadows and kept going, it was easier to stay hidden on foot.

"If they're dumb enough to enter the bakery, they're going to be killed," she worried as they slunk through shadows away from the sirens.

"Maybe not. Lance won't want any bloodshed to draw attention to what he's doing," Cash reassured her.

"We need to find what the demons are looking for before they do," Jax said. "If it isn't in your basement, where else would your father have kept demon artifacts? We searched Cash's place and didn't come up with anything."

"My mother?" Sachi wondered aloud. "She could have been hiding artifacts."

"I bet that's the first place the shadow demon looked, where do you think he got her cell," Jax pointed out.

"Damn," Sachi hissed.

"Who else did your father trust?" Jax asked.

Sachi froze, eyes wide, she turned to the men as an idea formed. "The fire demon!"

"Demon, Sach, demon!" Cash growled.

"So is my mother, apparently I am a little too," she grumbled and looked away from Cash, not wanting to see disgust there. "My father met with the fire demon on a regular basis, he was obviously helping her, what if she was guarding something for him?"

"She's here now to open the portal. She already killed

someone and tried to put her friend in its body. You're insane if you think we can trust her," Cash argued.

"She's right," Jax said calmly. "I don't say we trust a demon, but I think we need to know why her father was meeting up with it."

Nobody was excited about it, but they agreed it was the best next step.

They made their way west to the river, sticking to shadows and trying to look natural as they passed the vampires and other supes going about their normal business. The sirens had stopped, and she could only hope it wasn't because Lance had killed them. Neither man touched her, took her hand or made a move to outdo the other as they walked and Sachi couldn't help the little bit of hurt for it. Was their blossoming story already crushed? She'd been teased with the possibilities of two amazing men in her life only to have them reject her because of what she was?

The dark water of the river was before them. No one was on the beach of course since it was still considered a crime scene, which meant they were alone as they approached the flowing water cautiously.

"How are we going to find it?" Sachi whispered.

"I have a feeling it will find us," Jax said, putting a guiding hand to her lower back, he urged her forward.

They sat at the edge of the water for a while, waiting but nothing happened.

"Maybe if you put your feet in," Jax offered. "Maybe it'll sense your demon energy and come looking."

"Or eat me," she said, but she couldn't think of a better idea so she took off her boots and socks and stuck her feet in the water.

Nothing happened at first, but then the water warmed, and the flow seemed to reverse direction momentarily. Sachi pulled her feet back and the three of them scrambled away from the edge as a figure emerged from the water, a figure shaped like a woman. It was glowing from an internal fire and had black orbs for eyes and flowing red hair. Waves of heat radiated from it as it stood half out of the water. It flicked its gaze from one of them to the other but settled with an intensity on Sachi.

"You still smell like your grandfather," it accused. Its mouth was no more than a slit formed in what looked like a pane of glass that was its face, the sound it produced was high and piercing. The slit disappeared when it was done speaking, leaving a smooth flat surface with two huge black eyes framed in bright red hair.

It was terrifying.

Sachi tried not to cringe, the last thing she wanted to do was offend the demon. "Is that bad?" she asked carefully.

"It just is. Proof that his progeny escaped and procreated with a warlock. There are those who would be very interested in finding you and your mother."

Sachi didn't like the sound of that. "Is that why the demons are here?"

"Oh no, they're here to keep me from going back in."

Sachi was too shocked to respond, this demon wanted back in?

"In? You want back *into* Hell?" Cash clarified.

"I have been stuck in this horrid realm for fifty years and I'm sick of it!" She slapped the water that drifted around her hips. "Forced to survive in water! Fucking trapped," she snarled.

It made sense why she wanted back in Hell if she hadn't been able to leave the water in fifty years, but that didn't answer all the questions Sachi had. "Why are you up here if you can't survive on earth out of water?"

The demon settled herself into the water, sitting gracefully in the shallow with her burning internal light only held back by the lapping current flowing around her. Sachi wondered what would happen if the demon got cold enough, would she break easily like the glass she resembled, would her inner fire ever be able to get that cold? Somehow Sachi doubted it.

"I was the queen of Hell," she said after a moment. "I ruled with my husbands for millenniums."

"Husbands?" Sachi interrupted.

"Yes, demon females generally attract more than one willing male," she said with a laugh, "as you can see," she motioned to the two men beside her.

Sachi's face heated and refused to look at the men. She wasn't so sure they were hers anymore and she didn't want to see it written on their faces. "Oh, well… yeah I guess so. Sorry to interrupt your story," she hurried to add, wanting the focus back off of her and whatever was going on with the two men beside her. Was she some kind of demon femme fatale attracting men to her side? That seemed highly unlikely since she hadn't seriously dated anyone in years.

"Your grandfather was jealous, didn't agree with the way things had been done since the beginning of time, so he stole away one portal opening and dragged a poor butterfly back through the portal to be his second bride."

"My grandmother," Sachi gasped.

The demon nodded. "I wasn't keen on the idea and when the portal reopened, I thought to teach him a lesson. I slipped out fifty years ago thinking I'd claim a little earth treat for myself." She hit the water around her. "I was immediately aware of my mistake. The building I arrived in burst into flames, and I ran for the nearest water," she said bitterly. "And here I've sat."

"Is that what my father was helping you with?"

"I'll get there," the demon snapped.

Sachi nodded, lips pursed.

"My husbands missed me, it's lonely in Hell when the only woman for miles is kept locked in a cage in the king's bedroom. When she bore him a daughter there was great rejoicing among my husbands, thinking there might be another wife for some of them at least."

Sachi shuddered at the picture the demon was forming in her

mind. What horror had her mother endured all those years ago. How had she managed to survive? When had she escaped? She had so many questions she thought she was going to explode!

"Your grandmother saw the horrors that her daughter would endure, she sacrificed herself at the portal and paid the price for four of my husbands to take her across and leave her safely with a nice couple to grow up, she was just a child at the time."

"Not during an opening?" Jax asked. "So, they needed the blood sacrifice?"

The demon nodded. "They were supposed to help me go back through on the next opening and take my throne back."

"But they changed their plan?"

"They've gotten a taste for human flesh, and they have forsaken me." As she spoke angrily, the fire inside her body grew and started to flow through her glass-like form.

"We have to stop them," Sachi said, ready to go back and fight to save her mother and Fern.

"They won't open it tonight," the demon said, now calm again, the fire retreated to her center.

"How can you know that?" Cash demanded.

"Because I have the book that tells them how to do the spell," she said with a grin. "It was left with the babe. Your father sought me out when you were born and every time you got near the portal it lit up, recognizing your demon blood. He feared what you were, what you might do and although your mother hadn't ever told him, he figured it out, found the book and other artifacts that she'd kept hidden. I took the book and promised to keep it safe as long as he kept the portal closed and my husbands wouldn't be able to let any of their friends out to play. I may not be able to enjoy living up here, but I don't want to see earth destroyed."

"Why did you kill that human yesterday?" Sachi demanded. Wanting so badly to believe that this woman, this demon, was on their side, but she couldn't let go of the fact that it had killed someone, had tried to infect a human with a demon to reach her goal.

The demon shrugged. "Anadexius was the only one who stayed by my side all these years. He never left the water even though he could have. Never took a body to walk among humans. I took the woman and put him in it so that he could try and stop the others. I take it he was less than successful since he's yet to come back and tell me otherwise."

She spoke sadly and Sachi hoped she already knew that Anadexius was gone. She met Jax's gaze briefly and they shared a look of worry. They may have fed her favorite husband to a ghoul.

Sachi nodded slightly.

The demon dropped her gaze momentarily. "He was a good husband."

Apparently she already knew.

"I'm sorry for your loss," Jax offered.

"We knew the risk. There are still three out there, two trying to keep me from dragging them back to Hell and one on my side."

"Two," Cash said with a grin. "I broke the neck of whoever was inside Chief Rodriguez."

"A werewolf can't destroy a demon," she snorted. "Only the body it possessed. You've still got three demons out there."

That wasn't comforting news. "But they can't open the portal," Sachi reminded. "They don't have the book."

"No, they can't open it early. But it will still open tomorrow night if you can't do the spell to keep it shut." She rose up out of the water until she was standing on the surface as if it were solid. Her flaming hair and core bright against the night. "I can't let you do that. I *must* get home. I *must* kill the king and get my throne back." Her eyes were intense on Sachi as she paused, her gaze raking over Sachi and her mouth hole reappearing in a frown of discontent. "And they say there's only one thing destined to kill the king."

Sachi's breath was held, they'd all stood as the demon started to get louder, but they were frozen, staring into the fire of the beautifully terrifying creature standing on the water. "What?" she asked in the barest of whispers.

"His flesh and blood," the demon said darkly. "Lucky for me you walked right into my lap."

Jax and Cash dropped to the ground on either side of Sachi and strong arms wrapped around her from behind. She struggled but the body that was now firm against her back didn't budge. She kicked back and made contact but there wasn't even a grunt of pain.

"What the hell?" she hissed trying to turn her head enough to see who or what had a hold of her.

"His name is Bardbizt," the fire demon said with a smile. "My other faithful husband."

"Queen Ainu," Bardbizt said with a deep rumbling voice.

Sachi wrenched her head around enough to catch sight of who was holding her, feet dangling above the ground helplessly. She wished she hadn't. The sight was too terrifying for words, bright red eyes in a stonelike face twisted into a gargoyle. He had to be at least eight feet tall, and she could see long, black fur covering him in patches as well as leathery wings stuck out behind him.

"What the hell did you do to my men?" Sachi demanded and squirmed despite her fear and revulsion at the sight of the demon.

"I don't need them, I need you."

"Fuck that, I need them!"

Ainu sighed. "They aren't dead. Now get her out of here, Bardbizt, keep her until the full moon rises tomorrow night."

"Yes, my queen," Bardbizt said in a gravelly voice and turned with Sachi still gripped in his arms.

"Where the hell do you think you're taking me?"

"We will wait out the hours at your mother's house."

"Of course you know where that is because you've been stalking me?"

He snorted. "You aren't that interesting; I have been watchful of all the players."

Sachi wasn't sure how she felt about that, but she mostly wanted him to put her down. "Let me go, and you know that you can't just walk around unnoticed, you're a fucking demon that looks like it eats babies for breakfast."

"I don't eat babies."

"Doesn't change the way you look, and I can walk."

"If I put you down, you'll run away, and this way I can keep us both shielded from vision."

"Shielded?"

"Yes, I can cloak us so no one will see us, you are likely wanted for the murder of the human I was possessing, and like you said, I am a scary demon." His voice rumbled the last like he found the description amusing.

"What if I promise to stay close?" Sachi said with gritted teeth, she really didn't appreciate being heaved along like this.

He grunted but he let her go. She didn't try to run away, what would be the point, he obviously was willing and able to hurt her and at this point she was starting to think that staying with him and going along with Ainu's plan was the safest bet.

It was weird walking through town and passing people but getting zero looks or acknowledgement. The werewolves sniffed the air as if they smelled something they couldn't quite put a finger on, and the witches shivered as if they sensed danger they couldn't see. But none of them could quite figure it out and as Sachi and Bardbizt passed, it seemed they quickly forgot the odd sensations.

Sirens screamed and rounded a corner heading toward the center of town and, she supposed, her bakery. "Thanks for keeping me out of jail, I guess."

"No problem. Your boyfriends might not be so lucky if they don't wake up and move away from the river soon."

Sachi frowned and pulled out her phone. She dialed first Jax, then Cash, hoping to wake them up. Neither answered though and her worry increased. "Did you have to leave them there?"

"I couldn't carry all of you," he said simply.

"If they end up in jail for murdering the woman *you* killed, I'm going to have a hard time seeing your side of things, Bard."

He snorted at her use of a nickname and rolled his eyes. It was a disconcerting gesture on his gargoyle-like demon face. "They are far too smart to get caught and I didn't hit them that hard, they'll be up again soon. The police aren't even close to the river."

She hoped he was right.

When they got to her mother's house he assured her that he could shroud the entire house to look as if it was empty and quiet, no one would know they were there and they wouldn't have anything to worry about until tomorrow night.

"Great," she grumbled and pulled out her phone. There was a message from Jax.

> Where the hell are you?

And one from Cash.

> I can smell your fear, if something happened to you I'm going on a killing spree.

"Nice guys," Bardbizt said, peering over her shoulder as she plopped onto the couch.

"Mind your own business."

"You are my business."

She texted Cash back first.

> Don't kill anyone, I'm at my mother's with the demon that came out of Chief Rodriguez's body.

Then to Jax.

> I'm at my mother's with a demon, I'm fine. Watch for cops and find the damn knife!

"I'm going to bed," she sighed. "I suppose I'll see you in the morning?"

"You will," he assured her.

Her phone rang as she headed up the stairs.

"Hello Jax."

"What the hell do you mean you're with a demon?"

"Didn't Cash explain?"

"Cash is a wolf right now."

"Figures. Well, tell him that I'm fine, the demon that came out of Rodriguez is keeping me hidden and safe until tomorrow night so I can help Ainu. I need you two to not get arrested and to find that damn knife, we're going to need it."

"I don't like this," Jax grunted and she heard a growl in the background.

"It doesn't matter, this is what we need to do. We are Keepers," she reminded him. "The portal is more important than what we want."

"We are Keepers," he agreed grudgingly.

"Please stop Cash from doing anything stupid," she said. "I'll see you two tomorrow. Keep each other safe." She hung up the phone and closed her bedroom door, briefly wondering where Bardbizt was going to sleep, if he slept at all. She couldn't imagine the huge beast fitting comfortably in her mother's bed. He looked like he was most comfortable sleeping on the side of a church.

She undressed and crawled into bed, exhausted and dirty, but she was too tired to shower. She wanted to sleep, wanted to wake up and find out this was all a very bad dream. Well... everything aside from the pleasant memories of her father, she wanted to keep those.

"Take the good with the bad and do a good job because of what I am," she whispered. Her father had told her that many times growing up.

CHAPTER 19

Sachi woke up in her childhood bedroom. The sun was high in the sky and death was on the horizon. She lay there staring at the ceiling as tears rolled down her cheeks. She checked her phone, nothing from her men or Fern, and no updates from the hospital. Fear for everyone she loved overwhelmed her for a moment and she let the tears flow freely.

She was alone, and there was a demon somewhere in the house babysitting her. Queen Ainu wanted to drag her into Hell and use her to kill her husband, Sachi's grandfather, the current king of Hell. It felt like a fate worse than death in the moment and just as permanent.

She had no idea if Jax, Cash, or Fern were okay, and all she wanted to do was close her eyes and go back to not knowing anything about all this shit.

She didn't get up for a while, just stared at the ceiling trying to figure out how to save everyone without sacrificing herself. After a while she rolled over and stared at her vanity, still stacked with old makeup and lotions. When she was eighteen, she was ready to devote her life to keeping the portal closed. She'd planned to learn beside her father and take over when he retired, she never expected him to die so soon. She could remember now how proud she'd felt of the duty she would take on, the importance of being a part of such a monumental task.

She knew better than to try and leave the house, the damn demon could spin magic like a witch and had warded the house to keep her contained. She could feel it all around her. But she didn't have to stay in her room. So she shifted to a small butterfly and flitted out and down the hall to her mother's bedroom. She heard noises downstairs that sounded like cooking, and she could smell eggs and coffee, a very tempting smell.

She shifted back once in her mother's room and started searching. She didn't know what she was looking for, but if her mother was hiding something that could help them, it would be here. She scrambled to open every drawer, look on every shelf and under the mattress. She wasn't sure when the demon would decide to wake her up for breakfast, so she moved quickly.

She gave up after she'd thoroughly searched every possible space and walked downstairs cautiously.

"Good morning, sunshine," Bardbizt said as she stood on the threshold to the kitchen. He was setting the table with eggs, juice, and coffee. He was naked, but she assumed that was usual for a demon, he wasn't exactly shaped for clothing. He was tall and wide enough to have to need to crouch and go through a doorway sideways. He was all black and grey, his skin covered sparsely with patches of long, black fur. His legs were twisted, shaped more like an animal, goat perhaps, than human. Complete with hooves. His hands were huge and clawed, tusks jutted out of his mouth, a pig shaped nose and large eyes. Ears stuck out on top of his head in large triangles and moved independently. He had a tail with a pointy leathery tip and those wings. Huge leathery batlike wings that filled the kitchen when he stretched them out.

"Where are my men?"

"Your mates? They are probably still outside; they showed up just before dawn and wouldn't leave, but they can't get past my ward. You have picked strong husbands."

It sounded like a compliment, so she decided to take it as one. "Thanks." She hurried to the window to see if she could spot them.

"Last I saw, they were near the back door," he offered and pointed toward the laundry room.

She hurried to the back door and looked out. Jax and Cash were sitting on the grass staring at the door, she flung it open, and they both jumped up and stepped forward, stopping before they hit the invisible barrier.

"Sach! Are you alright?" Cash asked while Jax seemed to be eyeing every inch of her for signs of harm.

"I'm fine, are you guys okay?"

"Would have been better if we could have slept inside!" Jax yelled.

The demon huffed from the kitchen.

"He's keeping me here so they can take me through the portal tonight."

"Yeah, we can't let that happen," Jax said firmly.

Sachi bit her lip.

"What are you thinking Sach?" Cash demanded.

"Isn't it best to get the fire demon back into Hell?"

"Obviously," Cash agreed quickly.

Jax just narrowed his eyes at her, ready to argue.

"If I let her take me, she'll go, Bardbizt will go."

"And the other two assholes terrorizing the district?" Jax gritted out.

Sachi nodded. "We need to kill them still, it's the only way. I need you guys to find the knife. It has to be in the district somewhere. I'm going to search this place; I need you two searching Cash's place again. Without the knife I don't even think the fire demon has the upper hand."

217

"She doesn't," Bardbizt agreed, surprising Sachi with his close presence behind her.

"Do you know where the knife is?"

"Nope, but I can tell you it isn't here. I'd know if a weapon that could kill me was that close."

"Fuck," Sachi groaned. "Cash, it has to be at your place, my father trusted yours."

"We looked for hours last night and came up empty," Jax said, rubbing a hand over his face in frustration. "It wasn't easy with staying hidden but I think we looked in every drawer, every box."

"Nothing's been moved since he died." Cash froze, eyes wide. "Except a box of alpha items that went to Bernard when he took over. Sachi what if it was in there?"

"Get it!" Sachi demanded and Cash tore off to do as she'd ordered.

"Are you going to be okay?" Jax asked, looking at Bardbizt.

"I think he won't harm me; they need me." That didn't mean she was fine; she was scared, and she was creeped out and she wanted to leave the house. But there was nothing Jax could do about any of that, he was more useful helping Cash get the knife back. "Please just keep Cash alive."

He nodded and took off to follow Cash.

"Stay hidden!" she yelled, then turned to Bardbizt and frowned. "Looks like it's just you and me."

"Breakfast?" He said gallantly and walked back into the kitchen.

She followed and even accepted the offered plate of eggs, bacon and toast. He joined her, the kitchen chair creaking under his immense weight and they passed the time surprisingly pleasantly. Bardbizt turned out to be good company, witty and charming, if you could get past the way he looked and the fact that he had willingly killed Chief Rodriguez for a chance to walk around unnoticed outside of Hell.

"And you love her, Ainu I mean, enough to go back to Hell?"

Bardbizt took her plate and walked to the sink looking thoughtful. "I do, I always have, loved her. To be the husband of the Queen is a great honor that I took on happily when I was young. I served at her side along with the others for many years. I would do anything for her and if she had decided to stay up here forever and live in the water I would have served her there. But she is not happy with the constraints this world puts on her. I am glad she wants to return to our home where we can be ourselves and be together in our home."

"The others, they don't agree," Sachi pushed, even though Ainu had already told her as much.

"No, they have betrayed her and me, they have forsaken the vows of our marriage."

"You feel that you're married to them too, not just her," Sachi said surprised.

Bardbizt turned and faced her. "A marriage is a partnership, I entered into it second to last and I accepted all the husbands who came before me. I stood beside them and promised to keep them sacred the same as Ainu. And they promised the same thing to me."

Before Sachi could stop herself she stood and crossed the kitchen laying a hand on Bardbizt's chest. "I am so sorry that they have betrayed you, I am so sorry that even if you and Ainu do return, that it will be to a broken home."

Pain flashed in Bardbizt's large red eyes. "It was broken long ago and Ainu and I will rebuild what we have lost."

Sachi assumed that meant more than just marrying a few more demon males, but she wasn't sure she wanted to ask for more details. The thought of being there, of going down through the portal and being a part of whatever they were rebuilding, and destroying, made her stomach tighten.

Her phone beeped with a message and she was thankful for the distraction. It was from the hospital, her mother was awake. Another immediately followed from Detective Tyler saying her mother had been officially arrested. She wasn't going to be let out of the hospital for another day at least though, they had to keep observing and making sure she was okay, but when she was released, she'd be going into police custody.

"I can't let that happen," Sachi yelled at Bardbizt, holding up her phone to show the message. "Do you have a mother? Do demons have mothers?"

"Of course, what do you think, we spring up from a pit of lava?" he laughed. "We fuck, and we have babies like everything else."

She ignored his rude remark. "Please," she begged, an idea forming. "Help me get her out of there, I'd rather see her alive in Hell than rotting in a jail cell. She was only trying to save everyone from the worst scenario, the possibility of complete demon takeover." Sachi wasn't completely sure she was thinking clearly, but once the idea struck, her gut said go with it, anything was better than her mother in jail.

"The King's daughter," Bardbizt mumbled thoughtfully.

"I have to keep her safe, she's my mother," Sachi whispered.

Bardbizt nodded his large demon head. "I'll allow that taking her back would be beneficial to my love's plans."

Sachi didn't think her mother would be capable of helping with Ainu's plan, but she didn't say that; she needed Bardbizt to help her. There was still a demon threat to remove before they could get her mother safely.

"What about the shadow demon? He was there, threatening her last night."

"He can't move about during the day. As long as the sun's up he'll be hiding." Bardbizt looked thoughtful for a moment. "Just don't go near any mirrors in the room."

Her mood improved slightly with his cooperation, and as she let go of one worry, she circled back to another. She pulled out her phone and sent off a text to Cash and then Jax asking for an update.

"I imagine you care about who gets hurt, so how do you suppose we get your mother out of the hospital?" Bardbizt asked.

"I do care, I don't want *anyone* hurt actually."

The hospital was run by vampires because no one was better at smelling sickness or rooting out the cause of internal bleeding. Which meant that during the day it was a skeleton crew of mostly witch nurses in the building and that was going to make sneaking in and out possible. She'd have to call in a favor from Penelope and hope she could spread the word among the coven. No one did *disengaged and bitchy ignorance* like the witches. When the time came, they could all suddenly be far too busy to attend to any concern any officer might have over the whereabouts of a prisoner.

The trick would be getting her mother to agree to come. Sachi had a feeling the last place Helen would want to go is on a little vacation to see her father but it had to be better than the alternative which was surely jail.

Sachi dialed Penelope's number and bit her lip as it rang, hoping she wasn't going to wake up any of the babies, or disrupt naptime for their mommy.

"Sachi?" Penelope answered, her voice wary.

"Penelope, how are you?" Sachi hated to bother her, especially since the last visit had been to tell Penelope that she'd had a sister and that sister who she'd forgotten even existed, had been brutally murdered.

"I'm okay, I am taking my mourning time, even though it's been ten years, I feel as though it just happened."

Sachi nodded even though Penelope couldn't see her through the phone. There was the coo of a baby in the background, and she wished she could have gone to talk to her in person, she just didn't think Penelope would have welcomed a demon into her home and there was no way Bardbizt was going to let Sachi go without him. "How is your mother taking it, and your sisters?"

"When I called my mother and sisters, they acted like I was

insane, they had always known, had already made peace with it." Penelope sighed heavily. "But for me it feels like yesterday."

A lump rose in Sachi's throat. Remembering was so much harder than having known for ten years. Sachi wished she could be there for her friend, and she couldn't. "I'm so sorry."

"It's stupid to mourn now, I know that, but I feel like I was cheated out of it. My mother thinks its postpartum depression." Penelope sniffed back tears. "But I'll take my time and mourn because it's right."

"I think that's the right thing to do." Sachi had felt a renewed sense of loss for her father after getting her memories of him back from the demon Lance. If she wasn't so distracted by everything else, she was sure she'd be in a new cycle of mourning too. Maybe she would when this was all over, when she could finally sit and think over everything that she had lost ten years ago. So much more than a father, she'd lost ten years of love with Cash, ten years of magic knowledge and practice, ten years of really knowing who she was. She shook her head and got herself back on track. "Penelope, I called to ask a favor as well as see how you're doing."

"Is this about the human chief's murder? I will be your alibi, don't worry a moment about it," Penelope said firmly.

Sachi smiled, her friend was fierce and the fact that she was so willing to help with no questions asked made her heart fill. "Actually, I just need you to call in some favors with whoever is working the hospital today, I'm going to break my mother out."

"No problem," Penelope said without hesitation, making Sachi's shoulders drop with relief.

Sachi gave her the details and promised to visit soon. She really hoped she'd be able to, that she'd survive this whole mess and be on this side of the portal.

Sachi showered and fretted over her men, and checked her phone every ten minutes hoping one of them would respond with an update. Then she started going through every drawer and cabinet in the house to see if she could find anything demon-related.

"What on earth are you doing making all that racket? Your nervous energy is making me itch," Bardbizt snapped from the living room.

"My mother is half demon; I'm looking for demon things."

"Other than a murder scene in her laundry room and the remnants of her blood sacrifice on the kitchen table?" he asked.

Sachi eyeballed the area and frowned. "Why are the cops not here if this is a murder scene?"

"There's nothing to solve, they know the who and why."

She supposed he was right. Her mother was caught red handed and she'd confessed to the crime after she woke up in the hospital apparently.

Sachi settled into a chair and stared out the window to worry about her men. Her phone alerted to a message and she felt her entire body relax at Jax's name flashing across the screen.

> Been dodging police all damn day. Can't get close enough to talk to Bernard. We aren't giving up, there's nowhere else the knife could be.

Well at least they were alive and not in jail. So all she could do was wait.

CHAPTER 20

When the sunset was just an hour away, just a couple hours from moonrise and the start of the portal opening, Sachi stood behind a tree near the hospital with a demon she'd come to trust, at least a little. She was trying not to think about how she hadn't heard from either of her men in hours and what she was potentially going to face soon. She just had to save her mother. She'd never be able to live with knowing her mother was in jail, despite the fact that she'd killed someone for a spell.

"Fuck, maybe I'm more than a quarter demon," she mumbled.

"Nah, I can smell it on ya, just a quarter is all," Bardbizt said, obviously not sensing the rhetorical self-talk.

"I hope this doesn't take long," she said before shifting to her butterfly form.

"Better not or I'm coming in after you and I'll burn the fucking place to the ground to find you," Bardbizt warned.

"How gallant," she mumbled.

They may have entered into a sort of understanding truce, but that didn't mean he was on her side.

Sachi knew what room her mother was in after a quick phone call and was able to flit up to it quickly in butterfly form. A nurse had conveniently left the window ajar, allowing Sachi entrance and right on cue, the officer standing guard outside the room was distracted by a busty witch.

Sachi froze on the windowsill, staring in at her mother. Helen was pale and had deep circles beneath her eyes. She looked like she was sleeping but Sachi knew she wasn't in any kind of coma state anymore. There were machines beeping around her and she was cuffed to the bedrail. The smell of hospital filled Sachi's senses and she shuddered as she slipped all the way in and shifted back to human size and form. A quick scan told her the only mirror was in the bathroom and she hoped Bardbizt was right about the shadow demon hiding there and not in any actual shadows, like under the bed.

Sachi approached her mother quietly, aware that the police officer wasn't far away. She was going to have to convince her mother to come with her and she was going to have to get the charmed cuff off of her wrist or her mother would never be able to shift and escape.

That felt like a lot working against her.

"Mother," Sachi whispered near her ear, crouched beside the bed with one eye on the open doorway.

Helen's eyelids flickered before they opened, and she looked at Sachi with confusion before recognition.

"What are you doing here? You need to be at the portal! It's the full moon tonight."

"I'm busting you out of here first," Sachi whispered cheerfully.

Her mother frowned. "Why?"

"I need you to be safe, I need you to come through the portal with us," her voice hitched, and tears filled her eyes. "I can't see you in a jail cell."

Her mother's face turned soft, and she reached out with her uncuffed hand. "Sachi, love. I knew what I was doing when I sacrificed Kyle. I won't let the demons win."

Sachi nodded.

"Ainu, the fire demon. I went to her after the town meeting. I —I can't believe what I forgot," Helen looked ashamed and Sachi reached out to touch her mother's face gently.

"It was a spell, we all forgot, Mom."

Her mother nodded. "I went to the river, I knew that if a human had died there, it had to have been her. So I called to her, and she told me what I had to do to help you."

"You did help me. We found the shadow demon at the school, and we talked to Ainu, we have a plan to stop all this."

"She wants to take you through the portal to kill her husband," her mother scoffed. "That's not a plan, it's a death sentence."

"I won't let the demons stay here," Sachi said firmly.

"No, I don't suppose you will. You're just like your father. Willing to give everything for the sake of others."

Her mother's words filled Sachi with pleasure. She'd never felt very self-sacrificing but, in that moment, she knew she would give herself to save the district. There was no way she'd let the terror that the demons promised be unleashed on her friends, and there was no way she was going to let her mother be arrested for helping save them all.

"Let me save you," Sachi pleaded. "I can't live with knowing you're locked away."

"Kyle was a good man," her mother said sadly.

"So was my father," Sachi said. "So were Cash's parents and Jax's father. A demon killed them and more will die if he lets his friends out. Kyle was sacrificed for the greater good." Her words were firm, and she believed them too. Sacrifices were made in times of war, and that's exactly what this was. They had to fight to keep the portal closed or they would be invaded, and more than one innocent vampire would be taken from the earth too soon.

"Jax's father," Helen said with a smile. "He was my lover you know. Came around once or twice a year to discuss portal business with your father and we would spend a week or two together. Such a wonderful man."

Sachi froze, eyes wide and panic building. "You didn't have a child with him, did you?"

"No! Oh my Sachi, no. You are the only child I bore and when I smelled the taint of demon on you, I knew I couldn't have another." She shook her head sadly. "I would have liked to, but the risk was too great. I wouldn't want the stain of my father to continue into the next generation."

Sachi felt dirty at her mother's words, and her face must have shown it too because her mother's face shifted into pity.

"Oh not you, never you, Sachi. The blood in your veins may smell of demons, but it never reached your soul. Your father was too good a man for that. It's just a risk I wasn't willing to take again. Another child, another father, who knows what might have happened if their soul was tipped slightly the other way."

Sachi didn't feel much better. She was justifying the death of Kyle without remorse, or second thoughts and yet her mother said her demon blood didn't affect her. She shook the fear away. "Mother, we have to go. I need to get that cuff off of you so we can shift and fly out of here." They'd already wasted enough time and she didn't expect the witch was going to keep the officer distracted much longer.

"Oh this thing! Bah, can't hold a half demon with a little silver," she huffed and pulled her hand out as if it were nothing.

"Why the fuck didn't you do that already?" Sachi demanded.

"I didn't want to cause you any trouble, love. I wasn't going to let them jail me, but I figured it could wait until after the portal was closed up and everyone was safe again."

Sachi couldn't help shooting her mother a glare for the worry she'd caused, but they didn't have time to discuss it. She shifted and flitted out; her mother followed. The sound of cracking glass from the bathroom had her heart speeding up and she knew as soon as the sun set, they'd have a shadow demon on their trail.

They landed next to Bardbizt behind the tree and shifted back.

"Mistress Thyone, good to see you again," Bardbizt said with a little bow.

"I go by Pearl, Helen Pearl."

"Your adopted family name. Yes, I think I remember hearing that."

"You didn't forsake Ainu," Helen said with surprise.

"I love her! I would never," he said firmly. "Your daughter is going to save her, give us back our life together."

Sachi swallowed a lump at his words, more a threat than anything. She was going to do what she could to save everyone.

Back at her mother's house Sachi stared at her phone while her mother changed out of her hospital gown. She frowned, willing a message to come through from Jax or Cash, but there was nothing and fear started to spike. She was going to have to face this thing alone and she had no idea what she was doing, barely had an idea of how to close the portal, certainly no real fighting technique. Worst of all, she imagined Cash torn apart by Bernard and Jax too, just for being a bystander of the fight, or maybe trying to help when he shouldn't have.

Her heart ached for the perceived loss of the two men she cared about, one an old care renewed and the other fresh and full of promise. She wanted to explore them, find a relationship with them. She wanted a happily ever after. Did quarter demons get those?

"Ah, yes," her mother came into the kitchen mumbling, now dressed in her own clothes. She knelt down and knocked on a floorboard.

"What are you doing?" Sachi was sure she was watching her mother lose her mind, but the damn thing popped up as if on command and her mother reached in. She pulled out an envelope and blew dust from it with a grin.

"This is from your father," she said as she handed it to Sachi. "Instructions. He knew he was in for trouble that night and he had prepared, he just didn't think that it would be ten years before you were able to read the damn thing." She shrugged. "Maybe it'll help tonight."

Sachi took the letter and felt a glimmer of hope. She tore open the envelope and felt a stab of grief looking at her father's familiar handwriting.

> My Dearest Sachi,
>   I had hoped you would have years more to train with me but there's something wrong. I can feel it in my soul. I worry that I won't make it out tonight and so I am leaving you with clear instructions. Practice them and be ready in ten years to perform. If you feel you need more, contact Edvin Lintel, your mother knows how. He is a good man, I trust him with my life and he can help you with whatever you need. You've got Cash too, that brings me comfort, he's a strong man and that's what someone as unique as you needs.
>   I love you more than anything,
>   Dad

Sachi let her tears flow as she pulled out the small paper with instructions for a spell written on it. She could tell immediately that it was complicated, and she could see why he had suggested she practice it. "Too late for that," she mumbled.

"He believed you could do it," her mother comforted.

"He didn't know I'd be doing it from inside without practice or preparation," she said as she looked at Bardbizt.

"Hopefully not inside, but closed is closed," her mother said firmly.

"We'd better go." They were out of time. She hoped Jax and Cash would be waiting for them outside the bakery, and she hoped it would make up for the lack of time and training her father had recommended to have them by her side.

The hospital called for the third time, no doubt trying to tell her that her mother had disappeared, and the police station called for the second time, probably wanting to question her about possibly breaking her mother out of the hospital. Luckily Bardbizt's talents extended to cloaking the house so no one could tell they were in there, otherwise she had no doubt they'd have knocked down the door to get in already, or at least tried.

CHAPTER 21

As the sun set, Sachi, her mother, and Bardbizt made their way unseen to the bakery. Pretty easy for two butterfly shifters and Bardbizt cloaking them all. They were on high alert the whole time for the shadow demon and when they landed, they tried to stay hidden as they assessed the place. It looked dark and empty inside, but Sachi knew it wasn't. She could sense the demon energy within, and it was growing, pulling on something within her. "The portal is starting to open," she whispered.

Bardbizt just grunted in agreement and her mother looked as if she were restraining herself from going forward. The pull of the portal must be strong for her, this was why her father had kept her away and guarded during these nights. Sachi reached out to comfort her mother, not sure if it was fear or desire she saw in her mother's tense muscles. "Are you sure you can do this?"

"It's been too long since I was in my father's realm," her mother said quietly.

Sachi squeezed her mother in a quick side hug then turned to Bardbizt. "Will you be able to tell if the shadow demon is near?"

"With the amount of demon energy swirling out from the

building right now, I don't know," he admitted. "But my guess is he'll follow your scent to the house first, then here. We have a minute or two, the sun has just set enough for him to wander safely."

That wasn't reassuring.

"Shit!" Sachi hissed as a patrol car drove by the bakery slowly. "They're looking for us."

"They won't find us where we're going," her mother said confidently.

They all held their breath as the patrol car paused briefly, flashing a light over the parking lot and bakery windows before it moved away.

"What are we waiting for?" A dark, deep voice from behind had Sachi crouching and ready to lash out.

The shadow demon had tracked them quickly.

Sachi was frozen in fear as she looked into the red eyes of a shadowy shape, a gaping mouth full of sharp teeth, and hands that held a knife crusted with blood. Horns spread out of his head and large wings spread out behind him. He wasn't as tall or wide as Bardbizt but the way he seemed not quite solid made him equally terrifying.

"Sachi," it crooned, sending a shiver of fear down her spine. "I hope you don't think Bardbizt is going to stop me from slicing into that pretty flesh of yours and eating your heart."

Sachi backed away and shoved her mother behind her. "I don't need Bardbizt to do anything," she said with a false confidence. "No demon is going to stop me from doing my job," she hissed.

She called a ball of power to her palms and threw it at the shadow, remembering how her father had taught her.

The shadow dissipated and she had a small instant of satisfaction before the thing reappeared, shifting back into shape.

"Sorry, love. That won't kill a shadow demon," it drawled, then flew at her with arms stretched and knife out. The only solid thing about the demon was that knife and she had no doubt it would do what he wanted, slicing through her, ending her painfully.

Sachi's mother screamed and Bardbizt grabbed her, hauling her off and leaving Sachi to fight for her own survival. The damn demon only needed one of them for the plan and he didn't seem to care which survived. Asshole.

Sachi pulled another power ball and threw it, this time she aimed for the knife. The demon screamed as the knife dropped from his hand and Sachi dived for it, scraping her knees and elbows along the ground enough to draw blood, but she didn't stop to care. The adrenaline would cover the pain long enough for her to be killed or kill.

The shadow demon smashed into her from behind, solid despite the way he looked. He pushed into her back, his smoky essence surrounded her and filled her nose and mouth, choking her. Her hand gripped the knife, but she couldn't breathe, he was suffocating her with his essence and his dark laugh, so close to her ear, threatened to shatter her willpower to struggle for freedom. Her fingers were tight on the knife, it was her only chance, she knew, but she couldn't move. His hands were on her arms, his legs pressed into hers and she thought she heard her mother crying somewhere in the distance, muffled by the smoke engulfing her head.

"Sachi, fight!" her mother screamed.

That plea gave her a kick of willpower, she was not going to leave her mother to complete the plan because she couldn't kill one stupid demon. She focused and reared back, surprising the demon with her movement and he slipped slightly. She was able to gasp a quick breath before he was once again filling her mouth and nose, but one hand was free now and she reached back, hitting out at whatever she could. The damn thing couldn't hold her unless he was solid and if he was solid there was something to strike. She was suffocating and she was hurting, but she wasn't going to stop fighting as long as her heart was beating, and her mind was conscious. She was born to protect a portal and half trained or not, she would fight.

She was right in her assumptions, he dissolved into shadow to stop her from striking anything sensitive and she scrambled to her feet, gasping for air and held the knife up in triumph.

"Fuck you!" she yelled, not sure where the thing was going to reappear, she spun slowly, eyes searching shadows. Bardbizt was holding back her crying mother and he gave her an impressed nod. "And fuck you, Bardbizt. Why aren't you helping?" she snapped at him.

"If you lose this fight, how helpful would you be in taking down the king?" he shrugged.

He wasn't wrong and that just pissed her off more. She took a step toward him, ready to tell him where he could shove his opinion. Her moment of distraction was enough for the shadow demon to attack. She was pushed from behind and skidded across the parking lot on her already bleeding knees. Fresh blood ran down her legs as she leapt up and spun, but the thing was gone again already. Fight and flee was his new tactic apparently.

"Fight me solid, you coward," she hissed.

The demon laughed and she spun, he was floating close, and she stepped back into a fighting stance. "You can't win this, not alone, little princess."

"She's not alone," Jax said from behind the demon and Cash's werewolf growl agreed.

Sachi couldn't describe the wave of relief at knowing the two men were there and alive, but she didn't have time to appreciate it as they faced this demon together.

The shadow demon spun to face the two new threats and Sachi saw her chance. She didn't hesitate. She jumped forward, knife slashing down in an arc. She caught him in a moment of solidity and black blood poured from a neck wound.

The shadow demon howled, and Cash jumped on it before it

234

could dissipate, tearing into its chest, ripping at black flesh. The demon's claws tore at the wolf and reached deep, making Cash yip and fall back, bleeding.

The demon was shadow again and everyone moved slowly, waiting to see where it would reappear. Sachi felt it behind her a second before its arm was around her face, filling her once again with its smoke, choking her faster this time as it pushed deep into her lungs, forcing her to suffocate. She squirmed and kicked out, but he barely grunted as her boots hit his shins.

Jax attacked with a knife while the demon was in his weaker form. He drove it deep into the demon's back. The demon cried out and dropped Sachi, she sputtered and crawled away as Cash dove between her and the demon. She tried to gain back her breath and shake the darkness from her brain as her men fought the demon.

Jax pulled the knife out of the demon's back and struck again before the demon could react and disappear. The knife hit his neck and then his chest in quick succession. The demon froze, Bardbizt hissed, and everyone stared as the shadow demon shivered then exploded in a final puff of dust. The knife Jax had buried in his chest clattered to the ground.

"You found the knife," Sachi croaked, rolling to her back, still not able to take a full breath.

Cash whined and licked her face with his big, wet, wolf tongue.

Jax knelt on her other side, holding her face and looking into her eyes. "Are you okay?"

She nodded, not sure if she really was but it didn't matter because they weren't done with this fight, and she wasn't about to step aside over a little near suffocation. She hurt and she was more scared than ever to face what waited for them on the other side of the portal, but she wasn't going to tell them that either.

Jax kissed her softly.

Her mother tore out of Bardbizt's grip and rushed to flutter her hands over Sachi's bleeding legs. "Oh dear this is no good."

"I'm fine, Mom," Sachi said, sitting up with Jax's help.

Cash shifted to human and picked up the knife. "It worked."

"Where the hell have you two been?" Sachi snapped.

"Getting the knife from Bernard," Cash huffed. "It wasn't as easy as it should have been."

Sachi let her annoyance go, they were here now, and they had the knife. Everyone was safe, for the moment. She could hound them for all the details if they survived the next things they had to do. She didn't miss the way Cash looked at Jax with a bit more respect in his face though and Jax gave Cash an approving nod, some kind of male exchange Sachi didn't understand but hoped meant they had leaned on each other when necessary during the day.

Sachi got to her feet and put an arm around her mother. Their group was silent as they took in the gravity of what was ahead of them. A new pulse of power seemed to emanate from the bakery.

"The portal wants to open," Jax said. "It senses the spilled blood, and it hungers."

Cash growled. "I'm going to have to go in wolf, the moon's rising, Sach." He looked strained and she knew it was hard for him to be human even now and a new fear emerged. Would the pull of his pack running in the full moon take him from this duty he'd chosen? How could he possibly stay here when they inevitably called out to him?

"Do it," she said, giving him a quick kiss because all she could do was hope that his sense of duty to her and this mission would be enough to keep him here.

Cash handed the knife to Jax and Jax gave him a quick hug and gripped his arm briefly. The show of support made Sachi smile as she grasped the shadow demon's knife. She pushed away the nerves threatening to overwhelm her, straightened her back and stared down the back door. This was it, no room for anything but confidence and determination. She reached into her pocket and reassured herself that she had her father's instructions.

"That knife will kill the human body but not the demon," Bardbizt said, motioning to Sachi's knife.

"I can take care of the demon when it comes out of the body," Jax said with a grin, holding up the knife he and Cash had found.

"I can't go in there with you," Bardbizt said. "I'm going for my queen and I'm taking this halfling with me as insurance." He gripped her mother's arm tightly, eliciting a little gripe of pain from her.

"Just get her back here in time," Sachi hissed and gave her mother a quick hug, honestly relieved that Helen wouldn't be going in with them for what Sachi hoped would be the most dangerous part of the night. "I'll see you on the other side."

"You were always meant to do great things," her mother said tearfully. "I may have been saved from Hell, but it was all part of the plan to create you, so perfect." She ran a finger over Sachi's face. "You will keep doing great things after this."

Sachi wanted to cry but she held back the tears. Jax's hand was on her back and Cash's big wolf head was leaned against her leg offering comfort. She wasn't alone.

"I won't let you down," she promised.

"Couldn't if you tried," she assured Sachi, then Bardbizt was rolling his eyes and dragging her away.

"Watch for cops!" Jax yelled after them.

CHAPTER 22

Sachi squared her shoulders and stared at her bakery. It was pretty and pink and unassuming. There was a portal to Hell in the basement and that left a bad taste in her mouth.

She gripped her knife tighter. Beside her stood Jax, gripping a knife that could send a demon from the earth for good and on her other side, Cash in werewolf form with teeth and claws so sharp, he could tear through a solid body in seconds. They were not helpless, but one thing stood between them and the demon they needed to destroy.

"Fern," Sachi breathed. "We have to get Fern safely out of the way."

"We will," Jax assured her, and Cash nodded his big wolf head.

They moved forward, a force to be reckoned with. They crept into the kitchen and to the stairs leading to the basement. Noises drifted up confirming that the demon Lance was still down there with Fern.

There was no way to enter the basement unnoticed, so she decided striding in with confidence was the best bet. She hurried down, head high and a smile plastered to her face. Her men followed and she took in the scene quickly, assessing the well-being of her friend.

Fern was sitting on a pile of boxes looking pissed but fine. Her eyes lit up when she saw Sachi step down the stairs. Sachi was disappointed to see cages filled with Fern's brothers and sisters. Apparently, they hadn't been able to stay hidden this long, but they looked fine too.

The demon Lance stood over the portal looking like an emo god waiting to be worshiped, arms out and smile wide. The portal was gaping open, a black hole rimmed in red light. Something told her it wasn't complete yet, otherwise they'd be too late already, but it was close. "Welcome!" he said cheerfully. "You're just in time to witness the glory that is Hell unleashed."

"You've overestimated yourself, Lance," Sachi sneered. "You have no backup." She lifted the shadow demon's knife.

The demon Lance's eyes widened slightly at the sight. "You're better than I thought you'd be." He grinned too wide for his face and his sharp teeth showed in the eerie glow of light coming from the portal. "I like a challenge."

Cash started to edge out from behind Sachi. She hoped he was heading for Fern, she wanted Fern as far away as possible, and her siblings. Jax stepped to her other side. "There's no challenge, we have the power here and you can slip back to Hell, or we can kill you for good. Your choice." She was going for nonchalant, but she heard a quake in her voice and so had the demon, his eyes narrowed, and his lips twitched.

The demon Lance looked at Jax unconcerned by the threat there. He lifted a hand and a shot of white light burst out and across the room, hitting Cash and knocking him flat.

Sachi screamed, Cash didn't move from where he'd landed. Only Jax's hand on her arm kept her from going to Cash and completely ruining their plan of confidence.

"Demon bastard!" Sachi shouted and threw a ball of purple-tinted power at him. He ducked and it missed, crashing into the boxes behind him and knocking the fairy cages down. She cursed herself silently, she could have hurt them, she had to keep her emotions in control.

Jax reacted at the distraction, leaping forward and knocking into the demon's side. Sachi wanted to rush to Cash then, but she had a job to do. She hurried over as Jax was blasted off of the demon with a burst of light. She went in knife first and stabbed the demon in the arm as he tried to roll away, blood rushed out of the wound filling her with satisfaction.

"Bitch," he hissed and scrambled to his feet.

Jax pushed the demon from behind and knocked him right into Sachi. She rolled with him, grasping his shirt. She took him to the ground, straddling his chest, her knife to his throat. She had him at the edge of the portal now and she pushed his head down, watching an inky blackness swirl up from the space and move around his flesh, licking at it hungrily.

"Hell wants you home," she whispered with satisfaction as he struggled to push her off, but the portal was sucking him in, holding him down and she could see the moment he realized it. He panicked, she could see it in his eyes, he was too afraid to think straight then, and he didn't pull his power. He couldn't react right as the realization that he was about to lose overcame all reasoning. This powerful being was at her mercy and a sick satisfaction filled her. She slit his throat with the knife, watching the body he'd inhabited for so many years die around the demon inside it. Blood poured into the portal like a sacrifice and the portal flared with renewed energy. Sounds of lapping and sucking filtered up from the darkness and Sachi knew there were demons just there below her, right under that darkness feasting on Lance's blood.

Jax pulled her up as black, shadowy hands reached through the portal to drag the bleeding body in. "What did you do?" he demanded.

"I—I don't know," she admitted.

"She fed the portal with a vampire sacrifice," the fire demon, Ainu, said stepping into the room and filling it instantly with an otherworldly heat.

"Fuck, we have to get it closed." Sachi had to squint as the heat rolled off of Ainu and she could smell smoke, something was trying to light on fire.

"Not from here," Ainu snapped and the last thing Sachi saw before she was shoved down the hole was Jax's worried expression as he threw the demon killing knife to her. She was going through the portal, and she was going alone. She didn't know if Cash was alive, and she'd killed someone, well a demon-possessed someone. She had actually enjoyed it if she were being honest, taking the bastard out that had threatened her, her mother, her best friend, and her entire world.

But it was the demon inside him that had done it, and she'd only killed the vampire shell he'd been animating for all these years, tricking them all. The demon had been sucked down into this Hell hole and she had a feeling it had already been devoured by the shadows within.

Sachi landed on her ass in a dark cavern. Shadows shifted around her, and she knew she wasn't alone. All around her, demon eyes stared, and she could hear their breathing as they assessed what had fallen into their realm. The temperature was just below combustion and the smell was like nothing she'd ever experienced before. Sulfur and death.

She felt the walls closing in on her, she crouched and held her knife tight. She wouldn't go down without a fight. "Stay back," she growled into the pulsating darkness.

A hot light landed beside her, and the shadows screamed as they rushed away. Ainu was feared here. Bardbizt dropped to Sachi's other side with her mother still in his grip.

"They'll be alerting the king," Bardbizt said with a huff.

"Guard the portal," Ainu demanded.

"Of course, my love." Bardbizt took up a fearsome stance

under the portal. She hoped Cash and Jax were safe and guarding above, hoped they were letting the fairies out of their cages and Fern was flying home to safety. If she wasn't back out by sunrise, Sachi knew that Jax would close the portal himself, locking her in.

Sachi really hoped it didn't come to that.

"Time for a family reunion," Ainu said darkly and strode away.

Sachi gripped her mother's arm as they followed Ainu through a tunnel that stunk of death. Rock walls embedded with bones, some fresh enough to still have pieces of clothing hanging off them. Were they human bones or demon, she didn't want to know. She didn't dare get close to the walls, for fear that they would suck her into them, and she'd become a part of the structure that connected Hell to Earth. When they emerged out onto a city street, she was thankful to be out of there, but the shock of the modern looking road and buildings made Sachi gasp. The air smelled slightly fresher, but still unlike anything she'd ever encountered and not at all pleasant. It made her think of bad dreams and suffocating fear. Everything was dark, embraced by a red glowing haze, but it was recognizable as a downtown area complete with storefronts, only instead of supes and humans walking around it was all sorts of disgusting demon creatures.

When they spotted Ainu they ran screaming into buildings and slammed doors. Sachi wasn't sure how she felt about being with the creature that was making all those demons run and hide.

"Imbeciles," Ainu hissed. "They know they betrayed me, and they will get what's coming to them after I deal with *him*."

They walked down the street and whispers floated out of cracked windows. The demons were shocked to see the queen, but they were mostly interested in why Sachi and her mother were there.

It struck Sachi that she didn't hear any mechanical sounds, no cars, no hum of air conditioners and if she didn't spy the dim lights from inside buildings and a few flickering streetlights, she'd have assumed they didn't have any kind of electricity here at all. She wondered if it was just so small they didn't need vehicles, was this all there was, these few streets and handful of people. Hadn't Ainu implied there were no females.

Was this a dying species?

Sachi tried not to care, but something inside her ached a bit for the people here, those just trying to live a life and not trying to come up to earth and consume and destroy.

Ainu turned a corner and the buildings started to look more like homes than shops. Eyes peeked from behind curtains here too, no one was out on the streets and Sachi wondered if they had phones of some kind, able to spread the word to hide from Ainu who was stalking toward her husband for revenge. They stopped in front of a large black building with statues depicting demons killing other demons and naked humans worshiping them. They were uncomfortable to look at and Sachi stared straight ahead to a huge red door as they made their way down the path. The door swung open before they could step onto the porch, but no one was there.

"He's expecting us," Ainu said with a fierce smile.

"Maybe we shouldn't go in," Sachi whispered and tightened her grip on her mother's arm.

"As if that's a choice," Ainu said fiercely.

The steps creaked under their feet and as they crossed the porch, Sachi spied red eyes staring up at them from cracks in the planks. She hurried her step and they walked into a home and down a hallway. They passed rooms that looked like they could have been found anywhere on earth if you ignored the scent of sulfur and dead flowers that clung to everything. They were all decorated in dark woods and rich fabrics with large paintings hung on the walls. The pictures reminded her of what she'd seen in her art books in high school, but rather than humans they depicted demons on horseback or picnicking by the sea, all very human activities that she doubted the demons had ever done. She was struck by the variety in demon forms, no two pictures showed the same shaped demon and from what she'd seen before everyone ran and hid, these were only a few of the shapes they could come in.

Ainu led them confidently into a room with a huge fireplace and paintings of Ainu herself surrounded by demons all dressed in rich fabrics and looking regal. Sachi looked closely, recognizing the shadow demon they'd killed, Lance's demon form and Bardbizt too. She assumed the other was whatever had possessed the poor human girl and one was her grandfather, though she couldn't be sure which he was. She shuddered at the sight. They were all disgusting and horrifying and she didn't want to be a part of any of them.

"I'm surprised he kept that," Ainu said quietly, noticing her attention.

"My daughter!" A voice boomed and drew her eyes away from the painting.

A hulking red monster walked into the room. He had shining black horns that curled back from his forehead, bright gold eyes and black lips pulled back in a smile that revealed sharp white teeth. He wasn't wearing a shirt and she could see his chest was covered in black swirls and although he wore a black kilt. She could see enough of his legs to know he had human-like legs ending in horrifying clawed feet. A tail swooshed out behind him that looked like it belonged on a dragon and there was a smattering of scales along his arms.

Sachi felt her mother shrink back slightly. "Apparently," Helen said quietly.

"I can smell you, a perfect mix of me and my lover," he said with unexpected reverence.

Helen's eyes widened in hope for a moment and Sachi wondered if her mother was looking to find a connection here to her parents. That could make what they were here to do rather tricky.

The demon turned its gold eyes to her, and she felt trapped, her breath caught, and she was frozen in place.

"You," he sneered. "You smell far too much like your father. You are a Portal Keeper."

Sachi notched up her chin and forced in a calm breath. "I am."

His lips twitched and he looked at her as if she were nothing more than a stain on his day. "My own granddaughter siding with Ainu."

"Siding with humans," she corrected. "Demons don't belong up there." She gained confidence as she spoke and took a threatening step forward. He was a demon and fucking scary, but she wasn't helpless, and she had a job to do, or die trying to do.

"Your time of stolen rule is at an end," Ainu snapped, gaining his attention. "Step aside and take your punishment or we will destroy you."

"Is that what you're here for?" he mocked. "You think you can destroy me? Me!" His body glowed, and smoke rose from his shoulders. The already blazing hot room heated more, and Sachi wasn't sure how much more she could take before passing out. She was sweating profusely, and the air burned her lungs as she breathed. She'd give her soul for a glass of ice water.

"A challenge for the throne," Ainu said. "You have no choice but to accept."

"You know you can't destroy me," he said, suddenly his voice was soft, and he stepped toward Ainu with a smile and hooded eyes. "My love, you can come home. Come back to my bed and sit by my side."

"By your side," she scoffed. "I am queen, you will fucking kneel at my feet!" she yelled, and the house shook.

His eyes darkened and he frowned. "So be it," he hissed.

In a flash, the world shifted and she was suddenly standing in a field of burned grass surrounded by bare trees. The sky above was red, grey clouds floated over a full moon, and Sachi could smell smoke in the air.

"What the hell?" Sachi hissed, turning but finding no one else there.

"Granddaughter, you think to destroy me for her? She's not even your blood." The voice of the demon boomed around her.

She spun again and found him standing at the edge of the field. She was alone with the demon she needed to kill and she wasn't sure she could do it.

She straightened her shoulders and stared him down. If she was going to fail, she was going to fail fighting. "Blood forced upon a helpless butterfly shifter," she scoffed. "You were no father to my mother, and you are nothing but a demon in my eyes. I am a Portal Keeper trained by my father, and I will destroy the demons that I must, to keep that portal closed."

His eyes widened slightly, and his grin turned deadly.

"Fuck," she whispered as he stalked forward.

"I take no pleasure in killing one of my flesh, but the throne is mine, I won't kneel at the feet of a queen again."

Sachi crouched, ready to fight. She held her blade in one hand and in the other she called forward her power and a ball of light formed in her palm.

She didn't want him close enough to stab, so she threw the purple ball of power. It filled empty space as he disappeared. He reappeared behind her, shoving her. She fell to her already busted knees and spun, looking up at him from the ground, she threw another ball before she had any time to think. This one hit his shoulder and he growled as it sizzled on his skin, but the damage was minimal and Sachi started to seriously doubt her abilities.

"Your father taught you something before he died, I see. Too bad he didn't teach you enough."

Sachi scrambled back as he stalked forward. She threw more at him, each one hitting but it didn't stop him, didn't even make him hesitate. When she reached the edge of the field, she thought it was over, she had failed, and she was never going to see Jax or Cash again. What would become of her mother?

"No, please no!" she heard her mother's voice from somewhere beyond the trees. It distracted the demon enough that Sachi was able to scramble to her feet and move away.

"She is foolish to come here," the demon snapped, but Sachi could see a flash of sadness enter his eyes. There was something in this demon, some bit of humanity, but would it be enough?

Was he regretting that he might have to kill his daughter? There hadn't been any regret in his eyes as he faced down his granddaughter, she thought bitterly.

Sachi threw an energy ball at his head, and he easily dodged it as he lashed out. His hand smashed into her arm, claws sinking into her flesh. She screamed out, the burning cuts making her drop her knife.

"Sachi!" her mother screamed, coming through the tree line. "Don't hurt her!"

The demon turned to her mother, and Sachi took her chance. She threw a ball of power at his back. His tail whipped out and knocked her off her feet with seemingly no thought at all. Her face smacked into the ground, and she got a mouth full of dirt. She groaned but she'd landed near her knife. She grabbed it, ignoring the burn in her arm as she moved it. His huge hands ripped her off the ground violently and held her to his chest in an iron tight grip.

Sachi faced out and saw the terror in her mother's face. Helen froze watching them, her hands fidgeting in front of her. The demon's body was hot, burning Sachi where it touched. Sachi struggled but it was useless, her arms were pinned to her body, unable to use the knife she still gripped. She made a decision she hoped she wouldn't regret, she dropped the knife and pressed her palms to his body and pushed out power, hoping to shock him enough to loosen his hold.

He hissed and held her tighter, crushing her almost to the

point of broken bones. She pushed power again and he tightened more, she was certain he snapped a rib this time and she cried out.

"Stop," her mother demanded again. "I will kill you myself, you are no father, you are a goddamn demon, a kidnapper, a rapist. My mother suffered and died at your hands, and I will destroy you."

"Lies!" he roared and dropped Sachi to gasp and gag as pain rolled through her. She wanted to curl up and cry, wanted to let the release of passing out wash over her but she knew she couldn't, knew she had to fight. Jax and Cash and everyone else was counting on her.

But in that moment the pain was too much and Sachi could do nothing as the demon stalked toward her mother.

Helen stood her ground, hands fisted at her sides and glared at the terrifying demon. "You left the portal and stole her, dragged her down here, kept her in a cage and forced her to be your whore." Helen spat the words, letting years of anger and rage show.

"I loved her," the demon insisted, his voice strained. "I courted her above the portal and then I brought her here and offered her a life with me, I gave her everything!" His voice rose as he spoke until he was screaming the last, a desperate cry for understanding.

"You kept her from the sun, from her family. If she loved you so much, why did she send me away from you?" Tears streamed down Helen's face now as she confronted her father and revealed the hurt she'd been living with.

The demon looked away, hands fisted at his sides. Sachi forced herself to her feet, gritting her teeth against the pain. She stood on shaking legs, knife poised to strike but she hesitated, the look of pain on the demon's face was unmistakable.

"I loved her, and she was dying," he said with unmistakable pain in his voice. "She couldn't survive here but she wouldn't leave, refused to leave me. *I* sent you away, not her." He shook his head and covered his face with his clawed hands. "I couldn't take care of you if she died, I knew it would destroy me and I'd never be able to be a father to someone who reminded me every day of the lost love of my soul." He crumpled to his knees, shaking.

Sachi looked at her mother in shock. "What the fuck?" she whispered.

Her mother met her gaze with equal surprise. Neither of them moved as the enormous fearsome demon cried for his lost love. Helen crossed the distance to her father and laid a hand on his back. She leaned over him and embraced him as best she could.

"Step aside," Helen whispered to him. "Let Ainu have her place and I will stay here with you. Tell me stories of my mother and we will grow old together," Helen promised.

The demon looked up at his daughter and blinked in surprise. "Ainu would never let me live," he said bitterly then shrugged, resigned. "I know I've had my time, and seeing you has settled my soul." He reached up and gently engulfed the side of Helen's face in his huge palm. "I see that we made a fierce daughter and that makes me happy. I am ready to be reunited with my soulmate on the other side."

Sachi met her mother's eyes over the demon. She was shocked beyond speech.

"Tell my mother that I love her," Helen whispered, then held her hand out for the knife.

Sachi handed it to her and stepped back. Helen raised her hand and stabbed it down at the base of her father's neck. The spine severed, instantly killing him and the demon slumped.

Sachi rushed to her mother and held her as she shivered and cried for everything she'd lost, so many years ago and again today.

Ainu appeared in the meadow and looked down at the body of her husband. There was a touch of sadness on her face. "It is done," Ainu said with a nod. "I will make sure you have a safe place to live out your days here, Helen."

Sachi shook her head. "Mother, come back with me," she pleaded. "We can run away; we can live somewhere together." She didn't want to leave her mother here, not with all this sadness.

"No, Sachi, you are needed at the portal. I will be fine here." She looked down at the demon she'd killed. "I am my father's daughter, and I will find my place among his people. I want to know what it is to be in this place my mother chose over me." A bitterness tinged those words and broke Sachi's heart.

"You have a place with me," Sachi whispered.

Helen looked at Sachi sadly and touched her face. "My mother chose this place, this man over me. I am not choosing it over you, I am only choosing to know this place, it isn't forever, I promise, but I want to know," she admitted. "I've always been cold up above, it actually feels good down here," she said with a little laugh.

Sachi let a hysterical laugh slip and she wiped sweat from her brow. "Yeah, I guess you always did complain about the cold. As long as it's not forever."

Sachi pulled her mother into a gentle hug, ignoring the pain that spiked through her at even the slight squeeze.

"You're quite hurt," Ainu pointed out as they let go. "Let me help you back to the portal." Ainu held out a hand and after a quick kiss from her mother, Sachi took it.

"See you soon," Sachi said, her voice cracking with emotion and full of hope that those words weren't a lie. Then the world shifted and dipped and they were once again in the cavern below the portal.

Bardbizt stood there with a grim face surrounded by dead demons.

"You were successful," he said with surprise.

If Sachi had more energy she might have been able to think of something snappy to say, but she felt like she was barely holding on to consciousness now that all the adrenaline was leaving her body. "My mother was," Sachi admitted. "The king gave himself up for her, it was time." She was no hero in this, it wasn't a win, and she didn't want anyone saying her grandfather had been anything other than what he wanted to be. Maybe it was wrong, but she felt good about one last shot at Ainu who was only queen again because Sachi's grandfather had given himself up, lost without his lover and was ready to join her in the afterlife. Sachi had no love for the demon queen and the sacrifices she'd willingly made of humans for years. If there'd been another way, Sachi would have destroyed Ainu, but she wasn't strong enough, maybe in ten years she would be.

Ainu huffed and disappeared.

Sachi stood there staring up at a gaping white hole and the pain of the night overwhelmed her. Bardbizt lifted her gently and pushed her body up through the portal. Hands grabbed at her from the other side and pulled her up. She was soon laying on the floor of her basement and fighting back the darkness in her mind that wanted to take her to blissful nothing as Jax hovered over her looking worried and Cash in wolf form whined softly as he gazed down at her. The stink of decaying demons filled her nostrils. A quick glance around as the men carefully ran their hands over her obviously injured body, told her that the basement was littered with the bodies of demons who'd managed to get past Bardbizt.

"We did it," she said on a sigh and a tear leaked down her cheek. "My mother is not coming, close the portal."

Jax nodded and swiped at the tear. "I'll close the portal." He picked her up and placed her in Fern's arms. "Get her to the hospital," Jax demanded. He kissed Sachi's forehead, and she closed her eyes as Cash rubbed his furry head against her face. It was going to be okay.

Fern hurried out of the basement with Sachi clutched in her arms. Fern was surprisingly strong for such a small thing. Fairies were fluttering all around them, obviously no one had left the basement after being freed. "I'm so pissed at Lance," Fern said lightly as they hit the top of the stairs.

Sachi laughed, then groaned, as her ribs protested. "Just put me in bed, I don't want to leave them," she gritted out then gave up and let the darkness take the pain as she felt the pull of the portal lessen as it closed.

CHAPTER 23

"Sachi is in no condition to answer any of your fucking questions," Cash growled. His voice floated up the stairs and into the apartment above the bakery.

Sachi groaned as her eyes fluttered open and she looked up into the concerned faces of Jax and Fern.

"Hey," he said softly and pushed her hair off her forehead, his smile warm. "Do you want to go to the hospital?" Jax asked gently.

"No, I think I'm okay." She wasn't, but she really didn't want to heal in a hospital bed when she could heal here. There wasn't anything they could do to help her anyway. Somehow she'd made it out with cuts, bruises and a broken rib or two but nothing too serious. "Who's downstairs?"

"Police want to ask you why your mother is missing."

"Don't they know everything now?" she griped. "Hadn't all the memories returned with the death of the demon Lance?"

"Yeah, but she still murdered someone," Jax said.

"I think living in literal Hell is punishment enough, don't you?"

"Want me to tell them to get the fuck out of here?"

She did, but knew it wasn't the best idea. "Let them up, might as well get this part over with."

Sachi sat up with Fern's help, sweating and cringing in pain the whole time. "I'm calling a nurse in to look at you," Fern said and hurried out of the room as Officer Zeb Calin walked in with a stern look. Cash followed behind him snarling and Sachi could tell Zeb was fighting with himself in that moment wanting to obey this alpha wolf and at the same time, do his duty as a police officer.

"Cash, let Zeb do his job," Sachi said with a frown for Cash.

She wondered if it would be different if Cash really was alpha of the pack, if there wasn't a strained power dynamic between him and Bernard right now. Would Zeb have just turned and left the bakery as soon as Cash had told him to? That would be a handy trick if it worked, not that Sachi was planning to have a lot of run-ins with the police in the future.

Sachi spent the next hour answering questions and reliving the last few days. It was an insane story, but it was all true and now that the memories of everyone in the district had returned, it was a believable story. When Zeb was gone, a nurse was there to look her over. Pauline was a witch and mostly just rubbed her down with herbs and gave her some tea that fuzzed her head and asked if she needed a birth control tonic as she eyeballed Jax and Cash hovering protectively.

"Yes thank you," Sachi said, her cheeks heating a bit. There were no secrets in a small town.

"She'll sleep for a day and wake up weak. Make sure she eats when she does, she needs blood and food," Pauline said sternly to the men.

"I can handle that," Jax and Cash both said and Sachi smiled because she knew they could.

Pauline gave Sachi a sly grin. "I can see that. Call me if anything changes, she's banged up pretty good, but she'll heal quickly and nothing major is broken."

"Thank you," Fern said as she ushered Pauline out leaving Sachi alone with Jax and Cash.

"Don't leave," she whispered to them as her eyes closed and drugged sleep took her. They had a lot to discuss but it would have to wait, she hoped they would wait.

She woke up a few times with no idea how long she'd been asleep and unable to open her eyes but she could hear Jax and Cash's voices and knew they were there watching over her. She felt safe and loved and that allowed her to fall back into healing sleep quickly.

When she finally woke up for real it was the next night and she was starving. For food and blood. She was alone in her bed, but she could hear breathing, so she knew she wasn't alone in the room. It was dark and it took a moment for her to spot the lump in a nearby chair—Jax, and on the floor by her bed, a huff brought her gaze to a lump of fur, Cash.

Sachi tried to sit up, but her head spun and her ribs hurt. She couldn't use her injured arm to help at all, it wasn't broken but scratched up bad enough that it had been bound and strapped close to her body. She laid back with a groan. Instantly Jax was on his feet, tripping over Cash who was mid change and soon sitting naked on the floor with Jax sprawled across his lap.

"Christ man, what are you doing?" Cash grumbled and pushed him off.

Sachi couldn't help but laugh, but then regretted it when her ribs protested and she ended it with a groan, squeezing her eyes shut. "Don't make me laugh, guys, it fucking hurts."

"Yeah, you aren't healed up yet," Jax said and pressed a hand to her forehead. "How do you feel other than the sore ribs?"

"Hungry," she admitted.

"I can take care of that," Cash said brightly and shoved his arm in front of her face.

"She needs more than blood," Jax gritted out. "I'll go downstairs and make a sandwich, maybe some more tea, too."

"Thank you," Sachi said, her gaze meeting Jax's, she knew it couldn't be easy for him to just casually let her take blood from Cash, but if this weird relationship was going to work, they were going to have to get used to her feeding off them both from time to time.

Jax leaned down and pressed a quick kiss to her lips then left the room. Cash kneeled on the floor beside her, still holding his arm out in offering. She wasn't going to turn it down, she knew it would speed her healing process and she wanted out of this bed as soon as possible. So she grabbed his arm with her free hand and bit into the familiar flesh, letting the hot flow of blood fill her mouth and slide down her throat, quickly satisfying the craving. His other hand slid into her hair, encouraging her to take all that she wanted and making her groan at the pleasure of his touch mixed with his blood.

When she was done, she pulled away, licking the wounds and smiling at Cash. "Thanks, babe."

"Any time, love."

"You slept on the floor?"

He gave her a lopsided smile. "I wasn't going to leave your side and Mr. Magic fell asleep in the chair first."

"Mr. Magic," she said and tried to hold back a laugh, so she didn't hurt herself.

He shrugged and dragged the chair over so he could sit near her. He wasn't getting dressed though, she noticed, and her body liked that very much, too bad she was far too injured still to do anything about it. But she could feel the blood working its magic already, her energy was lifting, her headache was easing and the deepness of the ache in her ribs was lessening. She thought she might be mostly better in another day as long as she took blood one or two more times.

Jax came back in with three sandwiches and a cup of tea. She ate most of her sandwich before the tea started to pull her to sleep again.

"You'll both be here in the morning?" she asked, half asleep already.

"Since I can't get Wolf Boy to leave, I guess we will," Jax said softly as he took her plate off the bed and tucked the blanket around her.

"Good, I have questions," she said thinking of the day they'd spent apart and wondering what had happened with Bernard when they got the knife.

"I'll give you all the answers when you wake up again, now rest," Jax insisted.

"You're not leaving, now that your job is done?" she spoke her fear, emboldened by the fuzzy head the tea was giving her.

Jax gave her a stern look. "I am staying until you kick me to the curb," he assured her.

When she woke again the sun was shining and Cash was the only one in the room. She had a moment of fear and hurt before she heard the shower running. The way her heart eased knowing Jax was still here told her how much she really did care for them both.

"Sach, babe," Cash said, noticing her squirming to sit up. "Let me help you, glad to see you're awake again."

"Yeah, I must have slept like twelve hours," she said, feeling the passage of time in the way her mouth tasted like shit and her bladder was going to explode.

Cash helped her sit up against some pillows and she did a quick inventory of her aches. Everything hurt, everywhere, she felt like she'd been thrown off a truck, but it was less than last night so that was something.

"Do you need blood, or tea or food or anything?" Cash asked, eager and worried.

"Yes to all of that but first, can you help me stand up, I've got to get to the bathroom."

"Hey, Magic Man, get out, Sachi needs in there," Cash yelled as he reached down and pulled the blankets from her body.

Sachi glared at Cash but the water turned off immediately and Jax rushed in, water dripping down his delicious body and a small pink towel wrapped around his waist.

"You're up! Shit, I tried to wait but I really needed to get the demon blood and gunk off of me."

"He stunk," Cash agreed, earning a quick flipped finger from Jax.

"I didn't mean to cut your shower short," Sachi said as Cash helped her to slowly rise.

Jax came to her other side and the men worked together to get her to her feet and she leaned on them both as they walked with achingly slow steps toward the bathroom.

"I would happily forgo my shower to see you awake and upright," Jax said.

She sent them away at the bathroom door, and did her business alone and slow. Every movement hurt and she started to rethink her two day healing schedule she'd made up in her mind.

When she opened the bathroom door both men hurried forward to help her back to the bed. Jax was dressed in a pair of sweats and a T-shirt, she was a little disappointed.

"I made you some tea and cookies, well Fern made the cookies this morning, and there's some soup that Penelope sent over earlier I heated up," Cash said as she was settled onto the bed once more.

"And I am providing the blood today," Jax said with a grin and held out his arm.

Sachi looked from one happy face to the other and cried. Big horrible sobbing tears streamed down her face. They stared at her with shock while she blubbered and grabbed at her aching ribs.

"Stop that," Fern yelled, coming into the room. "What the hell did you two do?"

"Jax tried to give her his blood and she just started crying," Cash snarled.

"Maybe she didn't want your stupid tea," Jax snapped back.

"Both of you out!" Fern ordered and pushed the men out the door.

When the door was shut and she was at Sachi's side, Sachi had control of herself once again.

"Babe, what the hell? Are you okay? Want me to tell them both to go home? They've refused to leave, but if you want them to, I'll get them out."

Sachi shook her head. "No, I just feel so grateful that I'm alive and they are here, but then I feel guilty because people are dead and my mom is stuck in Hell."

Fern hugged her softly. "Yeah, it's been a shit couple of days, hasn't it?"

Sachi nodded. "I don't know what to think about all of this. I think I am just hungry and tired and them being so nice is freaking me out."

Fern laughed. "You should see how they treat each other when no one is looking," she whispered.

Sachi gave her a wide eyed questioning look.

"They are actually really nice to each other, treat each other like good buddies or brothers or some shit. I don't really get it, but when they aren't competing for your attention and they don't think anyone is looking to judge them, they like each other."

That made Sachi happier than anything she'd heard since waking up. She had Fern help her change her clothes which were still the ripped and bloody things she'd gone to Hell in, then told her to send in the men.

"I'll be here for a while if you need anything. The bakery is closed but I am making things for people who had ordered stuff so we aren't having to cancel on anyone's birthday."

"Thank you, Fern."

"It's the least I can do, shit Sachi, you saved the world."

Jax and Cash came back in, pushing to be first, snapping and snarling quietly at each other. But Sachi saw it with a new eye and decided she'd have to make it a mission to never show favorites with them so they wouldn't feel in competition for her.

"I am ready to eat," she said and pulled Jax's arm forward. After she satisfied that need, she ate the soup and asked for their story about Bernard and the knife.

"It's not resolved, not really," Cash said. "Bernard wanted an alpha challenge to solidify his place before he would listen to anything I said, but there wasn't time for that and the risk of not getting what you needed was something I wasn't willing to take. Jax is the one who finally convinced him to just give us the knife. Everything else could wait, but if there was no district, what the hell would the point of an alpha be?" Cash shrugged and gave Jax an appreciative look.

"So you're going to challenge him?" Sachi asked, her eyes already growing heavy again.

"Yes. I want my place. I want what my father wanted for me," Cash said.

"What about me?" Sachi asked as her blinks became longer and she struggled to keep her head up.

"I will always want you, no matter what," Cash said and kissed her forehead. "Now sleep, we will be here when you wake."

She closed her eyes then, satisfied that her men were not going anywhere.

CHAPTER 24

It was three more days before she felt well enough to broach the delicate subject of sex. Her arm was mostly healed, no longer strapped unmoving to her body and her ribs were nothing more than a bruise. Since she'd slept with both men already, it shouldn't have been an awkward conversation, but she wasn't sure how this was going to work. She knew what she would prefer, but she wasn't sure they were going to go for it. For the last few days they'd taken to sleeping in the room, Jax on the chair, Cash on the floor and even when she assured them she could share the bed with at least one of them, both were against it, saying she needed space to heal and what if they accidentally hurt her as they rolled over in their sleep?

She couldn't deny that was a risk, so she had nothing to argue, until now. Now she was fine aside from some remaining bruises, and she wanted them.

She'd gone through various scenarios in her head, she could try and find time with each man alone, but that seemed like a lot of work since neither was ever gone for long. She could just work seduction on them both and hope they were horny enough to go along with whatever might happen, but would that really solidify the relationship she was hoping to build?

So she decided to go downstairs, and bake. She made Cash's favorite—chocolate chip cookies—and what she had recently learned was Jax's favorite—lemon meringue pie. She set up a romantic dessert table in the apartment above the bakery and enlisted Fern's help to distract the boys while she got everything ready.

Sachi smiled as she looked at the little space she had created. The table she had was just big enough for three, as if it was meant for them and although she would likely want to get a bigger bed, she didn't see why they couldn't reside here together for the most part. Cash had his own house to go back to for space from time to time and they could set up the basement as a little place for Jax to call his own. She didn't want to get married, she just wanted a relationship, and damnit she didn't want to choose between them.

"Jax, Cash, can you guys come up here, please?" she called down the stairs to where they were currently arranging and rear-ranging the front shop sales racks for Fern as a distraction. The shop was already closed and as soon as the men were upstairs, Fern was going to lock up and leave.

Pounding feet told her the men were racing to be the first one up to her, or perhaps to get away from Fern and her ridiculous requests. Cash was first through the doorway, a big smile on his face and then a look of confusion at the candlelit table.

"Cookies?" he asked with a tilt of his head.

"And pie!" Jax said coming up behind Cash. "I thought I smelled lemon in the kitchen earlier, I thought you were hiding it so I wouldn't eat it all before you could sell it."

They rushed to the table and grabbed their favorites eagerly.

"I wanted to do something special, because you two have been so good to me during my recovery. Also, I want to talk about some things."

Both men froze with bites almost to their mouths. "Is this a, *'we need to talk'* talk?" Cash asked, shoving a cookie into his mouth whole.

Jax swallowed a bite of pie. "Feels like it," he said hesitantly.

Sachi clasped her hands in front of her and tried to keep her voice calm as her heart started to pound. She'd put on a nice light pink sundress and her feet were bare. Her lilac curls were perfectly shaped and laying around her shoulders but she'd decided on no makeup, these were her men and they didn't need to be impressed with a fake look. If they wanted her, this is what they would be getting.

"Have a seat, both of you, we need to talk."

"Shit," they both said as they dropped into seats.

Sachi took the remaining one and a deep breath. "I want to talk about how this whole relationship is going to work."

"But it *is* going to work," Jax said pointing his fork at her.

"I hope so, but I feel like we need a clear understanding. Don't you guys?"

The men looked at each other then back at her. "We already talked," Cash said. "We have no intention of making you choose."

That was a relief, Sachi's shoulders relaxed a bit, but she knew that wasn't all that mattered. "Good, but how willing to share are you two? Is this a Monday Wednesday Friday I'm with Cash, Jax gets Tuesday Thursday and we split weekends?"

"Why the hell does Cash get three nights a week and I only get two!" Jax snapped and dropped his fork with a clash onto the now empty plate.

"This is exactly why we need to talk," Sachi said, her voice high and strained. She wanted nothing to do with this confrontation, but it needed to happen. She couldn't let herself fall in love with these men any further just to have them tear her apart with their jealousy.

They just stared at her with looks of anger and fear.

"I won't pick, it's both or none and I'm not splitting my time either. You two are going to have to deal with each other," she took a steadying breath. "With each other in bed. I'm not saying you have to be all over each other, I'm just saying, I want you both in there. Most nights. And I'm not willing to schedule out my sex with either of you."

There, it was said, and the words hung between them like lead.

Jax and Cash both stared at her with shocked expressions.

Sachi felt her stomach turn and she steeled herself against the coming breakup. She tried to tell herself it was no big loss, that they weren't ever that involved anyway, it was fine. But it wasn't and she knew there was going to be a week of crying and too much chocolate cake in her future. She pushed her chair back and stood. "Well never mind then, take your dessert to go," she said, her voice thick with emotion.

"Babe," Cash drawled.

"What makes you think that isn't exactly what we want, or at least what we have decided to embrace," Jax said, standing and taking her into his arms.

Cash was up seconds later and embracing her from behind. Relief washed over her.

"We are in this," Cash assured her. "But we should think about moving into my place."

"No way, let's just get a bigger bed," she said, her face pressed against Jax's chest.

"I think that could be worked out," Jax said and lifted her chin, forcing her eyes to meet his. "I can't believe you doubted our willingness to follow you anywhere, love. Your inner demon allure is too much for us mortal men," he teased

"I just didn't know if being out of imminent danger would change things. Now it's just life."

"Life is what I want, with you," Cash said, licking her neck and giving it a playful bite. "Even if it includes Mr. Magic."

"Watch it, Wolf Boy," Jax said playfully.

"Watch this," Cash said and grabbed the hem of Sachi's dress, pulling it over her head.

Sachi flinched only a bit as her injured arm went straight up, but it was well worth it, she needed this, needed to feel like things were good with them.

Jax had a front view, and his eyes were riveted on her bare breasts, she hadn't bothered with a bra, or underwear. This was exactly the result of their conversation that she'd hoped for.

Cash ran his hands down her hips as Jax lifted his hands to her breasts and both men groaned when she let out a little sigh of contentment. Cash cupped her bare ass as Jax cupped her breasts and she couldn't keep the smile off her face. She needed this, wanted this and she planned to enjoy it, thoroughly.

"Are you certain you're well enough for this?" Jax asked, his thumbs rubbing over her tightening nipples.

"Definitely, just, you know, don't try to throw me around or anything," she said with a laugh.

Cash grabbed her hair and forced her head back, his mouth was hot on her exposed neck, nipping and sucking and sending tendrils of desire straight to her core.

"Oh you make her squirm so well," Jax said, his voice rough. His fingers pinched her nipples making her gasp at the bite of pain and then he was kissing them better.

Between the two, Sachi was helpless to do anything but react. Her body quivered, her thighs became wet and her mouth was emitting sounds of pleasure she wasn't sure she'd ever heard before.

Her ass pushed back and she felt Cash's erection straining against his pants. His hand went to her hip as she rubbed against him, desperate for more.

"She needs you lower," Cash said to Jax, his tongue flicking out now to tease at Sachi's ear.

Jax grunted and kneeled in front of her. His tongue dipped into her belly button and traced lower.

"Hold her up," Jax said and then grabbed her legs and Cash's arm was around her middle pulling her up and against this chest as Jax positioned her legs over his shoulders.

She barely had a chance to wonder at the safety of this position before Jax's tongue was darting out and flicking across her clit, and then she was lost. She didn't care of this killed them all, she was here for it. She arched and pushed herself closer to Jax's face, her heels digging into his back and urging him closer as her head rested on Cash's shoulder and his mouth continued its assault on her neck and ear.

She really hoped Fern was already gone because the cries of pleasure were loud then and she dug her hands into Cash's hair as her body twisted and shivered with a release.

"Oh my god," she said as she collapsed, boneless. If it wasn't for Cash, she'd have fallen to the floor when Jax moved her legs off of his shoulders.

Jax stood up with a look of pure satisfaction on his face. He grabbed her face and pulled her in for a deep kiss and the taste of herself there sent a spike of pleasure through her.

"Let's show our butterfly what else we worked out while she was recovering," Jax said.

"You guys talked about this?" Sachi asked.

"Oh yeah, what else were we going to do as you slept," Cash said with a deep rumbling laugh.

"I guess you didn't worry that I wouldn't want you after it was all over?"

Jax grabbed her chin and met her gaze. "I did, but I had hope too."

"I didn't," Cash said as he bit her neck. "I have known you too long to think you'd be so fickle."

Jax snorted and pulled her into his arms, sweeping her feet off the ground and walking to the bedroom. "A bigger bed will be a must," he said as he set her down then stepped back and started to undress.

"Are you ready for this?" Cash asked, stepping into the room and starting to undress as well.

Sachi could only nod as she watched both men, so beautiful, so strong and all hers. They came to her on the bed and arranged themselves as if they really had discussed how this would go. Jax positioned himself near the headboard and Cash crawled up at her side then flipped her to her stomach and pulled her up on her knees.

"Be a good girl and thank Jax for that head work back there," Cash said, slapping her ass.

Jax was on his knees and Sachi leaned forward slightly to grab ahold of his powerful erection and bring it to her lips. As she sucked him in she felt Cash's cock pressing for entrance behind her.

It was all so smooth, all so easy she couldn't believe it. They worked together perfectly stroking in and out of her, their hands caressing and guiding her all in perfect rhythm. It felt like they'd been doing this for years. Spirals of pleasure were coming from both men and meeting in the middle. She loved the way they controlled her, the way they played her body while taking exactly what they wanted.

This was everything she had imagined being with them could be and dared to hope for.

Jax was the first to blow, he pulled out of her mouth with a groan and lifted her chest to his so she was sitting up and riding Cash. Jax stroked his cock a couple times and then covered her lower stomach with ropes of hot cum. Cash immediately reached down and used it to lube her clit rubbing it just right to send her into her second orgasm and then as his body tensed behind her and he grunted his own release. Jax pulled her head to his chest and she bit into his body, drawing his hot blood into her mouth and her orgasm rippled into another instantly.

They collapsed. Jax on the bottom of the pile, Sachi laying on him with her head on his chest and Cash on top of her, his head resting on her mid back. The room filled with the sounds of their panting and the smell of their sex.

"That went even better than I expected," Cash admitted, breathless.

"So much better," Jax agreed.

The fact that they were in agreement kept Sachi from saying anything snarky about their male self satisfaction. To be honest she had no complaints though so she just smiled and patted them both.

"Someone needs to grab a towel," Sachi said.

"Cash is on top," Jax said and pulled her up so she was laying fully on him and Cash was now only tangled in their legs.

Cash growled but got up and went to the bathroom. When he came back he handed a towel to Jax and then used another to gently clean up Sachi. She didn't miss the look the two men shared as Cash swiped both of their cum off of her belly and between her thighs. No competition, no embarrassment and no regret, just a joint satisfaction and caring that made her heart flip.

Later, as Sachi lay cuddled between her two men, all of them still naked and satisfied, she couldn't imagine a better life. Cash kissed her back lazily and she smiled against Jax's chest.

They all froze as a howl ripped through the night, long and full of sorrow. It wasn't unusual to hear the wolves at night, but this sounded closer than usual.

"I have something I have to take care of," Cash said and moved out of the bed.

Something in his tone pricked at Sachi's nerves. "What is it?" she demanded, sitting up quickly and clutching the sheet to her chest. Jax put a soothing hand on her back.

"Don't worry," Cash said as he pulled on his pants and searched around for his shirt. "I just need to talk to Bernard."

"You mean you have to challenge him, don't you? You are going to try and claim your place as alpha now?" She felt a little frantic and it was clear in the crack of her voice.

Cash pulled his shirt on and sighed. "Yeah, it's something I need to do. I didn't want to do it while you were healing, I needed to go in without distraction."

"Because it's dangerous," she accused. She didn't like this, didn't want him to go risking himself, not when she just got him where she wanted him.

He shrugged and pulled his shoes out from under the bed. "It is what it is. I can't pretend I'm not alpha and if I try to stay under him, it will only make the pack weak with discontent. Half of them already want to follow my orders over his since the memories were unlocked. They are calling me when they should be calling him, and I know he's not happy about it. He's expecting this, the fact that he's waited out of respect for you is just lucky."

"I'm going with you," Sachi said and jumped out of the bed.

Cash grabbed her and pulled her in for a hug. "You shouldn't be there; it could be dangerous for you."

"Why?" she demanded.

"Because the mate of the alpha is supposed to be a breeding female, the other werewolf women are going to want to rip your throat out as soon as Cash wins his place," Jax explained. He'd moved off the bed and had begun dressing too.

Sachi pulled back and looked up into Cash's face. "That's true, isn't it," she whispered.

"It's a possibility, yes, but they'll settle once it's done and I've assured them that I don't plan to take a werewolf mate, ever. I do, however, plan to continue living this dream with you and Mr. Magic. Though, maybe I should change that to Mr. Relic," Cash teased and Sachi could have laughed if she wasn't so worried.

"You're just jealous," Jax teased back.

Sachi felt tears prickle her eyes at the easy banter between the two men. What if it was all about to crash though?

"I don't care. Jax and I are coming. He can keep me safe and I'm no weakling, I'm a goddamn demon!"

Cash smiled brightly. "True, and there's no rule against an alpha keeping a demon as a sex pet," he said gruffly.

"Don't make me blast you with a fireball, Wolf Boy," she growled back.

Still naked, Sachi looked from one man to the other, both now dressed and sighed heavily. She was going to have to defend this tonight, and beyond, she had a feeling. But she supposed anything this good was bound to make others jealous and with that jealousy came a desire to take it down.

She dressed in jeans and a pink T-shirt, pulled on black boots and brushed her lilac curls into a high ponytail. She added a bit of black eyeliner for the occasion and felt confident enough to face Cash's pack at his side.

Another howl ripped through the night, answered by more, very close this time. Bernard had issued a challenge and the pack was backing him on it. She stopped Cash before he could descend the staircase. "I don't care if you're alpha or not, just don't die, okay," she hissed and pulled him close for a deep kiss.

Cash cupped her face gently and smiled. "I am going to be alpha, and I am going to be your mate and I don't plan to die before I see you popping out little demon babies for me and Jax."

Sachi snorted at that but smiled, trying to feel as confident as him. "You know werewolves can't breed with butterfly shifters."

"But can they breed with quarter demon, half witch, butterfly shifters?"

Sachi opened her mouth and clamped it shut. She didn't have an answer for that and it made her wonder if that's why her mother had insisted she keep a birth control regimen going as a teen despite her boyfriend being a werewolf.

Cash gave her speechlessness a wink. "Keep her back," Cash ordered Jax then hurried ahead of them, down the stairs and out the back door of the bakery. Jax and Sachi were right behind, and they walked into a circle of wolves in the parking lot.

Fear for all three of them filled Sachi and her palm itched

with magic surfacing in reaction to her fear. "I'm scared," Sachi whispered and leaned back into Jax's chest.

Jax put his hands on her arms and kissed the top of her head. He leaned down and whispered in her ear. "Cash is strong and capable, he has a lot of support here, trust him to win and come back to us."

Back to us. Sachi felt tears sting her eyes at those words.

Fear swirled in her stomach as Bernard shifted from wolf to human and stepped away from the pack. He was a huge man. Long black hair, striking brown eyes and a body covered in scars. Proof that he was no stranger to a fight and came out alive every time. Sachi knew that a fight for alpha didn't have to end in death, but unless one of them submitted, which didn't usually happen, death was the only other option. She felt like she was staring the end of their happy threesome in the face and it pissed her off.

Jax's hands on her were calming but she still felt her power trickling over her palms, begging to take out the threat to her man.

"You have torn our pack," Bernard accused.

"The demon curse planted a seed that never should have grown," Cash said. "I am no longer content to let my father's legacy lay low. I cannot deny what I was born to be," Cash said confidently.

"So you will fight me for the pack?" Bernard snarled.

"If you won't step aside, then I will fight for my rightful place and make my father proud."

The wolves surrounding them howled in encouragement and sorrow.

Sachi felt power fill her entire body now, she wanted to lash out, to protect Cash.

"Don't," Jax whispered into her ear. "They will never accept a win that isn't unaided."

"I can't lose him now," she whispered back.

"We won't," Jax assured her. But she wasn't convinced.

Cash stripped quickly then shifted to his wolf form. It was huge, but so was Bernard's. A more even match, she couldn't imagine.

They circled each other, both baring their teeth and snarling. Bernard made the first move, rushing forward and trying to get a latch onto Cash's leg. Cash was quick though and he jumped at the last second, landing on the other side of Bernard. From there it was a blur of fur and teeth. The pack was loud, howling and yelping. Sachi wasn't sure what noises were coming from the pack and which ones were coming from the fighters. Blood spattered the ground, and she didn't know who's it was, she wanted to turn away, wanted to bury her face in Jax's chest but she forced herself to watch, to witness this moment that would again change everything for them. She was so tired of these moments, wanted something settled, something sane. She wanted their new normal.

Cash was thrown, skidded across the lot and crashed up against some of his packmates. Sachi screamed, seeing his bloody muzzle and limp body. She tried to pull out of Jax's arms but he held her tight, and as Bernard approached Cash's body, Cash twitched, snarled, and rose up, one leg bent, obviously broken, but he wasn't giving up. Bernard hesitated and that's when Cash took his chance. He leaped forward and, taken by surprise, was able to get a hold on Bernard's neck. From there it was seconds before Bernard's body was lying limp on the ground. The noise that erupted in the pack when Cash shifted back to human and stood on the defeated alpha's body in victory was deafening.

"I am your alpha!" Cash yelled to the crowd. Half of them shifted to human and cheered at his victory, the ones who remained in wolf form howled in misery at the loss of Bernard and cowered under Cash's gaze as he looked from one to the next. "Do any deny it? Do any wish to challenge me for my place?"

No one stepped forward in challenge and the noise cut off as Cash eyed each wolf in turn. Sachi was washed with relief as one by one the wolves shifted to human and kneeled under his gaze and then her fears turned to something new. She noticed the women, the ones who had turned with the first round of celebratory wolves looking at Cash with lust in their eyes. She glared at the naked women, how dare they!

"I am your alpha," Cash said again, quiet this time and more than one of those naked women took a step forward as if to congratulate him personally.

Sachi hissed and started to raise a hand but Jax gripped her arm in a bruising hold and held her even tighter to him. "No Sachi, trust him."

Cash noticed the movement of the women too though and he shook his head at them. "I am mated to Sachi, butterfly shifter, witch, demon, and keeper of the portal. I am mated to Jax, warlock, and keeper of the portal. Do any wish to challenge me in this?"

Sachi held her breath and she felt Jax stiffen behind her at Cash's claiming of him as mate as well, apparently this was something they hadn't discussed while she was sleeping. It made sense to her though, she could see that there was no way the pack would allow their alpha's mate to be in a relationship with someone else. But by claiming Jax as a mate as well, Cash had taken away any reason for the pack to come after her for cheating on their alpha. They have to accept her, Jax, and the whole relationship or speak now and challenge Cash's place and right to rule.

None came forward but more than one of the females sent her a quick glare before cowering under Cash's gaze.

"Then run with me this night," he demanded and shifted back to wolf. He loped to Sachi and licked her hand, meeting her gaze with love in his eyes. He nudged Jax's leg affectionately too, before running off, with the pack shifting and following behind him. Four pack members in human form remained and lifted the body of their fallen alpha, carrying him off for a proper, respectful burial.

When it was just Sachi and Jax staring into a dark parking lot she let out a relieved breath. "Do you think that'll be the end of it?"

"For now," Jax said and ushered her inside. "Let's make some tea, it'll go great with those leftover gingersnaps I saw in the kitchen."

Sachi let him lead her in and to a stool. She watched him move around the kitchen with efficiency, making tea and plating cookies. He looked at home in her bakery kitchen and that made her heart ache with happiness.

"What if I can't give him babies?" she said as Jax handed her a hot cup of lavender and chamomile tea.

He cocked his head and looked at her with a thoughtful expression. "Do you think you can't?"

"I don't know if I can, don't know if I want to," she added as she sipped some of the hot liquid.

"How about we worry about that when it matters," he said and handed her a cookie. "Honestly, I never really saw myself having children but I also never saw myself in a relationship with a quarter demon and her werewolf boyfriend."

Sachi laughed. "Yes, let's worry about it later," she agreed and took the cookie. They all deserved a little time of just being without worrying about anything more.

CHAPTER 25

Sachi stretched as the sun poured in the window. Cash whined and growled quietly in his sleep beside her and on her other side Jax slept like a log. It had been a year since she was dragged and pushed out of the portal with a broken rib, a mangled arm, and some new emotional damage. But she'd been embraced even stronger by these two men and her life was nearly perfect. They'd found a way to be together that felt good for all of them and although it didn't come without the occasional argument or disagreement, she'd found a strength in herself that held both men's dominant instincts in check.

She was part demon after all.

It was early, but she had to get up and downstairs to start baking. She was a Portal Keeper, they all were actually. Children of the three brave Portal Keepers who had died trying to protect this district eleven years ago. Sachi, Cash and Jax had succeeded where their fathers had failed and in that, they had found a deep love for each other. But that job only needed them once every ten years, when done right. Today she was baking cupcakes for Penelope's triplet's birthday party and full moon wolfsbane cookies for Cash's wolfpack.

She tried to move without waking either man, but just when she thought she had succeeded, she felt rock solid arms embrace her waist and pull her back down. Cash growled in her ear. "It's a full moon tonight, you know what that means?"

"I need to make cookies?" she teased. "And you'll need to shave about once an hour so I don't get beard burn on my thighs?"

He growled and Jax stirred beside them.

"It means I am hornier than usual." And to prove his point he shifted his hips and pressed his morning wood against her.

"Fern will be here soon."

"She won't come up here if we make enough noise," Jax said, coming fully awake and pressing kisses to her neck.

It was a normal morning routine for them. If she didn't make any real effort to get up and get going when she needed to, she ended up stumbling down to the kitchen with pink cheeks about an hour after Fern got in there and started baking.

She didn't want to argue and she sighed as she allowed the men to do their best at worshiping her body. It was a familiar dance; one they'd all come to enjoy without reservation or embarrassment over the last year.

With Cash chasing his full moon high he took the lead.

"On your knees, I want to watch you scream around Jax's cock while I pound into you," Cash said.

Sachi complied, all thoughts of the bakery gone as she moved, her face snuggling into Jax's lap as he laid across the foot of the bed, too lazy in the morning apparently to get up.

She liked that position though. It allowed her to lift her ass at an angle that forced Cash to hit her just right with each thrust. She wiggled her ass in invitation as she grasped Jax's hardening cock and licked it base to tip, one hand rolling his balls and the other working his shaft. She licked his tip as he groaned. "Oh shit, man, I am not going to last. You'd better get her going, Cash." Jax said, his hips thrusting up.

Sachi laughed and took him fully in her mouth. She wasn't sure what Cash's hold-up was, so she wiggled her ass again. She heard a drawer by the bed open and close then a click and cold liquid was dripping between her ass cheeks.

"Oh," she mumbled around Jax who laughed at her surprise. Sachi pulled back and looked at Jax. "Is this one of those things you two discussed when I wasn't looking?"

Cash leaned over her and kissed her cheek. "Just relax, love, trust us."

"I do," Sachi said and it was true, she trusted them with her life.

Cash sat back up and his fingers slid through the wetness, running over her ass all the way down to her clit and back up to the bundle of nerves that rarely got so much attention.

Sachi started to follow where this was going to go and she smiled around Jax's cock.

Jax put his hands in her hair and pushed her back down. "Don't worry, it's not time to move yet," Jax said.

Cash pushed one finger into her ass and she stiffened then shivered at the pleasure. She sucked Jax down to his base and pulled up slowly, swirling her tongue at the tip and making him pull her head off of him.

"Not fair, Sachi, we had a plan!" Jax said with a strained tone that made her grin. She loved the power she could wield over these two powerful men.

"Can't hold your load, Jax?" Cash teased.

"Not with her tongue swirling my tip and her hand gripping my balls," Jax said without shame.

Cash pushed another finger into her ass, stretching her out, then he pushed the cold rubber tip of a plug in as well. They'd been working up to this, with slow steps and apparently the men had decided it was time. Cash worked the plug and fingers in and out of her a few times, adding more lube, making sure she was stretched and drenched.

When Cash was satisfied that she was prepared he pulled out and she whined at the emptiness she was left with.

"Straddle Jax," Cash ordered and she moved quickly, in a hurry to get Jax into her wet core, every thrust into her ass had left her walls clenching and needy. She held Jax's cock and slid down onto it, her head thrown back she howled up at the ceiling.

Cash pushed on her back until she was flat against Jax's chest then he moved behind her and lined up his cock with her ass.

"Ready, love?"

"Yes," she said and looked into Jax's eyes. She held his face and kissed him as Cash pushed in slowly, filling her more than she'd ever been filled in her life.

"Oh fuck," Sachi whispered against Jax's mouth.

"I can feel your dick," Jax said.

Cash laughed above them. "I'm not going to lie, Magic Boy, I think this might be my new favorite thing."

Sachi laughed and then they started to move. Cash led, sliding out and in and that moved her against Jax, it really felt like Cash was fucking them both and Sachi watched Jax's eyes as he realized the same thing. She wondered for a moment if he would stop it, if he would try and take charge but he just opened his mouth on a quiet groan as Cash worked them both toward orgasm.

When they came it was a domino starting with Jax, triggering Sachi who screamed until her mouth was covered by Cash's arm in offer of blood. She bit into him as he reached his orgasm as well. All three of them shuddered and cried out and hands grasped and caressed each other. When Sachi fell still on top of Jax, she had one hand back on Cash's ass, one in Jax's hair. Jax had one hand gripping her arm and the other was farther above her, presumably on Cash. Cash had one hand on Sachi's breast and the other was gripping Jax's hair alongside Sachi's hand.

"You're on towel duty, alpha boy," Jax said and Sachi heard the slap of skin against skin as Jax slapped Cash's ass.

Cash grunted and pulled out of Sachi with an appreciative groan. "That is something I want to see again," he said and ran a finger between her cheeks where his cum was dripping, down to where Jax's cock was still buried in her.

"Next time I'm on top," Jax said.

"You will love it," Cash agreed and walked toward the bathroom.

"Don't worry about the towel for me. I'm showering, I have work to do." Her legs were jello but she managed to kiss each man and make her way to the shower as they toweled off and laid on the bed talking quietly. She imagined they were critiquing the position and next time it would be slightly improved.

How the hell had she gotten so lucky?

When Sachi finally made it downstairs an hour later, Fern was hard at work baking happily.

"Good morning, sunshine," Fern said with a wink. "Sounds like everyone's in a good mood today."

Sachi laughed as she put on her apron. "Full moon energy," she said with a wink.

"Don't forget what Pen said yesterday, bad moon for entertaining," Fern said with a wave of her spatula then laughed and Sachi was glad to see her best friend in such a good mood.

It had been hard, the last year, for Fern. Lance's betrayal had broken her trust of males, and some of her siblings had been seriously injured by the cages he'd put them in. "I went on a date last night," Fern admitted shyly.

"Oh! Do tell."

"You know the new gym teacher, Sara. She came in with the new elf clan."

Sachi nodded. Bardbizt had managed to kill off the entire elf clan to keep his secret when he'd been in Chief Rodriguez's body and a few months ago a new clan had moved into the woods. The gym teacher was a gorgeous tall thing with bright blue eyes and silver hair. Sachi wasn't surprised that Fern was attracted to her.

Especially since she was still swearing that she'd never trust another man again.

"She took me on a picnic by the river, it was nice," she said softly, and her cheeks reddened.

Sachi wouldn't point it out, but she had a feeling Fern was already falling in love and that made Sachi very happy.

Cash loped down the stairs and kissed her. "I'm meeting with the council about a group of young weres who want to take a field trip North, can I bring some cookies? They always listen better when I've plied them with your sugar first," Cash said.

"Are you taking Jax?" Jax had become an important part of the pack in the last year, especially where the youths were concerned. He had a soft spot for the gangly teens who were just trying to figure out how to exist in the world. Cash had always been so popular and amazing, he couldn't relate the same way to them and the young werewolves liked Jax more, though they were too scared for their lives to tell their alpha that.

"He's going to come by in a bit with the group, they've prepared a presentation I guess," Cash shrugged. "He didn't really tell me what it was about so I suppose we'll all be surprised."

Sachi gave him a kiss and Fern handed him a plate of lemon cookies. "Good luck," Sachi said and he rushed out the back door.

Jax was downstairs next, taking a plate of wolfsbane brownies with him to meet up with his little group of awkward werewolves.

"What kind of presentation did you come up with to convince the pack you're responsible enough to chaperone their kids out of district?" Sachi asked.

"I didn't prepare it, the kids did," he said with a smile. "I think it has to do with the health benefits of hunting some species of northern squirrel."

Sachi laughed. "Seriously?"

Jax shrugged. "They're kids, they just want to get away from their parents for a couple days, they can't think that deep."

"And you are sure you can keep them safe?"

"I can, and I already discussed it with Cash. I will be taking one of the fathers along as an extra chaperone."

Jax kissed Sachi and hurried out the back door. She turned back to her baking and busied herself with the daily tasks that she loved so much.

Sachi took a tray of macaroons to the front of the store, ready to display in the window. She flipped the open sign and looked out at the street, already starting to rush with supes, the first bus of humans wouldn't be in for another hour or so.

"Good morning, Dad," she whispered to the picture of him she'd hung by the door. He was standing beside a sign that proclaimed, *Moses' Bar*. She'd been embarrassed to display it a year ago, but now everyone knew he was a hero, and so was she. There was still a warrant out for her mother's arrest and once a week an officer stopped by to ask her if she'd heard from her mother. She had told them that her mother disappeared the night of the portal opening, it wasn't a lie exactly.

Sachi had to believe her mother was living a happy life with her demon kin and better off than what she might suffer up here, despite her having killed for the greater good. If not, Sachi would destroy Ainu for breaking her promise and Sachi planned to spend the next nine years training with Jax so she wouldn't be at a disadvantage if it came to that.

PLEASE RATE AND REVIEW

We hope you enjoyed
Butterfly Kisses by Courtney Davis.
If you did, we would ask that you please rate and review this title.
Every review helps our authors.

Rate and Review: Butterfly Kisses

MEET THE AUTHOR

Courtney Davis is an award-winning author residing in North Idaho with her husband and children — teaching, reading, writing and soaking up sunshine.

She loves creating creatures with a new spin and exploring human and inhuman interactions in a modern world. She hopes you find joy and an escape in her writing.

OTHER TITLES FROM 5 PRINCE PUBLISHING

www.5princebooks.com

www.ingramcontent.com/pod-product-compliance
Lightning Source LLC
Chambersburg PA
CBHW031111030726
47496CB00002BA/494